BUTTERFLY WEEDS

A NOVEL BY

LAURA MILLER

This book is a work of fiction. Names, characters, businesses, places and incidents are the product of the author's imagination or are used fictitiously. Any resemblance to actual events, locals or persons, living or dead, is coincidental.

ISBN-13: 978-1478321903
ISBN-10: 1478321903

Cover photo © Suprijono Suharjoto.
Title page photo © Suprijono Suharjoto.
Author photo © Marc Mayes.

To the Dealer of dreams,
For fairy tales

*We have but one dance
to a lifetime of songs.*

Butterfly Weeds

a novel

LAURA MILLER

Prologue

The evening was a Southern stereotype–warmer than comfortable, more humid than not, but then again, what more could I expect from a Charleston summer? I was learning very quickly that this was the only way they came–hot and sticky. Thank God for the breeze that made its way over the waves in the harbor and to our faces, though. Without it, I just know I would look like a soggy newspaper with all of its ink running down its thick, cemented pages. Minus the natural fan, my make-up and sunscreen, along with my cheery expression, would have taken off for the imaginary finish line at my painted toes hours ago.

With that thought, I caught a strand of my long hair that was being tossed in the salty breeze and secured it behind my ear as I took a step onto the city's shell sidewalk and waited.

"Now, where would you like to go, Miss Lang?"

It was as if his words had come from heaven. *Miss Lang*. Yep, that was my name. I tried unsuccessfully to replicate in my head the exact way he had said it. His voice had this thick, Charleston accent, where every word had more syllables than ever intended, yet each word seemed as if it had been carefully chosen and presented in a way that only a man born and raised in the heart of the South could–distinguished and from a different time. I smiled up at him, and he flashed a coffee-stain-free grin back at me. I was quite aware of just how rare his pearly whites were. This whole place ran on coffee beans and their fumes, though I hadn't figured out why. You've got the beach to your right, palm trees to your left. Do you really need a better pick-me-up? And on top of that, I had found out fairly early on that businesses here operated on a 32-hour work week. No one in this town worked on Fridays. No one. Here, Fridays were dedicated to the two Bs–Beach and Boats.

"Well, Miss Lang, where's our next stop?" he asked again, extending his bended elbow toward me.

Without so much as a thought, I slipped my arm into his.

Even when he was trying to act impatient, his smile was still gorgeous–almost debonair-like–to match his jet-black hair, sun-tanned skin and soft, brown eyes.

I put my roving thoughts on hold and turned my head toward the sky to instead marvel at my pleasant predicament. At the same time, I felt a smile unexpectedly escape my glossy lips, and I didn't even try to hide it.

The sights of downtown–the pier, the market, Marion Square–began cascading through my mind like an old-time slide show. There were too many places to choose from, though any place would do–as long as I had my company. And maybe life wasn't that complicated after all because wrapped up in my arm was Anthony Ravenel–first-year lawyer, quiet but deliberate. His office was a door down from mine at the firm, which seems now to be a pretty serendipitous coincidence–considering he had become such a close friend and that with his family's old money, he really never had to work a day in his life. But then, I guess much like all of us at 112 Broad St., unfortunately, law was his passion.

"How about…," I began, and then let my words trail off as I continued to ponder my great dilemma, our next grand adventure.

I could feel strands of my dirty blond hair being tossed in the soft breeze again, gently tickling the part of my sun-tanned back where my sundress began. I wasn't a true Charlestonian, so Fridays still involved me locked away in a small office with no windows to the world, but there was always Saturday–just enough time to get that Vitamin D that I used as an excuse to get a free tan.

My marveling continued then as I noticed that Anthony had been watching me intently, as if each word that poured off my lips held some precious, untold secret. I can't remember the last time I had this much undivided attention. Even my clients didn't pay attention to me this well. I made a mental note to choose my words carefully and to not mistake his psychiatrist-like listening skills for a therapy session. This was my co-worker after all. Though, I was starting to guess that on the flip side of the coin, it was a whole, different story. I was quickly getting the feeling that he wasn't seeing me as just a co-worker tonight. No, it definitely seemed like something a little more. And now that we were on the subject, he sure

3

didn't look like the same guy who shared a wall with me 50 hours of the week either. Tonight, somehow, he was the perfect kind of seductive and dangerous—the kind that could strike up a sweet conversation with you outside the hard walls of the courtroom but then murder you with dagger eyes and knife-sharp words during his opening arguments inside. And then, he was still different somehow. I hadn't figured out if it was that his future was more thought-out than anyone I had ever met or if it was somehow that his heart always seemed to know exactly what it wanted that made him inherently different from most guys. Then again, he was also straight and to the point—no drama, no jaded past. He was, no doubt, someone a girl like me could appreciate.

"How about we go…," I began again, recovering from my spiraling thoughts once more, but this time, a sound stopped me short.

Almost instantly, I halted and dug my sandal's heel into a soft space between the pieces of uneven sidewalk beneath us to keep my weight from tumbling forward. I could feel that Anthony halted too, bracing me as if to catch my fall. At the same time, I felt the corners of my mouth fall out of a smile as my eyes darted feverishly to the direction of a familiar, yet long-forgotten memory.

The adrenaline that rushed in waves through my body started at my heart and then sprinted to my fingers and knees, causing little, tingling sensations. And on the inside, I panicked.

The hum, which cut like a knife into my togetherness, was coming from an unfamiliar, dark-colored sedan resting at a stop light on the street directly in front of us. I noticed the melody first, but as I stood there, blocking out everything—the trotting hooves of carriage rides, muted conversations—I could faintly make out lyrics too.

"Julia, are you okay?" the beautiful man beside me echoed, sounding slightly concerned.

My heart was beating violently against the walls of my chest now. My breaths were quickening. My legs were struggling to hold my weight. The tiny heel of my sandal had, by now, become a part of the ground beneath me, and I was just merely an extension of this small piece of earth. And somehow, in what had only amounted to a matter of moments, my world had grown so small—and nothing mattered more than hearing that melody in the near distance. And yet, somehow, I managed to find a word. Well, almost a word.

"Hmm?" I asked half-heartedly. Even I could tell I was clearly distracted and disinterested in my company's, for now, unimportant question.

"Are you all right?" he asked again cautiously.

I tried to re-collect myself even as my senses were being drawn into the Siren's sedan-like lair.

"I'm sorry," I answered him in a soft, unusually preoccupied voice. The voice even surprised me. "I just… that song," I stuttered. My eyes were planted straight ahead.

He moved closer, and suddenly, I felt his fingers interlocking mine. I was aware enough to notice that they were larger than mine, a little rougher than mine, but I was too lost in something other than us to respond outwardly to his brave gesture, though I don't think he had ever touched me like that before. In fact, who was I kidding? Of course he had never touched me like that before. Co-workers don't hold hands.

"I hear the music. What about it?" he asked. He sounded puzzled, though his detective work remained patient and slightly curious.

"I know it," I whispered now as I struggled to still hear the lyrics from my past and the man's heavenly voice beside me all at the same time. I wasn't sure which one I'd rather be hearing at the moment. The beautiful man's voice was safe and predictable. The lyrics, on the other hand, were from a time when everything was perfect, but anything but predictable.

Anthony drew his face closer to mine without saying a word. I could smell the sweet hues of his cologne as his strong chest pressed against my shoulder. I was just beginning to realize how warm and strong his hand felt– maybe it was because there was such a sharp contrast between his and mine. My hand was growing colder and clammier with each pressing second. The whole moment was all so new, so foreign–my co-worker holding my hand, that sound–both of those events simultaneously. I mean, I would usually feel butterflies in a time like this–a first for us–the first move. Yet now, I just wanted him not to be near me, not to feel my ice-cold hands, my slimy scales for skin. And oddly enough, now, I just wanted him to stay quiet and still because regardless of how I wanted to feel or how I thought I should feel about him or his hand-holding or his cologne or his chest's close proximity to my body, it took a backseat to an unfamiliar, dark sedan and its not-so-unfamiliar echo in the distance.

"Is this one a favorite–the song?" he whispered, still trying to reel me in, I'm sure, and rightly so.

He remained patiently interested in what had so violently stolen me away from him. My eyes, however, continued to pierce my distraction as if I could physically see what the lyrics that poured from it meant.

"No, it's not a favorite," I lied. My half-truth was soft–almost in auto-pilot, the kind that was distant and low. It was still too early to let him in. And it wasn't completely a lie. The truth was that I didn't have the slightest idea of how to feel about it. Like him, I was hearing the song's entire version for the first time.

Having said my peace, I returned my full attention back to the sound as if I had no control over its pull.

Anthony paused then, but I still said nothing. I had barely noticed that I wasn't blinking. I guess I thought I might miss some of the lyrics or something if my eyelids lingered over my eyes too long. My glossy lips too were wrapped up in my body's so-called revolt, never touching each other as I stared longingly. And my chest rose and fell as if it took great pains to control its pattern.

"Do you like the artist then?" I could faintly hear Anthony ask me–almost as if from a distance.

I swore my heart stopped momentarily then as I unintentionally squeezed his hand tightly–tighter than one should squeeze a hand she was holding for the first time.

The artist. If he only knew.

I still said nothing.

"Are you sure you're okay, Julia?" he asked, sounding just short of worried.

No, was what I wanted to say, but I didn't, as a decade of memories and what seemed as if it were a heartfelt confession flooded my mind and lay heavy on my jaded heart. I could tell Anthony was starting to grow concerned by my short leave of absence and my sudden, distressed state. His voice held a lingering uneasiness, and I knew I wasn't being fair, but I still couldn't tear my stare away from that old sedan even as the traffic light turned a blaring green and the vehicle sped away, taking its melody with it.

I stared for long, drawn-out seconds until I was unable to see the car any longer. Then my eyes followed a conscious path from my elbow to my clammy hand to his hand and then up to Anthony's questioning, soft, brown eyes.

"Yes, I'm fine. It's nothing," I said, hastily, habitually tucking a strand of my hair behind my ear.

His big, chocolate, long-suffering irises made him look like an anxious puppy, waiting for its master to recognize its presence, waiting for her to say something, waiting for her to come back to him. He was so gorgeous–the mysterious, foreign kind of gorgeous–if you could call the South a foreign land. Really, he was the kind that you dreamed about–and here I was getting lost in some loud, old sedan. I knew that he probably didn't get this type of behavior very often. And he was so innocent, still so oblivious to my past and the people who had shaped it. And he looked as if he wanted me to say that I was fine and that my world hadn't just turned on its end, but I wasn't fine, and I wasn't ready to act like I was either. I wasn't ready to come back yet.

I took a second to take one more glance back at the cobble-stoned piece of the world where the old sedan had been resting just moments before. The car was definitely gone now, and by now a much larger, rusty pick-up truck with an early American flag plastered across its back window had replaced it. There was no music pouring from its speakers–no more lyrics, no more words. With the sedan, had gone the song, and it had left my world painfully quiet and eerily still.

I turned back toward the harbor as my eyes caught once again the surprisingly sultry creature still attached to my hand, still waiting unwaveringly for my reply. I counted it a blessing that he was still there, that he hadn't fled in my brief lapse of worldly consciousness. It was time to come back. After all, it wasn't his fault. He hadn't just dropped the entire weight of my past onto my chest.

"I'm sorry," I stammered. "How about the pier?" I both asked and stated with the best sincere smile I could muster up, forcing my attention back to him, back to us. I must choose my words carefully, I reminded myself.

"And, no, he's not my favorite artist," I softly said to him.

I took a deep breath in and then let it out slowly.

Then, I flashed another half-hearted grin back up at him just before taking one, last look over my shoulder.

"He used to be," I whispered.

Eleven Years Earlier

I could feel the fire warming my face as I stretched my bare fingers closer to its flames. The smell of burning logs filled the air around me and sunk deep into the fibers of my hooded sweatshirt and blue jeans. My eyes were entranced by the orange blaze, watching it sizzle and pop as it ate away pieces of the cedar's bark little by little. The night surrounding the fire was unseasonably crisp, but not altogether unusual for a Missouri summer, and voices echoed in my background over the flames' constant chatter.

"Hey, Julia," I heard one of those voices call out from behind me.

Before I could turn around, a lanky, teen-aged boy jumped over the log I was sitting on and plopped down next to me.

"Oh, hi, Jeff," I said cheerfully, after he was already making himself comfortable. "Getting a little chilly out there away from the fire?"

"Nah, I'm all right," he said shyly, then paused.

"Hey, I can go get ya some hot chocolate, though. That should warm ya up, if you're cold," he added proudly as the corners of his mouth rose slightly.

I started to answer him when a tall, athletic-looking figure squatted down behind the lanky boy. I could see in the bonfire's light the athletic boy's hand come to his face and cover his mouth as he whispered something into the lanky boy's ear.

Within seconds, the lanky boy stood up, dusted off his faded blue jeans and planted his eyes squarely on me.

"I'll be right back," the lanky boy announced. In his voice was an unspoken plea for me to stay exactly where I was.

Then, just as quickly as he had appeared, he disappeared back into the black night, undetectable by the fire's flames.

I stared down the tall, athletic boy in front of me, my green eyes bright and suspecting of mischief.

"Will Stephens, what did you say to him?" I asked, scolding him playfully.

"I told him his truck lights were on," Will said, grinning and taking a seat beside me on the log where the lanky boy had just been sitting.

"Are they?" I asked, somehow feeling as though I already knew the answer.

"No," he softly mumbled, grinning into the fire's flames.

A smile grew on my face as I caught Will's fierce blue eyes. He was boyishly handsome–that I could admit easily. He wore his usual–worn-in jeans and tee shirt– seemingly unfazed by the night's chill. He stood six-foot-four, had a medium build and a golden tan. His short, russet, slightly curly hair had been bleached by the sun to make the ends just a little lighter than the roots. It made him look like he belonged on a beach in Southern California, instead of in an old corn field in eastern Missouri. Though, his true origin was unmistakable. He spoke in that perfect Midwestern inflection–the kind where the words flowed faster than a Southern drawl, slower than a Northeastern accent–recognizable mostly by the way he drew out his short *a*.

"When are you going to say *yes*?" Will asked, without skipping a beat, causing my stare on him to break.

I turned my gaze back toward the flames.

"Depends on what the question is," I said slowly, with a coy smile, allowing my eyes to eventually meet his again by the time I was finished with my sentence.

"Same question," he echoed back–almost bashfully this time.

I paused for an instant.

"Then, same answer," I softly said, locking my eyes on his. My green eyes screamed that I was serious, but I still had a smile planted on my face.

"Come on, Jules," he protested. "I know you like me. And you're gonna love me, someday," he added in a playful, persistent affirmation.

My eyes grew big, just as the corners of my mouth turned up a little more.

"Love?" I asked. My voice held a natural surprise to match the rest of my physical state.

"Jules, just let me take you to Donna's," he implored–effortlessly resilient.

I laughed softly and shook my head.

"That sounds like a date, Will," I said, stuffing my hands into the pocket of my hooded sweatshirt to ward off the night's chill.

"Yeah, it kind of does," he admitted, smiling and nodding his head.

I paused to catch the side of his face that the fire was illuminating. His eyes were on the flames. His expression was happy but thoughtful.

"You're serious, aren't you?" I asked, keeping my stare on him, just in case he cracked.

His eyes cast down, but his smile remained. I watched him tug at a loose piece of bark on the log beneath us and finally pry it free and toss it into the fire's flames.

"Jules, I was always serious," he said, his expression never wavering.

I still stared at him, intent on beating him in his own game, though. I didn't know Will to be serious.

"Will, you threw rocks at me in third grade," I reminded him.

He glanced up at me for a moment and then quickly returned his eyes to the ground. I could see his even, white teeth through spurts of the dancing flames. I could tell he was grinning.

"It was out of love, I promise," he assured me, while meeting my eyes. "You could think of it like Cupid's arrows, only they were rocks."

I wrinkled my forehead and pursed my lips.

"No?" he asked and stated at the same time as if to echo my expression. "Well, I guess I just had a funny way of showing it back then."

"Will, you purposely got my favorite volleyball stuck up in the gym's rafters," I proceeded.

His eyes flashed sharply toward mine, and his smile widened. He even chuckled a little and shook his head.

"You still remember that?" he asked, with a surprised look on his face.

I glared at him with a callous, yet playful expression.

"It was last week, Will," I reminded him.

"Can I just take you to Donna's—to make up for all my past wrong-doings?" he pleaded as his hopeful, baby blue eyes met mine yet again.

Our gaze lasted just long enough for my straight face to unintentionally grow a smile. Yet, I continued to draw out the silent seconds while I tossed his invitation around in my head.

"You know, you kind of owe me," I softly admitted.

But before I could answer him further, several girls sprang from the darkness and proceeded to find places on logs on the opposite side of the bonfire. They were giggling, and their eyes were on Will.

"Will, sing us a song," a bubbly brunette finally commanded from across the flames.

The bubbly brunette was Rachel, my best friend—a self-proclaimed meddler, but loyal as they come. I met her the summer before our freshman year of high school at a volleyball camp. My first real memory of her was in the dorm room at the university where the camp was being held.

I remember the light was still on, and I could see through my tired, squinting eyes that Rachel was sitting on her twin-sized bed, wearing what looked like freshly pressed, silk, pink pajamas with tiny, fuchsia bows lining the tops of the pants and collar of the tank top.

"Hey, can you hit the light?" I remember asking her through my narrowed eyes.

"Okay, in a second. Some of my bows are coming untied," Rachel had replied.

The light was piercing, but my stare was curious.

"You know you're only going to sleep, right?" I had asked her, somewhat bemused.

"I know, but the ribbons will bother my face, and plus, I have to look cute. You could meet Prince Charming in your dreams, you know," she had said, remaining confidently unfazed by my comment.

I remember smiling, not even mad, just puzzled by her strange habits and too tired to reply.

We seemed to have been pretty inseparable ever since that night really. Wherever she was, I was. Wherever I was, she was–that kind of thing.

"Rach, I can't sing," Will protested bashfully, his head down, searching for another piece of bark to pull off of the log beneath us.

"What?" Rachel asked. Her voice went up in pitch as she said the word, and she pretended to look shocked. "Then why was THIS in your car?" she asked again proudly, picking up an object from the shadows behind her and passing it around the edge of the fire toward Will.

"My car?" Will asked in a deep, velvety voice– unusual for his age–as a six-stringed acoustic guitar became visible in the orange flames.

"Yep, your car," Rachel said, as if it had been perfectly acceptable for her to have retrieved it.

A surprised expression flashed across Will's strong features.

"Jules, remind me to lock it next time," he whispered to me, as his rough hands gripped the guitar that by now had reached him.

I smiled and shrugged my shoulders.

"Play us something," Rachel continued to demand.

Will, seemingly at a loss for words, found my stare.

"The girls want a song," I said to him smiling, offering him no escape route. By now, I was curious too.

He looked down at the strings of the guitar and grinned.

"Okay," he softly conceded, shaking his head back and forth as he began to strum the guitar's strings, eventually producing a soft, familiar melody.

I recognized the chorus to be the old song that comes to life through my jeep's speakers every time I turn it on. It surprised me how well he could play it. It was as if I were listening to the song being played on the radio in the jeep or on TV or something. He was good—really good even.

He tickled the guitar's strings a little bit more, almost as if he were prolonging the part where the words came in. But then, eventually his voice came, and he caught me off-guard yet again. His voice was deep, as usual, but his sultry hum made his usual deep voice sound even more soothing and kind of seductive. Will, seductive? Those were two words I had never put together. In fact, I almost choked on my own thoughts. And most surprising of all, he was good—way too good to be in an old corn field in the middle of nowhere, that's for sure.

His first words came out soft and timid, as if this were the first time he had ever had an audience, but as he continued, his protective walls seemed to shatter and slowly fall. And before I knew it, he was singing as if entertaining was what he was born to do.

I listened in a state of controlled awe as the girls on the other side of the fire joined in the next verse.

Then, Will grew quiet, as his fingers strummed the last chorus on the instrument cradled in his basketball-conditioned arms. And as his guitar fell silent a few moments later, Rachel and the other girls joined me in speechless amazement–our eyes on Will.

"Wow, Will," Rachel exclaimed first. "I'm not going to lie. I was really expecting a voice from the boy who starts a band in his garage only to still be in his garage 40 years later with a beer belly and a mullet. I wasn't expecting a rock star."

Will's eyes darted toward me, but quickly hit the ground by our feet again before they could catch my awestruck stare. His bashful smile was contagious, though, and it helped to break my frozen expression.

I glanced at Rachel with a face that held a million questions.

"Well, I can see that maybe you two have something new to talk about, so…we're just going to get some more hot chocolate," Rachel said before motioning for the other girls to follow her away from the fire.

Within a moment, Will and I were alone again. There was a slight pause before either one of us said anything, but it didn't last long. I just couldn't hold it in anymore.

"Will, that was really good," I gushed–near awestruck again. I was surprised at how easily the words just kind of fell out of my mouth. I was usually scolding him, not flattering him.

"Really?" he questioned me sincerely. I could tell he wasn't just fishing for more compliments.

"Will," I said, half laughing. "All these years…How didn't I know that you could play the guitar–or sing?" I questioned him. "And that good?" I added.

He continued to smile, and his eyes remained tantalized by the fire's flames.

"Not many people do know, I guess," he softly confessed. "I'm pretty good at keeping secrets around here." He winked in my direction as he rested the base of the guitar against the log next to him.

He still came off bashful, but I could see glimpses of his old confidence slowly coming back. I kept my eyes on him even as his attention turned back toward the flames. I knew I had a look planted on my face of something between intrigued and baffled, and I knew he could read me like a book, but I didn't care. I couldn't help it. He was good–really good, and I found myself fascinated by a side of Will Stephens I had never before seen.

"So, I see," I said, smiling wildly.

"Do you write songs too?" I asked. Maybe there was still more I didn't know about him.

"I try, when I get a chance," he said modestly. "Writing's the best part really. It's the words that change people's lives in the end, right?"

I paused to take in his question. He played the guitar, sang and wrote his own songs, and now he was talking about changing people's lives. I was beginning to realize quickly that in all the years I had known him, I had never really got to know Will Stephens.

"Hmm, I guess that makes sense," I said in reply to his question. "I've never really thought about it," I confessed.

I watched his eyes follow the dancing flames in the fire. I could see he was smiling.

"I'll have to write a song for you sometime," he said–almost inaudibly–as his eyes met mine again.

A smitten smile unexpectedly shot across my face, and I quickly hid it as best I could–purely out of habit. Will Stephens doesn't get smitten smiles.

"Do you write a song for every girl you have a crush on?" I asked sarcastically, trying my best to recover my poker face. I felt like I was coming unraveled. It was a completely new feeling for me—like someone had just released a million, tiny butterflies loose in my stomach, and they were feverishly flying up into my head and making me lose my mind.

"Well, I will once I write one for you," he retorted quickly.

I smiled—completely uncontrollably. I didn't even try to hide it this time. The truth was that I was kind of already getting used to the intrusive, little butterflies overtaking my being. They could stay, I resolved.

"I'm pretty sure it's brown-eyed girl though," I playfully added, in an attempt to railroad the subject as I now, under the butterflies' control, pulled off a piece of the bark and threw it into the flames before returning my hand safely to my sweatshirt's pocket. "In the song, you said green-eyed girl."

Will paused for a moment as if caught in his own mistake.

"Let me see," he said then, as he gently touched his hand to my chin and turned my face toward his.

Gone was the instinct or necessary desire to violently shift my face away from him or to get his hand away from my chin as quickly as possible. I simply just sat there—motionless, letting his hand take control of my movement. Who was this new person I had become?

"Nope, pretty sure it's green-eyed girl," he said assuredly.

A slight smile lingered on my lips.

"Will Stephens, what am I going to do with you?" I softly asked, as his hand slowly fell from my chin.

He remained silent then, almost as if he had lost his words, yet his piercing baby blue eyes remained on me.

"Jules, I'm sorry about the rocks, your ball and every other stupid thing I've ever done," he said sheepishly.

I laughed.

"It's okay," I said. "You get the ball down for me some day, and we'll call it even."

"Okay," he softly said, smiling and shaking his head, returning his gaze to the flames. "But I'm not gonna stop askin', you know?"

I looked at him—amused.

"I considered that," I said, laughing. "And what if I never say *yes*?"

Will looked to be pondering my question.

"Well, then I suppose I would have spent my life doin' something worthwhile," he said. "My parents can't be disappointed in that."

"Will," I said in protest, laughing again and lifting my eyes toward his.

He was already looking at me when our eyes met, and for a split second, my world mysteriously paused.

His wild, bright blue eyes were all I could think about then as I became completely and hopelessly lost in his world.

"Will," a voice suddenly shouted out from behind us. The voice was shrill and intrusive, elbowing its way into our little world—literally.

Both Will's and my attention jetted toward the direction of the sound behind us as we watched a lanky boy emerge from the darkness and plop abruptly down onto the log between us, forcing both Will and I to shift apart.

"Will, those were Ben's lights, not mine," he informed Will hastily–not ever giving Will his full attention.

"Here, Julia, here's some hot chocolate," the lanky boy announced, facing me and presenting to me a steaming, Styrofoam cup.

I removed both of my hands from my sweatshirt's pocket and cradled the cup as Will recoiled and shifted his weight away from the boy now wedged between us. I watched Will quickly divert his eyes to the fierce, orange flames again as he habitually ran his hand against his thigh.

"Thanks, Jeff," I said as the distracted, lanky boy found a stick and proceeded to poke at the fire's ashes.

I watched for a few, long seconds Jeff menacingly prodding what was left of the logs before my gaze turned up again.

What I glimpsed next made me smile. My own eyes had caught the bright, blue gaze of Will Stephens, and for the first time in the history of humanity, his eyes didn't look so juvenile–his stare didn't seem so mischievous.

Falling

"What's your favorite sport?" I asked.

"Uh, basketball," he said confidently.

"What's your favorite food?" I continued.

"Umm, I don't know. Uh…," he stuttered.

"Will, the game doesn't work if you don't answer the first thing that comes to your head. It's supposed to be the truth. You have to do it fast," I tenderly protested with a happy smile, though I tried to show him the most serious face I could conjure up.

"Okay, pizza," he said, grinning, yet slightly defeated.

"What's your favorite summer job?" I asked.

"Umpiring," he answered quickly.

"Okay, what do you want to be when you grow up?" I continued.

"Okay, Jules, that one I really don't know. You know that. Skip," he pleaded.

"Okay, fine," I said. "I'll answer for you—a famous musician."

He was smiling and shaking his head when he looked up at me.

I continued.

"What's a hobby not many people know you have?" I asked.

"Uh...playing guitar, I guess," he said.

Who are you going to marry?" I rambled off quickly.

"You," he answered without missing a beat.

I stopped suddenly. My expression went from almost blank to a wild smile in a matter of a simple second.

"Really?" I asked, just wanting to hear him say it again.

He smiled wildly also. "That surprises you?" he asked. "I've only asked you out every day I've known you."

"I know, but I guess I just didn't really think that far ahead," I said, smiling softly and bringing my legs to a bent position, halfway up the hood of his SUV.

"You really want to marry me?" I asked.

"Of course I do. Well, if that's okay with you?" he asked sheepishly.

I smiled a happy smile as I pressed my head against his muscular chest. I could smell the cologne that lingered on his tee shirt. It had become both a welcoming and comforting scent. It was attractive and familiar all at the same time.

"You want to grow old and wrinkly with me?" I asked.

"Maybe old, but not wrinkly," he said back. I could tell he was smiling.

I wore my best half-smile and squinted my eyes up at him.

"Oh, that's right. I was blessed with the good genes, so that means you'll have to grow wrinkly on your own," I retaliated as I gently pinched his side.

Laughing, he squirmed slightly and then pulled me closer to him. And for a moment, neither of us said anything.

Then, I breathed in the subtle smell of wild flowers as I slowly leaned back against the windshield again. Thousands of fireflies flickered in the deep ebony, open fields around us, while what seemed like a billion stars extended from the highest point of the night sky to the tip of the shadowy tree line.

"Do you remember the first time we officially met?" Will asked, breaking the peaceful silence.

I thought hard, staring up into the endless sky, almost as if searching for the answer there.

"Was it the first day of school?" I asked finally.

"Yes," he said confidently.

"Do you remember what you were doing?" he asked.

"Umm…no, I don't think I do," I replied, shaking my head.

"You were trying to get your duffle bag into your locker, and you were struggling so much that a book fell from your arms and hit your bare toes," he said.

"You were watching me?" I asked with a surprised smile lighting up my face.

"I noticed you," he said. "I don't know how I couldn't have. You were making such a fuss."

I laughed. "Why didn't you offer to help?"

"You looked too cute to interfere," he said. "Your nose was all scrunched up and your eyes were closed so tight."

"Oh gosh," I groaned. "That was your first impression of me?"

"Yes, and it was then I knew I wanted you," he said, smiling softly.

"Right," I said. "I'm sure that was the defining moment."

"It was," he confessed.

"You really are beautiful, you know," he said next, as his eyes returned to the heavens' sea of stars.

I smiled wider, surrendering to another warm breeze gently pushing across my face.

"You're not so bad yourself," I teased as I glanced up at him again before refocusing my attention too on the night's sky.

Moments went by before either of us spoke again. It was I who finally, yet reluctantly, punctured the quiet with my find.

"Look, a shooting star," I exclaimed, pointing to the vast west sky above, unable to control my excitement.

"Make a wish," I said as I quickly shut my eyes, causing my nose to rumple and forcing a happy grin to my face yet again.

Then, I peeked out of one eye for a second to see Will following my lead. His eyes were closed tightly also. I was happy he had played along. He wasn't exactly the make-a-wish-on-a-star type, like I had been raised to be.

I held my eyes clinched together until I recited a wish in my head and then looked back at Will. He was just opening his eyelids as well.

"What did you wish for?" I asked.

Will turned on his side and faced me. The moon was almost full, and the light reflecting off of it lit up his face just enough to make those blue eyes of his subtly visible. He really was gorgeous–the kind of subtle gorgeous that you found once you ripped away a childhood of rock-throwing, the kind of familiar gorgeous that could make you melt if you weren't too careful. And his smile–that was his secret weapon. It had always been–even if I had never let him know that I had thought so. I was pretty sure he could solve all of the world's problems with just that one, sweet smile of his.

I watched his eyes make a line from my lips to my eyes. Then, in one gentle motion, he carefully tucked the few blond strands of my long curly locks that had lain to rest on my cheekbone behind my ear. His soft touch attracted my full attention.

He paused then for a couple more seconds, presenting me with just enough time to take everything–his sultry lips, his warm, blue eyes, his seductive smile–and bottle it all up, for safe keeping, of course. Then, as if there were no turning back at that moment, our eyes met, and he leaned closer, and hovered over my lips. My heart pounded, and the now, welcomed butterflies flocked in by the millions. But this time, there was no lanky boy to interrupt them.

I felt his lips finally meet mine, and I surrendered to his soft, gentle kiss.

I smiled when his lips eventually withdrew from mine. My heart continued to pound as he kept his piercing blue eyes on me. He seemed to be taking in my joy, just as I was taking in his. I probably could have run a marathon right then and still have been standing at the end, smiling and unfazed.

"You gonna be my butterfly forever?" he asked me then, softly, almost a whisper—his voice raspy, but comforting.

"Your butterfly?" I whispered, smiling, though a little confused.

"Yeah, you're as beautiful as a butterfly. C'mon, you know you want to be," he playfully coaxed.

I laughed gently.

"Well, you've never asked it that way," I softly whispered. I was thankful that he probably couldn't see me blushing.

"Does that mean *yes*?" he asked, grinning.

I paused for a moment.

I felt his hand take my hand as he intertwined his fingers with mine. I surprisingly loved the way my hand felt in his—loved and safe.

"That means *yes*," I softly confessed, allowing a smile to span across my face.

"That's what I've waited my whole life to hear," he said, smiling, as he kissed my forehead and then retook his place beside me.

We returned to unreserved silence then, as if emptying our souls without a word. It was funny how the same lips that had always incited so much speech—usually scolding—could also take it away so effortlessly. And now, with the silence, I couldn't help but replay the previous set of moments in my mind over and over again—as if confirming their reality, as if verifying that it was, in fact, Will Stephens sitting beside me, the same Will Stephens who had been just another menacing boy a week ago—before I turned back toward him.

Yep, it was him—the same guy. He looked so different now.

"You still never told me what you wished for," I whispered into his ear.

He turned and faced me again.

"Well, since it came true, I guess I can tell you. That is how it goes, right?" he playfully asked.

"Of course," I whispered, nodding confidently.

"Well then, I wished for my first kiss—but only if it could be with you," he went on.

I refused to say anything then, as if a word would force us into the next moment, and I had no desire to do that. It surprised me at how much I wanted to inhabit our most recent minutes together and rerun his last words on a continuous loop for the rest of my days. Had I really fallen for Will Stephens?

Bringing our locked hands closer to my lips, I kissed the back of his hand and then positioned it so that it softly touched my cheek.

Will's eyes met mine then.

"What did you wish for?" he asked softly, curiously.

"I can't tell you. Mine hasn't come true yet," I confessed with a mischievous smile.

Will chuckled and kissed my lips again.

"Will you tell me what it is when it does?" he asked, after unlocking his lips from mine.

I thought for a moment.

"Yes," I softly said, smiling and gently biting my bottom lip.

"You promise?" he asked.

"I promise," I assured him.

He shook his head, as if satisfied with my vow.

"Jules," he whispered.

"Mm hmm?" I softly asked.

"I'm glad you finally said *yes*," he whispered again.

"Me too," I said.

"It was worth the wait," he said, smiling up into the heavens.

Masked Hero

Rachel and I arrived at Will's house in my jeep at five after nine. The sun was well on its way to making its exit from the world that day, and though it was still barely daylight outside, it would only be a matter of maybe minutes before the sky was completely swallowed by darkness.

"So, you have no idea what they're up to this time?" Rachel questioned me when we pulled into Will's driveway.

"No idea. Your guess is as good as mine," I replied as I slid the jeep into park.

"You guys are late," I heard Will protest just then, while marching vehemently around the corner of the back porch with a duffle bag slung over one shoulder. His two buddies followed close behind him.

I hadn't even had the chance to reach for my door handle before the boys closed in on my vehicle in a single-file line.

"What?" I questioned and then laughed. "It's only five minutes."

The three guys' faces screamed seriousness, well, except for one. One was giving everything he had not to smile, but in the end, wasn't being very successful at it. Though, all three of them looked very much like they had a job to do, and by the way it seemed, it was no doubt of an urgent matter.

"You got the camera?" Will questioned me.

"Yeah, I brought it," I said, trying my best to hold in my giggles.

"Good, you two are our press tonight." Will exclaimed, now smiling, as he threw the duffle bag into the back of the SUV.

Then, Will and the other two boys climbed over the jeep's sides and squeezed tightly into the backseat.

I watched them through my rearview mirror.

"Wow, you guys all fit back there?" I remarked, surprised.

The army of severe faces just stared back at me in silence.

"Okay, where am I going?" I asked, shrugging off their glares.

"To the windmill," Will announced, sounding very much like he was on a vital, secret mission.

The windmill?

Of course, I knew what he was talking about and where it was. Everyone did. At the edge of town was this huge, old windmill that hadn't been in use for as long as we'd been alive. What I didn't know was why we were going there.

I glanced over my right shoulder so that I could see the three boys now stuffed into my backseat like a Polish sausage in its casing. My puzzled expression did nothing to deter the boys' looming smirks across their mischievous guises. I turned around again and teasingly glared at Rachel, hoping by some sixth sense that she had come up with some answers in the last couple minutes, but Rachel only shrugged her shoulders and slowly shook her head back and forth.

"Don't look at me," Rachel demanded. "I'm only along for the ride–and maybe to save you from whatever mess these boys might put you into tonight."

I smiled and peered again at the boys through my rearview mirror as I slid the jeep into reverse.

"You guys better stay out of trouble tonight," I playfully said as I eased the SUV into drive and pulled out of the driveway.

"Don't worry, even if we don't, at least Spider-Man will save you," the half-smiling boy spilled to me as he tried desperately to wipe the devilish smirk off his face.

Will elbowed his chatty friend next to him.

"What does that mean?" I, now more confused than comforted, questioned the boy.

"Never mind him, Jules. Let's just get to the windmill," Will exclaimed, sending a stern glare in the direction of his blabbering partner in crime.

I shook off the boy's bizarre comment and continued down the street. In less than ten minutes, we arrived at the windmill located at the southeastern edge of town. The area was mostly unlit except for the little bits of moonlight that, by now, peeked through the passing clouds every once in a while. A small, chain-linked fence that wrapped around the windmill's base only promised to minimally ward off trespassers. The barrier standing four feet tall was the only thing that worked to separate us from the thirty-something-foot wind contraption.

As the jeep neared a narrow driveway, almost completely obscured by weeds, I tapped my brakes and slowly eased into the tiny, white-graveled area and brought the jeep to rest facing the windmill.

"Okay, now what?" Rachel asked, as she turned around to see the boys.

"Now, it's time," Will's friend said as he and the other boy spontaneously flung their legs over the sides of the jeep and hit the ground running, leaving Will behind.

"They are having way too much fun with this, Jules." Rachel said, half-seriously, and turning back toward me.

"I know, but we're bound to find out what this is all about soon, right?" I asked her.

"Let's just leave 'em and go get some ice cream," Rachel whispered.

"I can still hear you, Rachel," Will said, smiling from the backseat.

Rachel stared at me with eyes that looked like she had just gotten caught with her hand in the brownie batter. Her face made me burst into laughter, and soon both of us were giggling contagiously.

In the meantime, Will had evidently set out to put his plan into motion. Reaching into the back of the SUV, he grabbed the duffle bag, walked to the back of the jeep and dropped the bag so that the rays of the taillights made it ever so visible in our dark surroundings. Then, he marched toward the tall, once-wind-powered structure and scaled the fence, as his buddies looked on from the outside.

"Turn your lights off, Jules, and grab your camera," Will shouted to me. I was still sitting in the driver's seat next to Rachel, still giggling at the sight of the three, severe-looking boys taking immediate charge of the still mysterious situation.

"When are you going to fill Rachel and me in on this little conspiracy of yours?" I shouted back to Will as I switched off my lights and then turned off the SUV.

Seconds went by with no answer, and soon it became painstakingly evident that my question had fallen into the Great Abyss. I looked at Rachel, and then, as if we both had simultaneously surrendered, I begrudgingly grabbed the camera from my center console, and we both pushed open each of our doors and slowly made our way to the boys, now standing on the opposite side of the fence, next to the base of the metal-framed tower.

"Okay, you ready?" Will's friend asked, nudging Will's arm.

"Almost," Will said. He was staring at the duffle bag just barely visible in the moonlight behind the jeep as he answered.

"Ready for what?" I asked innocently.

We were just arriving with our so-called press materials when Will leapt back over the four-foot fence and darted toward the jeep again. I wanted to ask more questions, yet I suspected that they too would inevitably fall to the unforgiving ground beneath us. And at this point, I wasn't even exactly sure if I wanted to know the answers anyway. Instead, I remained silent, resolving to figure the rest of the mystery out on my own, as my eyes followed Will's path back to the jeep until he finally disappeared from my sight.

"Boys, seriously, at least tell me how long this is going to take," Rachel questioned impatiently. "I'm leaving for this trip to my grandmother's tomorrow, and I haven't packed yet–not like there's anything to pack. It's not like there's going to be anything to do there or anyone to impress…"

"Rachel," I softly whispered, elbowing her arm and interrupting what seemed like it was going to be an endless soliloquy.

I was staring at Will–or what had been Will moments ago.

In the moonlight, we all witnessed something straight out of the comic books. In spandex from head to toe, Will emerged from the darkness wearing a red and blue, webbed suit, complete with a spider-eyed mask. In seconds, Will had become none other than Spider-Man.

"Will, what are you going to do," I asked somewhat concerned, while trying to hold back wanting to laugh.

As I questioned Will, I watched the other two boys taking their positions on the other side of the fence. Spider-Man too soon followed, easily swinging his long legs over the barricade and landing on the other side as well.

"Will Stephens! You are not climbing that windmill," I scolded him as his scheme became more and more evident to me.

"Are you crazy, Jules? I'm not going to climb it," he said with a crooked smile as he motioned to his friends.

The boys hoisted Will to where he was just off of the ground, and Will grabbed a hold of a rusty, metal bar that connected the windmill's two, horizontal legs.

"Okay, Jules, you can take the picture now," Will shouted down from his perch. "And Rachel, watch for cops, will ya?"

My gaze went directly to Rachel, who rolled her eyes.

"Hey, like I said, I'm just an innocent bystander. You kidnapped me from my home thirty minutes ago. I'm seeing nothing, and when you drop me off at home tonight, I will have seen nothing," Rachel replied, smiling back at my questioning look. "How would I explain this anyway?"

I laughed at Rachel's remark and turned my eyes back onto my boyfriend illegally climbing a big windmill for no real, apparent reason.

"You look ridiculous," I said to Will as I playfully surrendered, reached for the camera in my jacket's pocket and aimed the lens toward Spider-Man. "Let's just get this over with."

I snapped several photos before Rachel's shrill frightened me, causing me to fumble the camera.

"I see lights. Someone's coming," Rachel shouted up at Will.

All eyes, including Will's, jetted toward the lights inching down the all-but-abandoned road as instant panic set in.

The old windmill sat secluded almost five miles down a deserted, gravel path. There were no other paths leading out except for the one that we had come in on, and we would have to hurry if we wanted any chance at escaping without detection.

"Will, get down," I shouted, turning my camera off and shoving it back into my jacket pocket.

Rachel quickly took off toward the jeep, while Will jumped from the boys' hold and off the metal frame. Within seconds, the two boys had scaled the four-foot fence and were darting toward the SUV as well. Rachel was already in the driver's seat, shouting at everyone else to get into the car by the time Will's buddies made it to the jeep. One boy grabbed the duffle bag sitting on the ground behind the SUV and jumped into the backseat after the other. Then, Will scaled the fence, grabbed my hand, and together we ran to our get-away car.

"Wait, Jules, my tennis shoes," Will said aloud. "Keep running. I'll go get them."

Within seconds, he had let go of my hand and was darting toward the back of the jeep, leaving me behind.

But before I could even realize what was happening, a sharp pain raced through my ankle, causing me to fall into a disheveled ball to the ground.

"Will," I screamed, grabbing my ankle.

"Jules," Will shouted as he paused at the jeep's door, shoes in hand. He had to have been able to see me. The jeep's lights were, by now, blinding me, adding to my misery.

"Go," Will shouted to Rachel through his mask, throwing his shoes into the back of the jeep. "Come back and get us in an hour."

"I can't leave you guys here," Rachel protested. "What if it's a crazy trucker and this turns into a horror movie?"

Will paused.

"You're watching too many movies. It'll be okay. We'll be fine. Now go," I heard Will say again quickly, as he tapped the jeep's hood and jetted back toward me.

Rachel glanced toward the lights in the distance and reluctantly put the car into reverse and then drive and peeled out of the rock-mixed-with-dirt, makeshift parking lot. And within seconds, she and the two boys were on the open road and out of sight.

When Will reached me, he scooped me up into his arms and hurriedly carried me over a raised piece of land on the far side of the tower, away from the gravel road. He laid me down on the ground, resting my back up against the dirt and grass-filled hill. Then, he found a place next to me.

"What happened?" Will asked, after he had successfully sheltered us from detection.

I squinted as I repositioned my foot and then turned my face toward him. Through my throbbing pain, I bore an awkward smile. I couldn't help not to.

"I stepped in a hole," I said, groaning. "I think I rolled it or sprained it or something."

Will grabbed a rock about the size of a bowling ball and gently lifted my foot onto it.

"This should help. Try not to move it for now. Does it feel like it's broken?" he asked.

"No, it's not broken. I'll be fine," I answered him, wincing.

The sound of tires rolling over loose gravel caused both of us to freeze then. Will turned onto his stomach and peered over the short levee and through its tall, swaying grasses, like he was in some kind of war movie. The clouds had completely covered the moon, and now, the only things visible were the rays of the mysterious car's two lights. I watched them creep slowly against the backdrop of the tall grasses. I lay against the warm soil with my back to the suspenseful scene, still frozen in my place, wishing I could see what was happening, my heart pounding.

Seconds drew out until I could no longer hear the gravel crunching underneath the tires' weight.

"Will, who is it?" I whispered nervously.

"I think it's Brian," Will whispered back.

"It had to be him working tonight, didn't it?" I whispered. "I still think he missed his calling as Oscar the Grouch's puppeteer."

Will's eyes stayed on the stalled car for an agonizing minute before the gravel began to give way again under the pressure of the patrol car's tires. Then, Will let out a sigh of relief.

"Red taillights," he exclaimed.

"Well, I think we might have just evaded danger once again, Mary Jane," Will, now almost giddy and, I'm sure, full of adrenaline, announced as he met my eyes.

I relaxed my head back against the grassy earth again.

"My hero," I said sarcastically, smiling and letting out an enormous sigh of relief also.

I felt exhausted and in pain, yet full of life, all at the same time.

"How is it that you climbed up and down that old windmill and cleared a chain-linked fence twice as I watched from the safe ground below, and now I'm the one who winds up injured?" I asked.

"Why, I'm Spider-Man, honey," Will said, while making himself comfortable on the soft, grassy ground beside me.

I laughed and rolled my eyes. I somehow found him utterly irresistible in that moment, even in his one-piece, full-body, spandex suit, still complete with its webbed mask.

"You know, Mary Jane got to kiss Spider-Man after he saved her," I reminded Will.

"Well, then, my damsel in distress, I must get a kiss," Will proclaimed, pulling off his face mask and leaning over me.

I raised my head and touched my lips to his. For a moment, I reveled in the feel of his unrivaled kiss. And butterflies welled up in my stomach as he eventually withdrew his lips from mine and gently kissed my forehead. Heaven must come with sprained ankles, I caught myself thinking.

Will was a great kisser. His lips were tender and soft and knew just how to fit perfectly against mine. I loved the way his kisses made me feel–like I was the only girl in the world that could complete him. And even while hiding from the law and lying in a dirt-filled ditch with a throbbing ankle positioned on a hard, rough rock, Will still managed, somehow, to make me feel safe and beautiful and happy.

"You know this was my plan all along–to get you alone tonight," Will announced proudly.

I turned my head toward him.

"This was your plan?" I questioned him, smiling. "You're plan was that we would come as close as possible to getting arrested, that I would twist my ankle and our friends would leave us out in the middle of nowhere? That was your plan?"

"Well, when you put it that way, that wasn't it exactly, but I still have you here next to me," he said sheepishly, sending a coy wink my way.

I laughed.

"I love your laugh, Jules," Will said, a little more seriously now.

"I love yours too, Spider-Man," I said back to him, still smiling.

"We're going to spend the rest of our lives like this, you know?" Will informed me then.

I looked at the dirt and grass stains pressed deep into my tank top and shorts and then at my leg propped up on the dirty rock at my feet.

"Oh, God, is this all I can hope for?" I asked as sarcastically as I possibly could.

Will hovered over me, smiling coyly.

"What do they call your kind?" he playfully asked. "Is it hopeless romantic?"

I looked into his beautiful blue eyes and smiled wildly as he continued.

"I meant, I want to spend the rest of my life under the stars, surrounded by life and everything that comes with it–twisted ankles, close calls, tree frogs and all– beside you, through it all," he said sincerely.

I could tell by his voice that he wasn't joking this time. And I was speechless. He was the songwriter for a reason. I was just his speechless muse.

"Will Stephens, I wouldn't want to be anywhere else with anyone else but you tonight. And when you put a ring on this finger, I will consider myself the luckiest girl in the whole, wide world," I said happily.

Will paused then, and his eyes found mine.

"Are you feeling lucky tonight?" he asked me, exposing his bright, wide smile.

"What?" I asked, giggling and a little thrown off-guard.

I watched him spin around and start gathering things from the ground behind me.

"Will, what on earth are you doing?" I questioned him, unable to see for myself.

"One second, my love," he reassured me.

He continued to fidget with something beyond my view.

"Okay, close your eyes," he said finally.

"Why?" I lightly protested.

"Trust me," he said.

I reluctantly closed my eyes, heard some rustling and then heard him speak.

"Okay, open," he said.

I opened my eyes to him kneeling beside me, a braided grass ring in his hands.

"What is…," I started.

"Jules, will you marry me…someday?" he asked, before I could finish.

He looked so sweet and innocent, and beautiful, with his dark curls shooting up every which way–the result of his head being pressed against the grassy ground just moments before.

I giggled happy giggles.

"Yes, Will, I will marry you…someday," I said, grinning from ear to ear.

Then, he slid the ring onto my left hand and kissed my forehead.

Just then, the ground in front of us was illuminated– this time, by another set of headlights.

Will turned and peered over the embankment. I held my breath until he looked back at me smiling.

"Our carriage awaits, My Future Mrs. Spider-Man," he announced happily.

Will stood up, brushed the dirt off of his spandex suit and helped me to my feet–or one, good foot, at least. And in one, solid motion, he scooped me up into his arms and made his way toward the lights.

The two boys in the backseat welcomed us with cheers and shouts.

"We thought the police had picked you up," one of the boys bellowed out.

I lightheartedly rolled my eyes as Will glanced at me and smiled.

"Not this time, boys," Will said.

He then set me gently into the passenger's seat next to Rachel, and then he too jumped into the backseat with his two buddies. When they were all tightly packed into the back of the jeep again, Rachel once again put the SUV into reverse and then drive and headed back down the gravel road toward town, leaving the site of the previous hour's commotion in the dust.

Two days later, I hobbled down the wooden stairs of my parents' rural route home. Will had rewrapped my ankle with bandages the night before, and I managed to get around fairly easily on it now.

Making my way to the kitchen, I spotted the weekly newspaper sitting as usual on the table. I glanced at it, looked away briefly, but then something caused me to take a second look. A photo had caught my eye.

I snatched up the ink-filled weekly as my eyes went directly to the image plastered on the front page below the fold and then raced over the words in the snapshot's caption:

Spider-Man makes his way up what is believed to be the old windmill southwest of town earlier this week. An anonymous source dropped this photo off at the Journal's offices Monday morning. So far, no one has come forward with leads as to who might be the man or woman behind the mask of the town's elusive hero. For now, we can only rest assured that New Milford is a little safer knowing that Spider-Man is in our midst.

I laughed out loud, unable to conceal my all-knowing smile.

So this was his scheme all along, my eyes now returning to the photo.

"What is it?" my dad asked me, walking into the room and interrupting my thoughts.

I jumped slightly.

I watched him make his way to the refrigerator, grab the orange juice, set it down onto the kitchen table and then face me, waiting for my reply.

I hesitated as my eyes feverishly darted to the photo again. It could be anyone up there. He'd never know, or at least, a girl could hope anyway.

"Did you see the front page today?" I asked in answer to his question.

"No, what's on it?" he asked, reaching in my direction.

I reluctantly handed him the newspaper, face up, then watched his features for his reaction. I could see his eyes widen as a gaping smile broke across his face.

"Well, I'll be. That's Spider-Man all right," he said, cracking a full smile.

He read the caption, and then I watched as his eyes returned to the photo again. He snickered some more and then continued.

"Crazy nut. Well, that's one way to get more dates. He might not be my hero, but I bet he's somebody's," he said, chuckling and winking an eye in my direction.

Oh, God, did he know?

He handed me back the newspaper and shuffled toward the toaster resting on the countertop at the other end of the kitchen.

Well, if he did know, at least he was going to let it go. I sighed a sigh of relief, and then I held the paper in front of me once again—my grass ring in view—and got lost one last time in its front page image and in the night I hoped I'd never forget.

Moments went by, and the memory just kept replaying itself in my head. And before I knew it, I was smiling like a goofy, little kid, lost in my own little world, until my dad's words from across the room suddenly jerked me back to reality again:

"By the way, you never told me what you did to that ankle of yours."

Snow Globe

I left Will wrestling with the patchwork quilt as I ventured to the edge of the bluff. I could see downtown beginning to come to life like someone had just shaken the summer version of a tiny snow globe. Little street lights were illuminating miniature figures that were making their way around the old, red-brick buildings and paved streets. Only this time, instead of the mini people donning tiny, wool coats, they wore shorts and tee shirts, and freshly cut grass took the place of fake snow, devouring the ground where the mini people walked. I wondered for a second if I shook it up, would grass fly everywhere?

Between a set of railroad tracks and the muddy Missouri River, a life existed—one of a more mature nature, if you will. Only several shops constituted New Milford's downtown—a dime store, a tiny, one-room movie theater, the post office, a bait shop and a restaurant that changed hands every so often. They were the lucky ones—the only businesses that had survived a levee break in the last flood.

A freshly red-painted train caboose had, for decades now, made its home on a green, little patch of the world outside of the one-room post office. Every small town that I had ever been to had had a caboose. It was as common as a water tower adorned with the high school's mascot or a lumberyard in the center of town, I guess. Although, now that I was thinking about it, the caboose did seem a little odd. What purpose did it serve—or was it just for decoration? Did the elders of all small towns really think it was ornamental—like a welcome sign or flowers? *Welcome to New Milford. Can I interest you in a photo next to our caboose?*

My forehead wrinkled slightly as I pondered to myself the great questions of modern times before my eyes left the caboose for more grass-globe images.

My gaze rested on a spot on the levee. Park benches and a small, white gazebo sat overlooking the river, begging passersby to pause from the world for a moment—to take in the way the current pushed its way south or the oaks that swayed in the wind on bluffs far off in the distance. The levee had always been my beach, the world beyond it, my ocean. That's as close as it got here, anyway. No waves, no dolphins, no white sand, no sea gulls. If you were lucky enough, though, every once in a while you did get to see a crane, or a beaver.

A smile crossed my lips. If you could be so lucky, I thought as I took one last look at the world below my high perch before making my way back over to Will.

I could hear the crickets and tree frogs starting their night song in the small, wooded area behind us. A faint smell of lilac filled the air. There was always lilac in this part of town. Where there were grandmothers, there was always lilac. And by now, a blanket of darkness had just swallowed up the sky, capturing us in its shadowy web.

"You need help there, chief?" I asked Will, as I avoided a small tree branch strewn across my path.

"Now, you ask, after all the work's done as usual, my dear," he playfully answered.

I paused and smiled at him.

"Get over here," he demanded with a grin.

I took a couple more careful steps and slid down onto the patchwork quilt spread out over the dirt and grass below it. Will scooped me into his arms and together we fell back onto the blanketed earth.

"How much longer do we have?" I asked him.

"Oh, probably about a couple more minutes," he replied, squeezing me closer to him.

"Sing to me then," I pleaded happily.

"What do you want me to sing?" he asked.

"One about us," I said.

We were both on our backs. My head was resting against his chest. I could hear his heartbeats.

"Okay then," he softly said.

There was a slight pause before he began, but when he did, his voice was almost a whisper–raspy and sultry– perfect.

Though you'd rather watch a sappy ending
Than a football game

And you're not very good at fleeing the scene
Without a sprain,
I wouldn't want it any other way
I'm yours forever, My Butterfly
So, looks like you're stuck with me
'Til the end of time."

I laughed.

"How romantic," I gushed sarcastically.

"I wrote it myself–just now–just for you," he said proudly.

"Thanks. I'll just do some creative interpreting, I guess," I joked and raised my head slightly off of his chest so that I could see his face. "But seriously, though, minus those passionate words, you can really get a girl's attention. You should sing, you know, for people, as a career. You've got a gift. You can't hide it forever."

"Why can't I?" Will bantered back, using his hand to nudge my head closer to his body again.

I followed his lead, and he kissed my forehead.

"Because someday, somewhere, somebody's gonna find out. Then what are you going to do?" I continued.

"Tell them I've got everything I need right here," he said, wrapping his arms around me.

I smiled wide and allowed his muscular arms to form around my body, though I was determined to get my point heard.

"Wouldn't it be a dream-come-true though?" I persisted. "Plus, you would be doing the world a severe injustice if you didn't."

Will lowered his face to mine and then brought his lips to my ear.

"Mine is a far simpler dream, my sweet Jules," he whispered in that sultry voice of his–the voice that only a year ago I wouldn't have heard the same way.

"See what I mean with that voice. I almost believed you," I said, laughing.

"Jules, trust me. My life's a dream already. I don't need to go chasin' something somewhere else," he said.

"But you're not at all attracted to the thrill of it all, the lights, the fans that would adore you?" I asked sincerely.

"Okay, okay, don't you think you're getting a little ahead of yourself?" he asked me, laughing softly. "Fans?"

"Well, you won me over, and I'm not easily convinced–you said that yourself," I reminded him.

"All right, my little Hollywood agent," he said, continuing to smile. "You're right, I've got you, and that's all the fan I ever wanted."

He softly kissed my lips, while someone went and let loose butterflies in my stomach again. He had won, and the butterflies were the sign to prove it. I was forced to surrender. I really didn't want to argue with him on that point.

I sighed–a content, happy sigh, as the first fireworks soared to our height over the muddy water below. Reds, whites and blues sprinkled the night sky and lit up the countering bluffs in the distance.

I could feel Will's hand caressing the strands of my long, blond hair now and laying each piece gently back down onto my shoulder.

"I love you, Jules," he softly said.

His words sounded like a love song in themselves– one that I had never heard before tonight. My heart raced, and little jolts of excited energy shot through my body faster than little squirrels upon realizing winter would come early and they hadn't gathered any nuts.

I followed the path to his lips and then met his eyes. I watched for a second as the red and white lights danced against the background of his blue irises.

"I love you too," I whispered back.

Then, I returned my head to his chest, listening to every heartbeat, as he squeezed me closer to his side, and I watched the lights dance in the night's sky—fully content with my happy, little, grass-globe world, caboose and all—praying those lights would dance forever.

Battling

 I plopped down onto the plush, beige chair in the living room of Will's basement. Will lay sprawled out lengthwise on a worn-in, auburn couch. The familiar video game controllers and cords, left abandoned, stretched across the cream-colored carpet in front of the entertainment center, and small, overstuffed pillows and colorful throws representing several different sports teams littered the chair and the couch that Will lay on.

"What are you up to?" I asked him as I made myself comfortable in the soft chair next to the couch.

Will remained quiet just long enough for me to sense that something was wrong, though I waited for him to speak first as I racked my brain trying to figure out what that something was.

"You didn't tell me that you were going away," Will finally said, accusingly.

"Away? What do you mean?" I asked. I had a slight smirk on my face. *Away* seemed so vague. It almost sounded criminal–or worse.

"I know you applied to Missouri," he charged.

"And?" I punched back, though I knew I would have more explaining to do later. I knew he would never settle for that answer.

"It's hours away, Julia," Will said sternly. "There's several good schools right down the road."

I paused for a moment, mostly to hold back my disdain for his disdain.

"Will, they're hardly just down the road," I protested. "And Missouri's a good school for me, you know that."

Will remained silent and used the remote to flip through the television channels rhythmically. I watched him continuously press the channel button, not even bothering to see what was on each one, while he stared expressionlessly into the TV's screen.

I moved over to the couch and took a seat on the piece of plush surface near Will's stomach that had not been taken up by his tall, muscular figure. I swiveled around so that I faced him and then gently took the remote from his hand, muted the TV and set the remote down onto the surface of the coffee table.

Taking away his distractive device was easy. Getting his full attention proved harder. His stare remained plastered to the screen.

"I didn't tell you because I'm not even sure that I'll even get in and because I wanted to avoid this," I said, opening up my hand and pointing it face up toward him.

It wasn't the real reason, and I knew I should have told him, but he, now, had given me a temporary leg on which to stand, so I stood my ground. Who was he to say where I could go to school?

"Avoid what? Me being a part of your life?" Will asked sternly. "Don't I get a say in anything? Does it matter where I want you to go?"

Confused by his line of questioning, I paused to evaluate the conversation and to manage the mercury in my anger thermometer, which by now, was rising quickly to *boiling*, before continuing.

"Will, I'm sorry that I didn't tell you, but at the same time, I should not have to ask you where I can and cannot apply to schools," I protested.

There was a slight pause.

"Well, if you're going to leave anyway, then what's the point of us staying together? We should just end it now," Will said coldly, still glaring into the muted television screen.

His cold words struck me hard and right to the heart. Sure, we had argued before–mostly about silly, little things like what time certain stores closed or how long it took to get to some places or what the real words were to certain songs, but this was different. I had never heard him hint at giving up on us before, and I had never heard words so cold come from the same lips that made me feel so loved.

"Will, you don't mean that," I softly demanded, growing more and more irritated with him.

I watched his eyes as they followed the figures dancing on the television set.

"Will," I said, demanding his attention.

His eyes made no movement toward mine. Furious, I grabbed my keys from the coffee table and made my way to the basement exit. I had nothing left to say, and even if I had, he was too stubborn right now to listen anyway.

When I reached the brass knob of the wooden storm door, I took one, last glance back at him. His eyes were still planted on the television's screen. I let out an angry sigh then, just before I pushed open the door and marched outside, letting the wooden entrance swing shut behind me.

Outside, the night sky had already blanketed the world, making everything pitch black, and the contrast between the bright, living room inside and the darkness outside at first shocked me, but in the end, did little to slow me down. Despite being blinded for several seconds while my eyes adjusted, I kept moving. I was livid by now, but there was still that crazy-person part of me that wanted him to follow after me. I wanted him to say he was sorry and hold me and make everything all better again, which I knew he had the power to do.

My heart stabbed at my chest when I reached my jeep, only to glance behind my shoulder and find that he wasn't there.

"Forget it," I whispered angrily under my breath.

I lifted the door handle, jumped into my jeep, swung my seat belt across my chest, heard it click and felt blindly for the key on my key chain that would start the ignition.

In the dark, my fingers shifted from one metal object to the next, feeling for the largest one with the rubber coating on top. While brazing over each key, I came to a strange, long piece of metal with what felt like a tiny hook at the end. When seconds went by and I could not so much as conjure up an image in my mind of what the object could be, I felt for the dome light above my head and switched it on.

"My luck," I whispered again as I gripped the steering wheel with both hands and laid my head against its rounded top, letting out an irritated sigh.

It had been a golf club attached to his set of keys—not mine.

Moments of dead silence allowed the argument to begin replaying in my mind again. He had been so selfish, so thoughtless. I hated his cold, cruel words, but they, at the same time, seemed so insincere. In fact, he almost looked scared. Could he have been just as terrified of me leaving as I was at the thought of leaving him? His words stung, but I knew that he had not meant them—could not have meant them.

Lost in my own meandering contemplations, I suddenly heard the front door of the house open, which forced my eyes to follow the sound.

Soon after, an outside light flickered on, and then I could see, standing in the doorway, Will, with a slight smile in his face that had been absent just moments before, holding up my set of keys.

I tried to hold back my own smile as he sauntered toward me, his eyes seductively piercing me. He had made me angry. I had to show him that.

His lips finally burst into a full grin as he edged closer and saw my own frustration uncontrollably waning.

After closing in on my jeep, he opened my door, unbuckled my seat belt and took my hand. I willingly stepped out of the driver's seat, planted my feet on the street along the curb and leaned my back up against the side of the vehicle. I watched him as he gently closed the door and pulled me closer to him.

"I'm sorry," he whispered into my ear. "I love you more than the world itself, and I can't imagine life without you."

He paused, kissed my forehead and put his lips to my ear again.

"You'll get in, and I'll be happy for you. And we'll find a way to be together—no matter what. If I have to sing songs on the sidewalks of New Milford to get to you, I'll do it," he said, softly laughing.

An overwhelming feeling of love overtook me then. It was as if he alone held the keys to my sanity and my safety and my happiness, and he had just used them to give me life again. So much for showing him that I was angry.

"I'm sorry too," I whispered back. "I should have told you. But let's not fight anymore. I love you," I said, nestling my head into his broad, muscular chest.

And in those three words, I felt like I understood then that life would not always automatically generate a perfect puzzle joined together by fireworks and fireflies. And though I had hoped that we would not fight like that again, I ultimately knew that life would not be that easy on us. Some jagged pieces that didn't seem to quite fit together were always going to be in the box—this, I somehow knew. But what is a puzzle without the hard to fit pieces? Why would people even bother to put it together without the challenge and the excitement in seeing the image slowly become one, united likeness? In the end, I had to believe that when all of the pieces were touching, they would leave behind a beautiful depiction of life. And I knew that if Will and I could somehow find a way to be together in the final act that we would always find a way to combine the jagged pieces to construct a beautiful ending. I held tightly to this assumption as I surrendered to his gentle embrace and hoped in his promise.

"Jules, we're gonna grow old and wrinkly together, you know that, right?" Will softly whispered into my ear.

I smiled as he squeezed me tighter and seemed to take in the flowery scent of my hair.

"I know," I whispered.

Chasing Fires

"Hey, good lookin'," Will called out as he snuck up behind me, took the couple of books from my hands and put his arm around my waist.

I jumped slightly, but quickly recovered when I realized who it was.

"Hey," I said, smiling. "You scared me."

"Just waking you up, my sweet Jules," he said in his sultry voice.

The voice was cheerful and comforting.

"I mean, today, it's calculus and physics, but tomorrow it's the presidency," he continued, giving me a wink.

I smiled at him coyly. Then, I grabbed my backpack and duffle bag, closed the jeep's door and turned toward the lingering figure towering over my much smaller frame.

"And are you prepared to be the First Gentleman yet?" I asked. A sarcastic smirk lingered on my lips.

"Sure, but only as long as I can turn the backyard into an eighteen-hole golf course. Oh, and I would like to be addressed as *Will, Will Stephens*," he said in his best James Bond impression.

"What?" I asked. I shook my head slowly and squinted my eyes for effect as I spoke.

"It's just one, measly, little golf course and one, measly, little name request. I don't think the American people would mind," he said with a mischievous half-smile. "Roosevelt got a zebra," he added.

My bewildered stare caught his.

"What?" he asked. "I was listening in history the other day."

I stared into his baby blues for a second longer before speaking.

"You're ridiculous," I said, smiling up at him.

Then I turned and started making my way to the small school building at the bottom of the hill. Will followed after me.

"Lady's first, my love," Will said as he suddenly reached in front of me and grabbed hold of the metal door with its two, tiny, glass windows. "I know you'll come to your senses eventually."

I faked a laugh and then walked through the tall doors.

It took me two tries to manipulate the latch that freed my sticky locker door from its base, but on the second try, the slender door popped open.

"You walking me to class today?" I asked Will as I slid a couple of textbooks onto the locker shelf above me and grabbed two others.

"Is today any different than any other day, Jules?" he asked rhetorically and in a voice that made him sound as if he were being put out.

"Of course," I said, chiming in on the opportunity. "Today is the day you realize that you can't possibly live without me," I said, grinning in his direction.

"I thought that was yesterday," he said, smiling back, pleased that he had beat me at my own game.

My grin grew as I shut the stubborn locker door and stepped toward Will three lockers down.

"Okay, let's get goin'. I've gotta stop by Coach's office before class too," Will said, taking the couple textbooks from my hands.

"Okay," I replied. "Why do you so urgently need to talk to him this morning?"

"I don't. He's got a cookie jar," he said, sounding as if I should have known. "You have so much to learn about life, my dear."

I rolled my eyes again as we set out down one of the two hallways that made up the small high school building. We reached the tiny classroom seconds later, and Will followed me in and set my books down onto a small lab table next to a life-size, plastic skeleton.

"Thank ya, hon," I said, smiling.

"Just remember. I want it to be eighteen holes, and maybe we can have a press conference, just so everyone knows how to say it. It's *Will, Will Stephens*. It doesn't have the same effect if it's not said right," he reiterated.

"Okay, 007," I said, humoring his ridiculousness.

"Oh, and have fun in your next quote, unquote class, otherwise known as study hall," Will jeered at me as he quickly kissed my cheek before the teacher in the front of the room could turn around. "I've got to quote, unquote, check some English answers after this hour," he said in a hushed tone, at the same time, making quotation marks with his fingers.

"Okay, my little scholar. I'll see you later," I said, smiling back at him.

"By the way, I've decided what I want to be when I grow up," he said before he turned to walk away.

His words came out so casually that I almost didn't notice he had said them at all.

"Really?" I asked, slightly delayed, and I'm sure looking somewhat shocked by his announcement.

"What?" I asked.

"A firefighter," he announced proudly.

"A firefighter?" I asked. Was he serious? Was he joking? I was trying to figure it out.

"Yeah, it just came to me last night when I was driving by the fire station," he said. "You know, I drive by that building every day and never think about it, but last night, I thought, I can do that. I could do that for the rest of my life and be happy."

He was smiling. He looked like a boy who had just won an all-day access pass to a theme park.

"You sure about this?" I asked him earnestly. My expression was as blank as the chalkboard in the front of the tiny classroom.

"Never been surer. Well, except when I met you," he said, sending a wink my way.

I paused for a second, while a smile resurfaced on what was my vacant face.

"That's great, honey. I'm really happy for you," I said, not being completely truthful. Though, I forced the corners of my mouth to turn up even so.

He smiled back at me as he turned to go.

"Wait," I said, stopping him. "Does this mean you get to wear those sexy firemen outfits?" I asked in a hushed tone, half-teasing, half-serious, trying not to show him my hesitations.

Will looked at me, still smiling, not completely surprised by my comment. Then, he nodded his head slowly in confirmation, while raising one eyebrow.

"Then, you've definitely got my vote," I said, smiling wider.

"Good, well I'm gonna be late. Don't let Mr. Bones over here sweet talk ya too much," he said, elbowing the life-size, plastic skeleton.

And then, he was gone.

My stare slowly faded from the doorway then and landed on a spot near the skeleton's ribs. Thoughts cascaded through my head–lots of thoughts, from all directions.

His news left a bitter-sweet taste in my mouth. Firefighters were heroes–I knew this. Everyone knew that. But at the same time, there were always costs. Costs I didn't even want to imagine.

My smile was fading when I noticed that I was still staring at Mr. Bones. I quickly turned my gaze down before anyone could misjudge my meandering thoughts for an odd obsession with the plastic figure.

Couldn't he have decided to be an accountant or a banker or a teacher or something safe like that–anything but a firefighter? Didn't he know how dangerous the job was or what it all entailed?

And sure, I was thrilled that he had found something he was passionate enough about to pursue as a career. He had fought the questions and pressures of classmates, teachers and the school's counselor about choosing a livelihood for so long now. It must have meant the world to him to have finally found his calling–his heart's desire. And he would be great at it. There was no doubt in my mind about that. He had always had that kind of connection with the community. Of course, camp counselor and little league umpire would never prove to be quite as dangerous, one would hope.

And what about college? I had always marveled at its intriguing nature–a new place, new faces, new experiences and most of all, independence. But then again, Will had never really bought into the whole college scene's allure either, I guess. He hadn't ever been too interested in anything new at all really. And when it came down to it, I guess, his choice was, after all, honorable and courageous, even if he didn't see it that way, and despite my own reservations, it wasn't, after all, my choice to make. And he had already planted his heart and had made up his mind, and there would be no changing it. I knew this much. Beyond that, he had been smiling–that little, goofy smile of his when he thinks all the world is right. That's what really mattered in the end.

I shuffled to a chair behind the lab table and fell into it.

He had been smiling, and now I was smiling again too thinking about him and his decision and my decision to support him–reservations or no reservations–because in the end, I knew that our lives were about to change. And I had already promised myself that I would spend the next several months bottling his smiles for safe keeping–for a time when they wouldn't be an arm's length away.

Remember

By Thursday morning, I had my worn-in jeep packed with the essentials–clothes, TV and CD player–and I was just about ready to set out on my new adventure when something in the distance caught my attention. While searching for an available space to stuff the last of my treasured possessions, I heard a car treading over gravel on the county road just up the hill. The sound caused me to look up from the dusty floorboard.

Through the leafy oak trees that lined the rock-covered path, I could see a red SUV kicking up sand-colored dust and gravel as it hurriedly made its way to the edge of my driveway. As a wave of excitement jetted through my body, I quickly found a tiny crevasse on the jeep's floor and squeezed the final duffle bag into the last available space inside the vehicle. Then, I brushed the strands of my hair that had fallen into my eyes away with the back of my hand and waited anxiously.

The SUV came to rest behind my jeep moments later, and the boy in black basketball shorts, a cut-off, red tee shirt and red and white tennis shoes stepped out and stood rigidly in front of me. His tee shirt made it possible for me to see his tan muscles protruding from his biceps, and I couldn't help myself from noticing that his calf muscles, left exposed where his basketball shorts stopped, were just as defined. I wondered for a second if he had planned his outfit especially for today, yet quickly tossed the idea out. Will didn't plan, and besides, this was his usual attire. Maybe I was just now realizing how much I was going to miss it, miss him.

Today, he also wore his favorite hat bearing a popular brand of golf clubs across the face of the cap's crown. I always thought the cap gave him a certain ruddy and handsome look that was completely irresistible. Today, as always, and even after three years, butterflies danced in my stomach as I watched his still figure watch me.

"You all packed?" he asked finally, through a half-smile.

"I think so," I said, taking a glance inside the jeep.

Will watched as I then took two tries to close the passenger's side door, leaning against it with all of my might.

"I told you you'd get in," he softly said.

I paused and smiled up at him.

"Well, we can't all make it into the fire academy," I said.

Will's eyes fell toward the dusty ground at his feet, and his cheeks turned a slight reddish color.

"I brought you something so you remember to remember me," he said.

He stood stiffly in front of his driver's side door, still facing me.

I gave him a gentle smile that froze into a half-smile as I spotted the sadness in his deep, azure eyes. My heart leapt out of my chest for him as I slowly made my way toward his motionless body. I never took my eyes off of his as I neared his figure, and when I was close enough to touch him, I swung my arms around his neck, brought his face down to mine and pressed my nose against his.

"How could I forget about you?" I asked. "If I forget about you, I've lost three of the happiest years of my life."

His lips gradually formed a smile, while his eyes lingered in mine for a long second. Then, he pulled away and reached inside his open window, grabbed an object from his passenger's seat and slid it in between our embrace.

I slowly pulled away from his warm body when I noticed the bright, orange-petal flowers resting in his hand. I smiled affectionately and reached out for the flowers' emerald stem, marveling at their beauty and the love that I knew was held within their petals.

"It's a butterfly weed," he softly said, releasing the flowers into my hands.

My stare was on the flowers.

"It's pretty for a weed. I've seen it before?" I asked.

"Yeah, along roads and in fields, pretty much everywhere around here. They keep cuttin' 'em down, but they always grow back. They never give up," he added softly but confidently.

I stared into the flowers' bright centers. I was smiling again.

He then kissed the part of my forehead where my hairline began as I happily examined my new bouquet and took in his words.

I could see now and even feel that the bloom's willowy stem wasn't soft or textured or even alive, but instead was mere plastic and its petals, silk. Will had given me plenty of flowers in the past–I admit that he had spoiled me. But none had been like this one.

As I stood quietly, tracing the flower's design and pondering his flower selection, I glimpsed a small, hand-written note attached to the flower's stem by a fine, white ribbon. I gently grasped the note in one hand and allowed my eyes to float over its hand-written words:

I'll love you until the last petal falls, Jules.

My heart instantly melted, and I immediately wrapped my arms around his neck again and kissed his lips. He was successfully chipping away at my brave, outer shell that I had miraculously crafted and had hidden behind throughout this whole leaving process. It had been the first time that I had seen him truly beside himself. The loneliness in his eyes made it seem as if he had already begun to miss me. I wanted to heal his abandoned expression. I was excited to start this new life, but now, all I wanted to do was hold him forever in my arms and never let him go.

"Do you know why they never give up?" Will asked me softly. He was looking down at the sandy-colored dust surrounding his restless feet.

I shook my head.

"No," I whispered.

Will paused for a moment and then met my eyes again.

"Because they want the butterflies to come back to them. They need each other to survive," he softly said.

My sad eyes, full of love, remained on his.

"Julia," he said again, almost in a whisper.

"Hmm," I replied. I could feel the waterfall welling up behind my eyes.

"You'll be my butterfly, right? You'll come back to me?" he asked sheepishly.

My eyes then filled with salty tears almost instantly as my own butterflies in my stomach fled my body and were replaced by an overwhelming flow of emotions springing up from my chest and resting at the base of my now aching throat. I wanted to tell him so much, but through my tear-filled eyes and racing mind, I could only manage to communicate one, complete, yet wholly honest thought.

"I love you, Will Stephens, and I'll never forget you. I'll be your butterfly. I'll always come back," I said.

Will held me tightly in his embrace, until my parents came out to say goodbye. I left Will's grip for an instant and wiped my tears with the back of my hand before hugging my mother and father. Then, I let Will walk me to the driver's side of my jeep one last time before I left home.

I pulled him close, and he gave me a kiss, and then he hesitantly opened my door and watched me climb into the driver's seat.

"Drive carefully, Jules, and call me when you get there," Will said, leaning into the driver's side to kiss me again.

"I love you," he said to me, with what I could tell was the best smile he had at the moment.

"I love you too," I said, giving him the best smile I had also, through my drying tears.

Then, I backed my SUV up and then slid the gear shaft into drive before stepping on the gas pedal and slowly making my way up the long, curving driveway. At the top of the path, immediately before the start of the county road, I tapped on the brakes and blew Will a kiss. Will spotted my familiar gesture through the passenger's side window, and like clockwork, put his fist up in the air to catch it. Then, I waved goodbye one last time and then bravely reset my focus on the county road in front of me. But no sooner had I got a half of a mile down the road, the sadness from the pit of my stomach welled up into my throat again, and the tears returned. The salty wetness gushed from my eyes as his figure grew smaller and smaller in my rearview mirror. My heart ached at the thought of him no longer being by my side to comfort me, and I missed him already, but I knew I had to go. This was the first step toward my dreams. I forced myself to think about my new adventure and the new things in store for me where I was going.

And I focused on rebuilding my hard, outer shell again, trying desperately to stop the tears that poured onto my now cherry-colored cheeks as I continued down the rocky path, my butterfly weed on the seat next to me.

College

College kept me busy, for the most part, and fairly quickly, but without knowing it, I had fallen into a pretty consistent routine that would ultimately involve me rushing home at the end of my day to call Will. I had decided very early on that this had become, by far, the best part of the routine. My happiest moment came when I heard his deep voice on the other end of the line for the first time since the night before. Just the sound of his sultry words sent butterflies racing through my stomach, and tonight was no exception. In fact, tonight, three years ago to the day, I had finally said *yes* to our first date.

"Jules," Will exclaimed.

"Hey, honey. Happy anniversary," I said, bursting with excitement.

"Happy anniversary to you too, babe," he said. "I really wish that I could be there with you right now."

"I know, me too, but I'll be home in two weeks, and we can celebrate it then. I promise," I said, trying to remain as optimistic as humanly possible.

"I still think that you should skip practice this weekend," he said, chuckling. "Who has practice on a Saturday anyway?"

"Crazy people who can tolerate running in circles just a little more than the average person," I playfully countered. "But if you skip your exam Saturday, I'll skip practice."

"Okay, you got me, but you better believe that two weeks from now I'm going to be about all the Jules-deprived I can possibly be and still be breathing, so you better get your cute butt out of Columbia as soon as you possibly can that day," Will playfully demanded.

I could tell that he was smiling on the other end of the phone.

"Don't worry. I've already got a list of things that I need to pack, so as soon as class is done, I can throw everything into a bag and head out the door," I informed him proudly.

"You and your lists," Will teased.

I laughed.

"That's why you love me, honey. You need an organized mess like me to keep your life together. How was your day, by the way? I never...," I started but then stopped.

"Hold on, Jules," Will said abruptly.

I could hear the dreaded set of tones ringing in the background through the receiver. The sound made my heart sink.

"Jules, I'm so sorry, but I've got to go. Can I call you later?" he asked.

I hesitated but then gave in.

"Sure," I said somberly–out of pure habit.

I realized, like many times before when those same set of tones went off, that a response of *sure* was my only option. I knew he had to answer the call. I knew someone else needed him more than I did at the moment, but I couldn't help but wish he didn't have to go. I had come to dread the high-pitched succession of tones that signified his district and that sent him scurrying for his keys and then out the door.

"Thanks, Jules. I love you. Bye," he rambled off hastily.

Before I could say goodbye as well, Will was gone, and the other end of the phone was dead.

Taking a deep breath and then slowing letting it out, I stared at a spot on the beige-colored wall in my dorm room, feeling defeated. Then, after a long minute, I set the phone down onto the bedside table beside me.

I understood his position. I understood what his job entailed–what his dream entailed. Yet a selfish part of me still wanted back that time when he didn't have to leave at a second's notice.

I sighed, lay down and pulled my covers up to my face. Rolling onto my side and curling up, I reached for my cell phone on the nightstand and brought it close to my chest. He would call me later, I knew, and I would be waiting. I might not hear the call, and on the slight chance I did, I probably wouldn't remember the conversation. Nevertheless, I would be waiting.

Shifting Paths

I pictured myself standing on one side of a cliff, and him on the other side, as I unconsciously scanned the words on a page in my textbook. I couldn't reach him, but I was trying. He was there. I could see him, but there was no way to get to him. In between us stood only two, towering walls of rock just far enough apart that a jump across the dark, bottomless cavern was surely not in either one of our best interests. But if I could only reach him, my world would be perfect again, I pleaded as the letters on the page blurred to unrecognizable blobs.

Though I had tried desperately to ignore the extra miles and the new, abbreviated visits and phone calls, I knew that my fears were slowly but surely catching up to me.

I saw the possible end a little more each day, and the more I thought about it, the more the thought pierced my heart. I ran the idea over in my mind, over and over again, yet I couldn't quite believe wholeheartedly that it truly was the end. Will had been my prince charming, my only desire. I had never pictured myself with anyone else, and I still could not. I felt desperately heartbroken and lost for the first time in the years that I had known him because, deep down, I knew, somehow, he had slowly faded away from sight in my rearview mirror–like the rest of my high school life. I wanted him back, and even though I believed that he continued to dwell in my heart somewhere, I also feared that quite possibly we had outgrown each other. Can you do that? Can you outgrow someone?

I felt lost in my racing thoughts at my small, dorm room desk when my cell phone burst to life.

Startled, I set my pencil down onto my economics textbook and glanced at the phone's screen. My eyes caught his name stretched across the display window, and my heart fluttered and then sank. I took a deep breath, and then I carefully pressed the small, emerald button. I both feared and knew what I had to do next.

"Hey," I said, sounding unusually heavy-burdened.

Despite my somber tone, Will started the evening conversation as usual.

"Hey. How was your day?" he asked.

"Same old, same old," I replied. "How was yours?"

"You know, pretty much the same too," he said but then paused.

"Is there something wrong, Jules?" Will asked.

The tone of his voice customary to our usual conversations had by now lost its luster too, and I cringed when his lukewarm words reached my ears.

I wondered for a moment if I should say it—say everything that I was thinking. Did I really want to? Was I prepared for where it might lead? I had no idea, but finally, I just bit the bullet and opened the floodgate.

"It's just that I feel like we've grown apart, and I know that sounds really cliché, but I don't know how else to say it," I gushed, without holding anything back.

I stopped, waiting for Will's response. It surprised me at how easily I had spit out the words, but what surprised me even more was that with the feeling of brokenness and uneasiness that followed also came a tremendous sensation of relief for having finally voiced my thoughts to him out loud. Nevertheless, I waited, hoping he could convince me that it was going to be okay and that we would make it, even though I feared that, this time, even he might not be able to convince me.

His sigh shattered my cascading thoughts.

A sigh?

His simple exhale was worse than a shot right to the heart. Instead, it was a white flag—as if he had just admitted defeat, had just given up on us—and half-heartedly at that.

"It hasn't been the same, has it?" he questioned me then. "I know it's been hard."

He sounded solemn and, at best, disconnected as the words fell out of his mouth. My heart sank further inside my chest. He knew too, I knew then. But what was it that I knew again exactly? What exactly had gone wrong?

"It has been hard," I softly agreed. I was motionless, stunned.

And then there was silence–until I couldn't take its deafening sound anymore.

"It's just that I've been busy with track, and you're doing your training, and when we do finally see each other, I feel like you aren't really even that excited, and…," I said, letting my words trail off.

Oh, gosh. I had said it. I had administered the first strike. I stopped and waited in terror for his rebuttal.

"Jules, I'm tired," he interrupted. "You don't have to answer to fire calls at two in the morning just to go back to bed and answer another one at five."

I jumped right in then without hesitating.

"You're right, I don't, and I understand that," I said slightly angered. The terror was melting into blind confidence. "But since you've been doing this, you never found a way to make it work. You never found even the tiniest bit of energy for me. Will, I may not be answering fire calls, but I'm working my butt off up here. Plus, I'm the one driving home to see you every month. You're never here. I feel like I'm the only one trying anymore."

"I try," he softly said.

"How, Will? How do you try?" I pleaded.

"I stay up and watch movies with you," he protested.

"First of all, you don't stay up. I know you're sleeping. Secondly, I don't want to always watch movies. I want to get dinner. I want to go dancing. I want to do things," I continued to plead.

"I have a job, Julia. You'll understand how that works someday," he said coldly.

My anger was hitting its peak.

"Really? Will, this has nothing to do with me going to school or you having a job, and you know it–and I can't do this anymore," I protested firmly.

The words just fell out of my mouth as if I only had this one, last chance to say everything. I kind of thought that I would feel liberated having said them, and I had, but that moment had come and gone. Now, I just sat there terrified—of my own words—not really sure if I even believed them myself.

Dead seconds went by and neither Will nor I said anything. Then, Will finally spoke.

"What does that mean for us?" he asked as straight-forward as a person could say those words.

His lack of passion stabbed my heart strings yet again and forced me to try out another set of words for the first time. I almost hoped, in a weird way, they would somehow salvage our past or, at the very least, fire up his fervor.

"Maybe we should take a break or something," I replied.

"You mean break up?" Will asked me firmly.

"Well, just to give us some time to think about it," I offered.

"Julia, you and I both know that there is no such thing as a break. There is only a break up. Is that what you really want?" he asked me sternly.

No, but that word would never reach his ears. My heart was breaking, but I remained confident in my confessions. The past several weeks had been hard on both of us. I knew this. Life had torn us into two, different directions and only because I felt I had already lost him, I found the nerve to fight against almost everything in me and answer him bravely.

"Yes," I stuttered finally, after a long pause.

My eyes began to fill with tears and the back of my throat ached now even as I tried to remain strong in my persuasions.

"Yes," I said again softly but with more conviction.

I had come too far to turn back now. The truth was that I wanted to see what life without him would be like– no arguments, no missing him every day, no letdowns when he had to change weekend plans with me last minute. I hated the words that rolled so easily off my tongue, but I sensed again a small bit of freedom in them as well now, and I held onto that freedom for courage, even while I secretly waited for him to convince me that my imagined liberty wasn't all it was cracked up to be.

"Well, I guess that's it then," Will said resolutely, without a waiver in his voice.

There was silence for a long second. Was this really it? Was this really happening?

"I guess so," I said in an almost whisper, responding to what I saw as his final, white-flag surrender to our relationship.

"Take care," Will said softly, yet his words still cold.

"You too," I whispered.

I pressed the red, *END* button, set the phone down gently onto the surface of the wooden desk and stared at it vehemently as if it were a ticking time bomb and I could deactivate it if I weren't careful enough.

Years in the making, and that's all it took. Sad and angry, my heart ached and stabbed at the walls of my chest. He had not fought for us like I thought he would have, and I was crushed. I wondered if he had thought less of me than I believed he had. What did I really mean to him after all of these years? Why wasn't he calling back and apologizing?

I sat there surrounded in my swirling thoughts, not able to escape the fact that now, suddenly, my world was eerily different. It was almost as if someone had put me in an unfamiliar room and had turned off all of the lights.

What happened to growing old and wrinkly? What about the fairy tale? He was the one who made me believe that a fairy tale even existed. He was supposed to always be there, but now he was nowhere to be found, and I was left imagining a world without him in it. It all seemed so cold and sad, and I blamed him for it.

I fought back the tears that welled up behind my eyelids as I picked up my pencil again. A piece of my heart wished that I had time to sort through the conversation that I had just had with the boy I had loved unswervingly for the past several years, yet that piece of my heart nevertheless could not outweigh the whole of my head that told me that there was no time to think about what was the past now—what wasn't probably even real in the first place.

My head forced my thoughts back onto my economics homework in front of me and back onto the sociology test I had the next day, for which I still had to study.

And with a single tear winning the battle and dropping to my textbook below, I turned the page and began to slowly read its blurry words. At the same time, I slid off the grass ring that had for so long graced my finger and set it carefully next to the ticking time bomb.

Resolutions

I threw my lip gloss and cell phone into my dark brown, leather purse and flipped off the light to what used to be my bedroom. Now, it hardly resembled anything that I would call mine. My mother had, just months after I had left for college, converted the room into a "guest quarter," as she so blissfully called it. The "quarter" even came complete with its own theme. Yes, what was once the shrine that paid tribute to my entire childhood, had now become "the country room," painted light emerald and decorated with white, lace curtains and a mammoth picture of a field of purple flowers that hung over the bed. It was as if she had been planning it for years. I could even picture her dancing about the room and listening to some old, 60s record as she stuffed my prized 4-H trophies and band posters into a box and hid it away for good. I cringed at the thought of my precious bands being wrinkled and crammed into an eternal box as I made my way down the hallway, anticipating each creek in the hardwood floor.

It was New Year's Eve. The holiday had never really been my favorite, mostly because it was at the wrong time of the year. How were you supposed to get excited about starting anything when it was ten degrees outside and all you could really think about starting was a vacation in any place south of where you were?

Christmas had been all right, though. My mother had decorated the place to the hilt, as usual, right down to the little ceramic Christmas mice that she would adhere to the banisters. Each mouse extended across a tiny sled and donned a miniature stocking hat and colorful mittens. The figurines made the normal and natural walk down the stairs awkward and slightly dangerous, but through the years, I guess I had come to look forward to their meandering presence during the holidays. With the mice, came Christmas.

Thinking about how I had grown to love the expected consistency of my Christmases at home, my thoughts turned to the one, obnoxiously missing piece. It had been my first Christmas without Will in years, and I had found it cruelly evident that he had not been by my side. I had survived, however, and now, I was just the tiniest bit excited because this New Year's Eve would be different too—a good different or at least I hoped it would be anyway.

It had been a couple of months since I had last spoken to Will, and though I didn't expect a love reconnection, I was excited to catch up. I missed his friendship, and honestly, a piece of me still hadn't healed from our last conversation. He had been my best friend for more than three, amazing years, and now, where his friendship had been was left a void that I had not even thought about filling yet.

After forcing my limbs through the arm holes in my favorite, worn-in wool coat, I jumped into my jeep and turned the key. I hated the months from December to February with a passion. Last night, it had dropped to a chilling 14 degrees, and now, the air temperature pierced the thinnest parts of my nose and ears. My teeth chattered as I struggled to pull my pale pink scarf around my neck, waiting impatiently for the heat in the vents to grow warm and then hot. It very rarely occurred to me to warm up the jeep before actually getting into it like everyone else in this great state did.

I'm on a beach. I closed my eyes and rubbed my hands briskly together. I'm basking in the warm sun. It's 85 degrees and perfect.

I opened my eyes and caught a leafless tree glaring at me from outside my so-called beach. Long icicles clung to its branches–they too seemed to be mocking me. The world out there looked dead and lifeless. I was surely in a British film.

Who was I kidding? It was cold out there, and it was cold in here, and even a warm image was too hard to conjure up tonight.

After several, painful minutes, and when the inside of my jeep was at least bearable, I forced it into drive and made my way into town.

When I arrived in town, I could see Rachel waiting for me at the place we had nicknamed *The Elle* years ago. It had gained the name because of its most eye-catching feature. A big *L* in the lumber yard's sign, nailed across the front of the building, had obnoxiously overshadowed the rest of the letters in the business' name for decades. The *L* gleamed bright cherry red, as opposed to its counterpart letters' deep chocolate brown. Further, the big *L* had always been slightly crooked, in contrast to the painstakingly straight letters that followed it.

I slowed the jeep and pulled up next to Rachel's deep emerald sedan and motioned to her through the sealed passenger's side window to get in.

Rachel grabbed her purse and gloves, crawled out of her car and dived into my now, warm nook on wheels.

"Hey! How was your Christmas?" she excitedly shouted over the drone of the heater still on its highest setting.

"It was good," I answered, omitting some of the truth, as I pulled away from our meeting place. "It was pretty much the same as usual. Uncle Ben wouldn't stop talking about his awful Jayhawks and Aunt Sharon and Mom spent half the night exchanging recipes of miracle creams that promised to fight aging and the other half of the night trying to get Uncle Joey and Uncle Mark to stop talking about football."

"What about yours?" I asked.

"Pretty much the same for me too, except that Lucas brought home his pet ferret and Aunt Kim's daughter accidentally let it out, and we spent half the night looking for Artie the ferret in the air ducts."

I tried to hold back my snickers. My friend looked so disheveled as she told her Christmas story.

Rachel turned and looked at me with a scowl.

"Julia, it really was horrible," she said with a perturbed look on her face. "It was Christmas, and I was looking for Artie the ferret."

I tried to stifle my laughter still, but it only seemed to make it worse.

"You're awful, you know?" Rachel said, laughing now as well.

Within a couple of minutes, I turned down a narrow, one-way street. I could faintly hear the voices and see the warm light coming from within the house, which looked to be full of life. I pulled next to the curb and put the jeep into park.

"Okay, Rach, we'll go on three," I said.

"Okay," she said, squeezing her gloves over her fingers and taking a deep breath.

"One, two…three," I counted.

On *three*, we both flung open our doors and flew out of the jeep as if our lives depended on our quickest exit. Stung by a frigid gust of air, we, decked from head to toe in scarves, coats and mittens, both sprinted to our friend's house in a world-class-athlete kind of manner–or at least, that was the manner we were going for.

When we reached the wooden entrance, still bearing a festive holiday wreath, Rachel knocked on it. And within seconds, Kathy greeted us at the door.

"Come in," she said cheerfully, giving each of us a hug. "Make yourself at home."

Kathy had always been one of those people who was far beyond her years. She always seemed to know the right thing to say, and she was always, without falter, well-mannered and extremely polite. And could she throw a party? Kathy's house had been the New Year's Eve party every year since I could remember.

Rachel and I quickly stepped into the warm house, and it was just short of heavenly. Finally, my beach.

I took off my coat, hung it on the wooden coat rack next to the door and made my way to the living room, while Rachel stayed behind in the entryway talking to Kathy. I didn't have time to talk; I was on a mission.

I squeezed stealthily past the bodies that inhabited my path. I saw everyone but the person for whom I was searching. He's here, I know. I saw his SUV parked outside.

I continued to scurry through the horde, acting like I wasn't on the quest of my life–only being stopped a couple of times. I did the normal, *Hi, how are you?* and kept moving.

I eventually made it to the living room, and when I looked up, I swore I had been transported to some romantic movie set–because our eyes met, and for a moment, we were the only two people in the bustling room.

He looked like his handsome self, although he had a strong five o'clock shadow now, and his hair had grown out just enough that small, wavy tuffs of it lingered on the tops of his ears. The look worked for him though. It was different, but a good different. I stood frozen in the doorway.

After taking a deep breath and letting it out, I gradually made my way through the throng toward Will, but as I did, I noticed something else that was different about him, but this time, the difference was just short of unsettling. And immediately, I knew then that this couldn't possibly be a romantic flick that I had just been transported to–more like anything but it.

I swallowed hard, and restarted my heart. Whose hand was he holding? A knife had just pierced my body. I had not expected this emotion. I expected excited, maybe even nervous, but not this.

I felt hurt and then awkwardly thrown off-guard, until that turned into a silent rage. But I knew I had no case on which to stand. That was the worst part. I could say nothing. There was nothing really for me to say. I wanted to turn around and walk back through the living room door in which I had just come. But of course, we had just had that weird, eyes-meet movie scene just moments before. And now, I had no other option but to move forward. So, I took another, cautious step toward him.

A couple more forced steps and I had already reached him and the unfamiliar one attached to him. I immediately introduced myself to the new, curly-locked brunette on his arm. I shook the girl's hand, making sure I forced myself to smile and to be polite and friendly–do everything that I was supposed to do. The girl looked nervous, but she smiled as well. Then, after the brief introduction, I met Will's eyes again.

"Hey," I softly said. "How have you been?"

He looked nervous too. Good.

"Good," he said, nodding his head slowly.

He kept it short and to the point, as if saying too much would cause him to wilt away.

I caught myself wondering if him wilting away would be all that bad.

"That's great," I lied, continuing to force my smile.

"So, did you go to Will's high school?" the girl interjected, interrupting Will's and my stare.

Both Will's and my attention turned to the girl, who had been fairly invisible in the last couple of seconds. He hadn't told her. The girl's innocent question struck me hard and made my heart sink to the pit of my stomach. It hurt, but of course, it had only been two months. I'd be surprised if he even knew her middle name.

I looked at Will, searching for a response that would make our chat a little less awkward than it already was. Then, the answer came.

For a second there, I thought that I saw a faint request in his puppy-dog eyes. I could almost see him begging me to answer the question simply, but I desperately wanted not to. I wanted to inform the girl that I was the ex-girlfriend. Just the word *ex-girlfriend* has such a stinging ring to it. I feel like it says that I've already won the game in play–as if it were a game to win. And now, it seemed like such a good word to use and such a perfect time to use it–but instead, I humbly took his hint and bit my tongue. He would owe me later.

"Yes, I did. I went to Will's high school," I said, refusing to elaborate.

"Julia," Rachel interrupted then. She had appeared out of nowhere. "Chris wants to ask you something about track and find out how outstandingly well you're doing," she continued, pulling me away, while staring straight at Will with her dagger eyes.

"It was nice to meet you," I said to the girl over my shoulder. I was smiling and polite–just as I was supposed to be.

"You don't mean that," Rachel whispered, whisking me away.

"I know," I whispered back to her, sounding defeated.

But before Rachel could steal me away from the scene permanently, I glanced back at Will one last time. I saw his eyes were still on me. He mimed the words, *Thank you.* I could also see that the gesture remained undetected by the girl who sat next to him, and I chose, against everything in me, to keep it that way. I managed a half-smile and then turned my head away from his gaze and exited the room with Rachel.

"It's a rebound, Jules," Rachel whispered to me. "I don't know what's gotten into him. Just don't pay any attention to him tonight and remember when life gives you a hundred reasons to cry, show life that you have a thousand reasons to smile."

I habitually nodded my head in reply to my friend's words, but not even everything in me could have forced my mind to think of anything but him then. He was with someone else. He was holding hands with someone else, and I wasn't the one sitting next to him. How had my world changed so drastically in such a short amount of time? I was all but crushed now, in pieces on the floor in the other room, yet I compelled my lips to smile as I greeted another friend in the dining room with a hug.

New Year's resolution—try not to cry.

An Invitation

$\mathbf{A}$s I threw on my gloves and flipped up my jacket's hood, I stepped outside and immediately felt the cool, spring air cast a chill over my exposed skin. I hate being cold–almost as much as I hate ex-boyfriends–I found myself thinking as I crossed my arms around my body.

In the end, it had taken several months to get over my New Year's Eve experience. And for now, I was over wanting to tie Will to that old caboose downtown and pay what tourists there were to pummel him with tomatoes. I thought it would be more fun than a photo.

And I guess I had eventually found a way to turn my bitterness into not-so-bitter bitterness as well–I found it's called *time*, and it seemed to be the only thing that really worked.

"Time makes everything better," I could hear Rachel saying in the back of my mind—in that little voice of hers that often overshadowed my own thoughts.

The outdoor track across the street was, at best, a five-minute walk, and within no time I felt the bounce and cushion of the track's red, rubber surface under my feet as I stepped onto its eighth lane.

"Nice gloves, Julia. I must have missed the snow storm through all of the green on my way in," a voice called out from inside a huddled group on the other side of the track. The voice was deep and carried a slight Northeastern accent.

"I haven't heard that one in a while," I said, sending a playful smirk in the direction of the chiding voice.

"Okay, okay, let's get going, guys. Enough chitchatin'. Warm up well. We've got a six, five, four, three, two, today," shouted a man with a clipboard and a stopwatch.

Lovely, I thought to myself.

"Hey, Julia, remind me to ask you something after the workout," the Northeastern accent softly said as I neared him. It sounded like he knew something that I didn't, and it peaked my curiosity.

"Ask me what?" I asked.

"Just remind me," he answered back, smiling.

"Okay, sure," I said as I tugged at my gloves, found an open eye in the wire fence, stuffed them into it and then joined the group already starting to jog around the track.

91

The workout came and went as usual—nothing out of the ordinary, and yet again I had survived. I reveled in my small joy as I fell onto the track's rubber surface to pry my spikes off of my swollen feet.

"Phew, that—was—pain," I said to no one in particular.

"Tired already?" the six-foot-one sprinter with the Northeastern accent taunted me.

I looked up from my disheveled state and smiled at the seemingly cool and collect figure staring in my direction. He had muscular arms and legs and strawberry blond hair and looked as if he were totally unfazed by the trial we had just endured. He was a year older than me, a sophomore, and he had become a good friend of mine in the time that we had known each other. A pre-med student and standout athlete, Brady had many alluring qualities that attracted my close friendship. Yes, I said *friendship*. Despite being coerced by the girls on the sprint squad to take him seriously, I was convinced that any relationship beyond a friendship with my now, good friend was completely out of the question. Even if I wanted a relationship right now, I was sure that Brady and I had crossed into the *just-friends zone* a long time ago.

"Tired. Never," I said with a crooked smile in answer to his question. I tried with great pains to slow my breathing so it wasn't quite so easy to see how out of breath I really was.

Brady laughed.

"Hey, you wanted to ask me something. What was it?" I asked. I had almost forgotten.

"Oh, yeah, there's a concert tonight at the Blue Star, and I have an extra ticket. Do you want to come?" he asked.

"Who's playing?" I questioned him.

"The All-American Saints. It's a new band. You probably have never heard of them, but I thought we could try it," he said, almost sheepishly.

He wasn't acting his usual confident self. What was different about him?

"Okay," I said, shrugging my shoulders. I didn't really have anything else to do later that night, and I had already caught up on all of my homework over the weekend. Besides, it sounded fun–even if he was acting weird.

"Who else is going?" I asked as I successfully forced one spike off of my foot and watched it fall to the rubber surface in front of me.

"It's just me and you. I'll pick you up at seven," he said as quickly as he could get the words out of his mouth.

And before I could ask anymore questions, he had disappeared behind the swarm of jumpers huddled together in the middle of the track. I paused from untying my other shoe and stared bemused in the direction in which the tall figure had just been standing. Just me and you? I knew that I had a puzzled look superglued to my face. We never did things as *just me and you*. It was odd, but I guess it wasn't that odd. And it surely couldn't be worth too much thought. Right? I had learned that guys were odd creatures many years ago, and besides, Brady probably bought the tickets only to find out that everyone he had asked was either too busy to go or didn't want to see a band, the likes of which they had never heard. That was probably it.

I went back to untying my spiked shoe.

When I finished, I slipped on my tennis shoes, stood up, threw on my jacket, un-jailed my gloves from the wire fence and headed for the box I called home to get ready for the concert that I had concluded would just be part of another night with a good friend.

Secret Crush

"I like 'em," I said, almost shouting, so that Brady could hear me over the drums and constant hum of the crowd. At the same time, I was trying unsuccessfully to drape my jacket over the back of my chair, while also juggling my phone and breathing in a combination of old building and a dozen perfumes and colognes. Aah, night life. Was it strange that I actually kind of liked the combination of juxtaposing smells? The scene and its attributes kind of reminded me of what life would look like—and smell like, I guess—if you bottled it up and kept it for a long time. I would bottle up tonight, I guess. Why not? I was watching a band with a good friend, who just so happened to be easy on the eyes, I might add. Life could be worse than tonight.

"Here, I've got it," Brady said as he helped me force the jacket to latch onto the opposite side of the chair.

"Tha-nks," I said–almost as if it were a question.

My eyes tracked his expression. I was waiting for him to make fun of my inability to perform a simple task–as if the endless banter never got old. But nothing came. He simply steadied the jacket on the chair, caught my stare, smiled and refocused his attention back onto the band.

A smile?

His reaction made me giggle quietly to myself. He must love this band. It had him acting…well, smiley.

"Where are they from?" I asked, straining my voice. I was sure he knew and would be eager to tell me.

"Memphis," Brady shouted back.

"Hmm," I said, nodding my head. "They're pretty good. I wonder why they haven't been discovered yet."

"They're an alternative rock band from the Midwest. It takes a while, I guess," Brady replied, a permanent smile planted on his tan, chiseled face.

"Yeah, I guess you're right," I said, smiling also and following his gaze to the four-member band on the tiny, worn-in platform.

The band just barely fit onto the modest stage that was maybe three feet off the ground. People, mostly in their teens and twenties, lined the wooden edges of the raised area, holding out their hands in hopes of touching the hand of a star–well, before he was a star anyway. Of course, they might as well have been famous. They had managed to captivate the attention of the entire hall of young adults, which each had an attention span of no more than 30 seconds.

And I wouldn't have taken my eyes off of them again either if it weren't for my own depleted attention span. My electronic distraction, also known as my phone, and its obnoxious glow suddenly caught the corner of my eye. My hand instinctively darted toward it and scooped it up.

But before I tossed it like a hot potato into my clutch, I glanced at the name on the screen.

Will.

My heart raced for a split second. I hadn't talked to Will since New Year's Eve. What could he possibly have to say?

"Do you need to answer it?" Brady asked, taking his attention away from the band as well to flash me a gentle smile.

Another smile?

"No," I said, the corners of my mouth rising, forcing my heart to slow again.

"Okay," he said, nodding his head and returning his attention back to the band.

My eyes followed his lead, but my mind fell onto some kind of misguided safari. And by the time the band was wrapping up its last song, I had already jumped off of the safari and had entered an imaginary dream land– complete with time machines that allowed you to go back and forward all at the same time.

And on the outside, from my corner of the playhouse, I was methodically dissecting the way each member busily unplugged amplifier cords and took swigs out of water bottles and exchanged glances with fans that just knew that he was going to be the next big thing someday. But on the inside, and for a fleeting second, I imagined it were Will doing the same things. I imagined his deep, soothing voice and crooked, half-smile and his new, scruffy facial hair.

My eyes followed a band member to the corner of the stage, and I watched as he took a napkin and a pen from a brunette with long, silky hair. It was the girl from Kathy's New Year's Eve party. Well, it wasn't, but it was in my head anyway. And suddenly, Will's voice didn't seem so smooth and his facial hair just made him look lazy and like a bear.

"Are you ready?" I heard Brady ask me, breaking my stare, my lapse from reality.

"Yeah," I shouted, noticing for the first time that I no longer had to shout. "That was fun," I added, forcing myself back to where I actually was.

I was smiling when I caught Brady's gaze. And for a strange moment, his peculiar smile–that he had been displaying all night–appeared mesmerizing, as if no one was moving around us, no one was pushing out chairs or brushing past us or trying to get the band members' attentions. For a moment, the room seemed silent and completely calm. Maybe I was still in Dream Land.

"Hey, do you want to get some hot chocolate at the shop down the street?" Brady asked me eventually, puncturing the vacuum that I or he or we had just either created or had just so happened to find ourselves in for the last several moments.

"That sounds like a good idea," I said, nodding my head.

It only took a couple of minutes for us to walk down the street and find our way into a small, local coffee shop. It was three stairs down and we were completely underground, surrounded by drawings of bridges and tall weeds and roads that wound into fields of clovers–images that would fit pretty well in "the country room," I noted. The drawings were all signed and for sale by local artists trying also to make their big break. The narrow, small room was cozy, dimly lit and full of soft, leather chairs. Brady and I made our way to a small counter with a chalkboard displayed behind it and planted our feet.

"It's on me," I said to Brady after I decided on a triple chocolate hot chocolate and he chose the regular hot chocolate.

"No, no, no," Brady said, reaching for his wallet in the back pocket of his dark jeans.

"No, you bought the tickets," I said, trying my best to persuade him.

"Your money's no good here, Julia. Plus, ladies don't pay," he replied, smiling and pulling out a bill from his wallet.

Ladies? Brady had never referred to me as anyone but "one of the guys," much less a lady. The gesture seemed kind of misplaced, but then again, he had always been pretty gentleman-like, almost like an old soul.

"Thanks," I said, smiling, opting eventually to give in and let him pay.

The barista handed us each a steaming cup of hot chocolate within minutes, and then we made our way out of the coffee shop and to a small, downtown city park that wasn't too far down the street.

I could feel the smooth hot chocolate glide down my throat as I took short, frequent sips to ward off the night's brisk air. The smooth chocolate felt good after a night of shouting over the band.

"How about here?" Brady asked me as he pointed to a small, wooden bench under a maple tree just starting to grow back its big, green leaves that the winter had stolen from it.

"This is fine," I said cheerfully, taking a seat and resting my back contently up against the back of the bench.

"Thanks for asking me to come. It was fun," I said, after I had turned toward my friend now sitting beside me.

"It was nothing," he said, resting his hot chocolate cup on his knee. "I'm glad you said *yes*."

His comment set me back for a second. I had heard that phrase before. It had come from a bear–a scruffy-faced, lazy bear. I guess I was still working on the bitterness. I shook it off and kept my eyes on my friend. There was something different about him tonight. Maybe it was his hair. It had gel in it. I rarely saw him with gel in his hair. No, maybe it was the way he was dressed. He was wearing dark denim jeans and a black, long-sleeved shirt under his dark leather jacket. It seemed to complement his deep brown eyes exceptionally well, and it was a far cry from sweats and a tee shirt. Though, he could hold his own in either outfit.

Just friends–It would always be a blessing and a curse, I thought, smiling slightly. I looked away and took another sip of hot chocolate.

"Julia," Brady said then, taking a deep breath and letting it out slowly.

I could hear the breath escaping through his lips. I looked up at him with a concerned expression. His whole demeanor had changed, and I wondered what had caused it. Was there still something he had to ask me? Was everything okay? My breaths quickened then. Were there still more surprises? I waited on my answer as he continued.

"I've liked you for awhile now," he sputtered and then paused, awaiting my reaction.

I swallowed quickly as my eyes darted back to the ground in front of me. I wasn't completely sure what I had heard. I sat frozen, puzzled and shocked. A foreign excitement churned in my stomach, though I still wasn't quite sure where he was going with all of this.

Moments went by in silence. I slightly panicked.

"And I like you too, Brady," I said, smiling.

I had taken the safe road, not really knowing if there was even a different road to take.

Brady smiled and shook his head back and forth as he looked toward the ground, seemingly at his shoes, seemingly frazzled.

"No, I mean, I like you, Julia. I like you, like I-want-to-take-you-on-a-date, and I-want-to-kiss-you like you," he confessed sincerely.

My heart stopped, and as if a smile restarted my frozen beats again, the corners of my lips rose. I was sure I had heard him right this time, and though I kind of felt guilty for making him elaborate, I loved what I had heard–twice. Who wouldn't?

His words were both reassuring and electric all at the same time, and as if my expression had given him the response he had longed for, Brady leaned over and kissed my chocolaty lips.

After he withdrew his soft lips from mine, he took my hand in his. His hand wasn't really soft, but it was warm.

I smiled and rested my head against his strong shoulder. I was still trying to fully grasp what was going on. What had just happened? Who was this guy beside me? Just moments ago, we had been two people who had long ago crossed over into the doomed *friend zone*. Now, we were holding hands. A million questions were running around dizzily in my head, bumping into each other and raising havoc, but at the same time, the moment didn't feel wrong or awkward. It felt right.

And with that revelation, I wrapped my free arm around his arm closest to me and felt the perfect contours of his bicep. I had always wanted to do that.

I was very much aware that the arm wasn't Will's, and the thought slightly stung. But I was quickly lifted with my next thought—No, these muscles were much too big to be Will's. I smiled.

It was all still so surreal to me. I had to have been dreaming. I was, for sure, back in Dream Land. This kind of stuff didn't happen in real life. Inside, butterflies burst forth from my stomach in all different directions toward my limbs. Inside, I was dancing crazily and doing cartwheels. Outside, I stared in utter amazement at my hand in my friend's as I tried to grasp the reality, the newness of the moment.

And as my thoughts continued to crazily run amuck, I gently squeezed his bicep again and smiled.

Just friends wasn't all that bad, but this—this, I think I like a little more. Yep, I could get used to this.

A Blink of an Eye

"Julia, is that you?"

I looked up from the teacher's desk to see a short, bubbly woman standing in the classroom's doorway. Before I could say a word, the figure spoke again.

"Well, how are ya? It's been so long," the woman exclaimed.

Then, I watched her scurry into the classroom and finally take a seat in one of the small, student desks in front of me.

"I heard that you were back in town, and I've been hoping that I'd run into you when I was over here sometime. What have you been up to these days?" the woman asked again before I even had a chance to answer her first question.

Will's aunt, who was also the elementary school's nurse, had always been a favorite of mine–mostly because of her inquisitive nature, which did some work in the town's most illustrious industry–its rumor mill.

"I've been substituting, trying to stay busy," I replied, happy to be in the presence of someone older than twelve for the first time that day.

"How has it been going?" she asked. A concerned look rose to her face, but I wasn't exactly sure why. As far as I knew, every kid had made it through first hour. Though, I quickly remembered that it was just one of her two, usual expressions. There was either a smile or that same I'm-sorry-to-hear-that look. There were only two options. That's all you got with her.

"Well, so far, no missing children, no injuries, thus far, knock on wood," I said.

I knocked on a corner of the old wooden desk a couple of times.

"Good, Good. So, what are you working on there?" she asked, straining her neck slightly in my direction.

She was craftily skimming the rumor mill even as we spoke, but how could you fault her? She was a curious soul–like a fly just before it gets stuck in the butter.

"Oh, this?" I asked.

I looked down at my stack of papers.

"I'm looking for apartments," I said. "It might be tough to find places to rent out there, so I figured I'd better get started now."

"Out where?" the woman asked abruptly, displaying a puzzled look–one slightly more severe than the usual concerned look–on her rosy, round face.

I had just assumed that she had known about my leaving for school in the winter. I knew that New Milford had not grown that much in the four years that I had been gone. Perhaps there were exceptions to the small-town rumor mill after all. Was it possible that not everyone knew everyone else's business and that Will's aunt was living proof? The thought was surprisingly refreshing, though I refused to take it as fact. I knew better.

"I'm moving to San Diego," I said. "I got accepted into a law school there."

"San Diego?" she stated and asked at the same time. "That's so far away."

Her reaction seemed slightly somber, which wasn't quite the expression that I was expecting. But before I could explain, the forty-something-year-old woman continued.

"Well, to be perfectly honest, I heard that you were coming back into town, and I had half hoped that you and Will would get back together," she elaborated. "But now that you're leaving, I guess that's out," she said, smiling softly and turning her face to the tile floor in between her desk and mine. A sad disappointment lingered in her eyes.

Will's aunt had a way with words. Her words weren't always the ones that you wanted to hear, but they were always the ones you needed to hear. Though, I wasn't quite convinced I needed to hear those particular words just now.

Her confession, though unsettling, brought it all together, however, and it was both flattering and heart-wrenching all at the same time. I loved Will's family, and I hated to disappoint any one of them, but in the end, it was life. People separated. They moved on. Fairy tales faded. New ones formed. Life kept going. And my life wasn't the only one that had kept going. Will's had too. I had learned through the ever-present grape vine that Will had went on, while I was in college, to pursue his dream he had first confessed to me that day in high school. He became a full-time, active duty firefighter about a year and a half ago and moved to St. Louis. Though he rented a place right outside of the big city, he also bought a house in New Milford. I had heard that he kept the house in our hometown so that he had a place that made him feel like he had never left–a place to fish and to run around and to do whatever it was that small-town men do that never quite grow up, I guess. It sounded like him anyway.

"How is he, by the way," I asked, smiling, continuing the conversation, yet still not exactly sure how to respond to the nurse's confession.

"He's doing well," she said, nodding her head. "Although, he hasn't quite seemed himself lately. In fact, he hasn't quite seemed himself for a long time now, and we're a little worried about him."

She paused, and then as if an imaginary light bulb went off in her head, she dramatically continued.

"Hey, maybe you could talk to him while you're here. He has a house outside of town next to Cedar Lake, and he'll be back there this weekend," she explained.

I smiled and nodded my head. I suspected the seemingly spur-of-the-moment idea was not so spur-of-the-moment.

"I could try to do that," I said, still smiling.

"Oh, I'd love it if you could. He'd love it," the woman said happily as she shot up from her desk and scurried back to the doorway–as if her great mission had just been accomplished, and now, she was off to solve the town's other great impasses.

But just before she reached the door, she turned and faced me again. I watched her as she took a deep breath and then let it out before she spoke.

"Don't count him out, Julia. He hasn't given up on you," she said resolutely and then quickly disappeared into the hallway.

A Visit

It was Saturday evening, and I had a nagging desire to see Will. His aunt didn't have a bad idea. She might have had ulterior motives wrapped up in it, but it wasn't a bad idea. And sure, I probably wouldn't have attempted to make the visit on my own initiative, but now that a request had been made, I was slightly intrigued by the notion. And after all, it would be good to see him again, catch up and say goodbye before I left town. What could it hurt?

I threw on a jacket and searched the desk for my keys, bypassing the phone on my nightstand. I could call him first, but I was kind of in the mood for a sneak attack. Those were more fun anyway.

I grabbed my keys and headed for the door.

In my jeep, I paused only to crack the window and to find a radio station playing anything that wasn't the sound of an old man rambling about the price of soybeans.

In less than ten minutes, I pulled off of the only highway that meandered its way through town and drove a short distance to a small farm house at the end of a narrow gravel road. I had known it was this house when his aunt had described it the day before. I had passed by the little white, two-story building almost a million times in my lifetime, and I had no trouble finding it again today.

As my jeep closed in on the old, wooden home with blue shutters, I spotted Will's SUV in the white-graveled driveway. Then the nerves set in. They weren't overwhelming–just enough to be annoying. I had run into Will a time or two while I was home from college and even a couple of times while I was at school and he was visiting a mutual friend. Those times had been short and the conversation even shorter. We had never spoken of the New Year's Eve night. We never talked much about what was really going on in our lives. What each of us knew about the other was, of course, from the rumor mill. I often wondered what his mysterious call was about the night of that concert years ago, but surely, he had said what he was going to say by now. And for all I knew, he had called me by mistake.

And now, I wasn't entirely sure of how he would react to my sneak attack. I knew he had his fickle moments–those moments when I had no idea what he was thinking. All those years we had been together, I had really thought I knew him. These days, though, he was as unpredictable as an alley cat. One minute, he's purring on your lap. The next, he's scowling at you from the window sill, and you're left wondering if he's plotting your demise over there, just waiting for you to fall asleep. That's Will. One minute, he's fine and civil; the next, he's reserved and cold.

I wondered what today would be like when I turned the ignition off moments later and stepped out of the jeep. The small house had an unattached garage, which led to a concrete sidewalk and three tiny, concrete stairs that I took to the house's front porch. The wooden slats of the tiny porch gave way slightly under my feet, making low-pitched creaky noises, as I made my way to the door.

I let out an excited and slightly nervous sigh before pulling open the screen door and knocking three times on the solid, wooden, storm one behind it. I regretted for a short second not calling him first. What was I thinking? Everyone calls before stopping by. What did I have to gain in a sneak attack anyway?

When no one answered, I felt a small piece of relief. Maybe he wasn't home.

I waited a minute and then followed the miniature wrap-around porch to the back of the house. I figured I would just look to see if he was out back. If he wasn't, I was out of there.

At the same time, a tiny piece of sadness replaced my nervousness. I was, oddly enough, looking forward to catching up with him. I have Rachel to thank for keeping me connected to my past, and believe me, she does a good job of it. But Will holds a different connection to that time. I was kind of looking forward to getting lost in it for an hour or so.

I turned the corner of the wrap-around porch, lost in my own regret, when I saw him. He was there, just sitting in a chair next to the lake about the size of a football field, with a thin, dark fishing pole resting in his hands.

I smiled.

I could really only see his back, and he was wearing an old baseball cap, but I could still tell that he looked good. And not a good for the circumstances *good*, but a good, *good*. And I suddenly remembered how I could have fallen for him years ago.

I paused for a moment before I took another step or made my presence known and gazed around the backyard. Golf balls littered perfect, freshly cut, green grass. Trees lined the lawn and the back of the lake, and everything was still, peaceful, quiet–perfectly still. Gone were the nerves and the regret for not calling. This was home, and I loved that I could see it in its natural state for even just a moment.

"Will," I eventually called out from the porch. There was a smile in the way I had said his name.

Will turned in his chair toward the direction of my voice.

I noticed his bright, blue eyes first. They seemed to smile even before I could see his lips rise at their corners.

"Hey," he said, immediately setting his fishing pole onto the ground, rising up from his wooden lawn chair and making his way toward me. He had a surprise in his voice.

I kept my eyes on him, uncovering one memory at a time about the way he assembled his steps–smooth, long strides, his right foot slightly turned out, something the average glance would never notice–as he made his way toward me.

"Your aunt said you would be here this weekend," I said, starting to explain my presence, while I leaned into his embrace when he reached me.

"Well, here I am," he said, gesturing toward the lake. "Pull up a chair."

I followed him to the edge of the water again and sank deep into an oversized, handmade lawn chair. Then, I shoved my hands into my jacket's pockets and crossed my legs to ward off the late evening, September chill and made myself comfortable.

"Are they biting?" I asked, thankful that he had taken my unannounced visit well so far.

"A little, but I haven't caught any yet," he said. "It's probably getting too cold. I heard you were back in town—for how long?" he asked. He was still smiling.

The rumor mill was still alive and well. The thought was oddly comforting.

"I'm here for a little more than a month," I softly said. "I'm substituting up at the school."

I noticed his smile begin to fade. I suspected it had something to do with me leaving again, so I continued in hopes of distracting him.

"I don't mind it. I actually kind of like it, and it gives me something to do in the meantime," I finished.

"I see. Then where are you going?" he asked hesitantly.

I hated telling him that I was leaving. Suddenly, I felt as if we were in high school all over again and I was telling him for the first time that I was going away to college. And strangely, I could tell he felt the same way—whether it made sense to or not.

The truth was that I still cared a great deal about him, and I would still do anything to protect his heart. Despite the fact that our relationship status had downgraded years ago, his friendship meant the world to me—even in its infrequent and sometimes irregular forms.

"I'm going to school in California, and then we'll see from there," I finally managed to get out.

"California?" Will blurted out. "And more school? What are you going for now?" he asked somberly, and now with a hint of sarcasm in his voice.

His whole demeanor was beginning to change–quickly.

"Law," I replied.

"Law," Will said to himself. "Well, that's your dream," he continued, forcing a smile and nodding his head.

I was relieved to see a smile again.

"But why California?" he asked. "That's like a whole, different country. You know there's no grass or trees out there. Isn't there something closer?"

I laughed.

"It's warm though," I confessed with a grin.

Will laughed.

"So, if I find a way to get rid of the winter here, you'll stay closer for once?" he asked, still smiling.

"I'll stay forever," I promised.

"What about palm trees?" he continued. "What if I plant some palm trees, would that help?"

I smiled and shook my head.

"Yeah, I didn't think so," he said, smiling also.

There was a brief silence as the tree frogs started their nightly song in the thick brush behind us.

"Well, I guess you've got the arguing thing down already," Will blurted out eventually, somewhat changing the subject. "You know, for the whole lawyer thing."

I hesitated for a second.

"Yeah, I guess," I said. "Thanks for that, by the way."

"Happy to help," he said, chuckling.

Our smiles again faded and were replaced by a reflective silence. It was just enough time for me to wonder if I had been wrong to come tonight. He didn't seem like he was in the mood for reminiscing or even talking, for that matter.

"Happiness is like a butterfly, you know?" Will blurted out then, interrupting my thoughts.

I looked back at him with a puzzled expression infused across my face.

"What?" I asked. There was a slight hesitation in my voice, though I was slightly intrigued. Where was he going with this?

"The more you chase it, the more it will elude you, but if you turn your attention to other things, it will come and sit softly on your shoulder," he recited.

"It's Thoreau," he added.

"Hmm," I said slowly. I wasn't quite sure how to respond to his seemingly out-of-place statement, and I definitely didn't have a clue as to what he was talking about.

I nodded my head in mostly apathetic agreement and then quickly changed the subject. Maybe this is what his aunt was talking about him not being himself lately. I reminded myself I would take his friendship in all of its forms. Then, I smiled warmly.

"So, how have you been? What have you been up to these days?" I asked excitedly.

"Working, golfing, fishing," he rambled off. "You're looking at it."

His words had grown somewhat cold.

I nodded again as I watched him bob the fishing pole up and down so that the bobber methodically bounced in the water, causing circular ripples.

"How's living in St. Louis? Do you like it?" I asked, trying desperately to keep the conversation going. I felt like I was trying to row a johnboat against the Missouri current.

"It's fine. It's all fine. Are you seeing anyone?" he blurted out softly, changing the subject unexpectedly again.

I cocked my head to the side so that I could see his shadowed face under the bill of his cap. He looked mysterious and almost seductive under that baseball cap of his–kind of like a famous country singer who was a model in his past life. Okay, that might be a stretch, but there was still something about him that didn't make him look like he belonged in this one-horse town.

When he continued to stare into the water, I slowly returned my gaze back to the lake as well. I should have been more surprised by his question, but I wasn't. He had a wonderful habit of throwing that same query into every one of our conversations since our own demise. I hated it, and I hated answering it too. I wanted to get lost in the past for awhile–not the present. And I had no idea how he would react to my reply each time. In the end, I wanted to tell him that I had found someone really special, and I wanted him to be happy for me, but then I knew this hope was in vain. No matter his relationship status, he never reacted positively to my response. But, in the end, I understood. Of course, I understood. I wouldn't exactly jump for joy at the mention of his love interests either. So why did he always ask about mine?

"I am," I finally said in answer to his question. "I'm still seeing Brady."

"Uh-huh," Will said slowly, continuing to stare at his bobber, still bouncing up and down on the water's surface.

Now, it was my turn to ask him, I guessed.

"What about you?" I asked, trying to stay positive, a forced smile reappearing on my face. I didn't really want to hear the answer.

"What about me?" he asked.

"Well, how's Miss New Year's Eve?" I asked. I couldn't help but grin, remembering the commotion that was that night. Now, it felt like a lifetime ago.

"Gosh, you still remember that? Jules, that was years ago. That whole thing was just a bad idea," he admitted, shaking his head.

I let my laughter out of the hold I had had it under.

"Didn't work out?" I asked, now trying to stifle the remaining giggles.

"Did you expect it to?" he asked, smiling too now.

I paused for a second.

"No," I admitted, shaking my head and smiling softly.

"Me neither," he said.

For a moment, we sat in silence again, watching the ripples soothingly bunch together and then disappear into the outer edges of the lake.

"Jules, I'm sorry about that night. I...," he started, turning toward me.

"Will, it's fine," I stopped him. "It was a long time ago," I said, smiling and catching another glimpse of his baby blues.

His eyes went back to the bobber when I finished. He wasn't smiling, but he was nodding his head.

Then, as if a silent timer had gone off, he reeled in his fishing pole, set it beside his chair and stood up.

His movement forced me to turn in his direction. Where was he going? What was he doing? In a moment, he had just transformed into an alley cat again. And now,

I felt more like his trapped mouse than his alley-cat friend. It was times like these, though, that helped to remind me that the two of us were just simply two, different people–two, different people who had taken different paths in life and had changed along the way. He was an alley cat now. I was the predictable one. I no longer understood him and he no longer understood me, and that had become evident throughout the years.

I watched him dust off the back of his jeans.

"Well, I have to go to my parents' house for dinner tonight," Will said, now stretching his muscular, long arms and towering frame to the sky. "Mom's making her specialty. I promised her I'd be there."

I hesitated for an instant, nodded my head and then spoke.

"Okay, yeah, can't miss that. I'd better get going then," I said, taking his awkward cue. "It was nice seeing you again."

I rose from my chair then, fiddling with my jacket and somewhat dissatisfied by our conversation and my decision to see him at all. Because now, my phrase, *What could it hurt?* looped across my mind like it was on a digital billboard continuously mocking me. I was quickly realizing that seeing Will might not have only hurt our friendship, but also my chances of having a nice, drama-free Saturday evening. I was silently admitting defeat when Will's alley-cat voice threw me off again.

"Come," he blurted out in his deep, raspy tone.

I instantly stopped adjusting my jacket and looked up at him. I wasn't exactly sure what he had meant by his sudden outburst or even sure if I had heard him right.

"What?" I asked softly, hesitantly–confused.

"Come with me," he propositioned me again.

I smiled, and my eyes darted to the ground near my shoes. Had anyone else asked me the same question, I would have politely declined. However, it wasn't just anyone who had asked me. It was Will, and I had nothing to do that night, and I loved his family and hadn't seen them in a long time. A dinner couldn't hurt. I bit my tongue. Well, it couldn't make it worse. In fact, a dinner with his family might salvage my Saturday night.

"Okay," I softly said, while nodding my head and smiling back at him.

Will smiled too.

"Let's go," he said, seemingly happy again, grabbing his fishing pole and making his way back to the small porch.

I watched him walk away for a second, temporarily paralyzed, stuck on a tiny patch of dirt and grass, wondering what I had just agreed to.

"You coming?" he called out cheerfully, turning his attention back to me.

I smiled, nodded and followed after him.

A Promise

I followed Will to his parents' house in my jeep and walked with him up the stone walkway to the door of his childhood home–something I had done so many times before.

I was a little hesitant at how Will's family members would react to me being there, but each one greeted me with hugs and smiles as usual–just like I had never taken a four-year leave of absence from their lives.

The meal too played out as if I had never left. Then, after dinner, I followed Will, glass of lemonade in hand, out to the deck that overlooked a piece of the Uptown. I immediately spotted a familiar, cushioned lounge chair that hadn't seemed to have moved an inch in four years, and I fell into it. The chair felt safe. I was home again.

Satisfied, I took a deep breath in and with it, inhaled the autumn smell of fallen brown, saffron and yellow leaves mixed with burning logs. The air was still somewhat warm, but the breeze was cool. I took one more sip of Will's mom's homemade lemonade and set it onto the floor beside me.

When my eyes returned to the horizon, they caught the flash of several businesses' lights that were just starting to come alive along the main highway that stretched through town. And in the west, the very last piece of the crimson, setting sun neared the edge of the earth as a quiet darkness slowly crept across our sky.

My eyes followed the lines of the sunset until I noticed a familiar-looking object in my view, resting up against the wooden banister.

"Do you still play?" I asked. There was a curious excitement in my voice. I could even hear it myself.

Will followed my eyes' path to the six-stringed instrument. And without missing a beat, he sauntered over to it, picked it up and took a seat in a chair next to me, laying the guitar gently in his lap.

He was smiling as he slowly and methodically swung its strap over his head and wrapped his other arm around its base.

"This song is all yours," he said with a boyish grin now planted on his face as he slid a pick out from underneath the guitar's strings.

More surprises from the alley cat.

"Mine?" I asked, strangely flattered. A smile battled and eventually won its way to my face as well.

"Yep, all yours. Everyone needs a song–this one will be yours. I'll never use it for anyone else," he vowed as he began leisurely plucking its strings.

I laughed.

"Okay," I said, smiling, agreeing to play along with his little vow.

The melody was slow and soothing, and immediately, it captivated me, almost seeming to transport me to a beautiful and enchanting place in a world where nothing ever seemed to go wrong. I remembered that world. I was seventeen in it and the muse of a talented seventeen-year-old, small-town boy. I let myself believe I was in that world again as I took a deep breath, exhaled and then watched religiously as his fingers gently tickled the guitar's strings, and his same, familiar, soothing voice softy came to rest at my ears.

The voice was home too, and I hung onto each word, lost in my past:

"It's a summer night
And I can hear the crickets sing
But otherwise, all the world's asleep
While I can only lie awake and dream
And every time I close my eyes
A butterfly comes to me

It has soft, green eyes
A sweet soul
Brave wings
And each time, it hears me sing…"

Will stopped singing, yet he continued to play the melody on the guitar a few more measures before his fingers stopped strumming as well.

I hesitated before I spoke. It might have been because I was slightly tongue-tied. It might have been because I was hoping that there was still more.

"Where are the rest of the words?" I asked, smiling softly. "What does the butterfly hear you sing?"

"I'm, I'm still working on the rest," he said, smiling his coy, alley-cat smile. "You can hear it again when I'm finished. I promise."

"Well, when will it be finished?" I asked curiously.

He paused, and his eyes found a place on the wood floor before meeting my eyes again.

"I'll find a way to get it to your ears," he said, smiling coyly. "Don't worry."

I smiled at him softly.

"Okay," I said, nodding my head, my gaze still on him, watching him almost suspiciously. "I'll wait if I have to, I guess."

I brought my knees up to my chest and wrapped my arms around my bended legs.

"You should play–for people–you know. I might even do you the honor of being your biggest fan," I added, urging him on with a smile.

Will's face lit up, but he was shaking his head.

"You never give up, do you?" he asked, chuckling.

My eyes caught his. I didn't say anything, though my expression was telling.

"Nah, work keeps me busy," he said, eventually shaking his head. "Besides, I don't mind just playing like this–for friends, for you."

I could definitely tell that my cheeks were blushing now as my eyes darted directly to the engrained lines on the floor again. I prayed that it was dark enough now that he couldn't see the fire in my face.

We were both quiet for a long minute, while my eyes traced those lines in the wood floor over and over again. Then, something brave came over me. I was still seventeen–for now.

"Will," I said, breaking the silence. "You know you've got a piece of me always, no matter what this crazy world has planned for us, right?"

He shook his head slowly, taking in my words, almost as if it were perfectly normal for me to have said them.

"Yeah, I know, and you've got the other half of me, damn the luck," he said, chuckling softly.

I laughed.

"How are we ever gonna function separately?" he asked.

"I'm sure we'll make do," I said, smiling, watching him stroke the strings silently on his guitar.

After several seconds, his eyes met mine again. I continued to smile, yet I quickly forced my gaze to the horizon in the distance.

"I probably should be going," I said then, softly, shifting my eyes back to him.

"Okay," he whispered, nodding his head slowly, as if he were being forced against his will to agree.

Now, he was the one who focused on the engrained lines on the wooden porch floor. My eyes settled on him again. It seemed as if he had something else to say but was afraid to say it or didn't know how to say it or something. And I wasn't sure if he would hold onto it forever.

I took a deep breath in and exhaled slowly. Then, I reached down to grab the glass of lemonade on the other side of my chair. But as I moved, I suddenly felt his hand gently come to rest on my opposite hand.

My face quickly darted back toward his. At the same time, my heart quickened. His hand was so familiar, yet something told me that it should be foreign to me now, and everything else told me that it shouldn't be on mine. But my hand was cemented to the wooden chair underneath it, and it would hurt too much to even try to move it. I knew this, so I simply let it be, as my eyes settled on his own baby blues. And for a moment, neither of us said anything. It was almost as if this were the last time we would ever see each other–like this, anyway.

"Promise me you'll come if I ever change my mind about the singing gig," he whispered finally. "Promise you'll come and listen to the rest of the song."

My heart slowed and the corners of my mouth rose slightly. I paused, dragging out the seconds, though consciously refusing to get lost in his sea-colored eyes, like I had done so many times before.

"I promise," I softly said.

My eyes lingered on his and his on mine for a second more, but a sudden thought of Brady led me back to my path, and I pushed myself up from the lounge chair, slid my hand out from underneath his and walked to the glass door that led to the inside of the house. I was no longer seventeen–or else, I wouldn't be walking away.

Once in the kitchen, I set the glass in the sink, quietly slipped on my sandals and made my way to the front door.

My hand rested on the brass door knob for a second before I paused and turned back toward his tall silhouette standing several feet behind me.

"Thanks for tonight, Will," I softly said.

"Don't mention it," he whispered, with a half-smile escaping from his lips.

I smiled too, and then I slowly turned back toward the cherry chestnut door, twisted the knob and slid through its frame and back into the chilly, evening air.

A Letter

When I reached the stack of metal mailboxes, I used the smallest key that dangled from my overly cluttered keychain to open the tiny compartment. Then, I pulled out two envelopes–one was most likely junk mail and addressed to April, my roommate; the other was smaller and hand-written and bore my name across its front. I smiled when I saw that the return address on the small, ivory envelope was Brady's. I paused for a moment to rip open its seal.

Brady had made it a point to send me letters sporadically during our time apart. Though his letters were never very long or in-depth, they were very sweet and never failed to make my day. Smiling, I hastily pulled out a piece of cream stationery and allowed my eyes to carefully browse over the words:

Dear Julia,
Though I miss you like crazy, I'm kept afloat by the thought of us.
At times when I think that I cannot wait another minute to see you,
I think about a time when our lives will no longer keep us a world
away—a time when forever is ours. I love you, Julia.
Waiting on forever,
Brady

My smile grew. Brady had a way with words. He was quite possibly a man after my own heart. I appreciated the fact that he could take a piece of paper and pen and transform them into a mini work of art. He was my own, little Shakespeare.

Folding the stationery over itself and sliding it back into the envelope, I reached for my phone in my back pants pocket of my jeans and found Brady's number on speed dial.

Within seconds, I heard his Northeastern accent pouring through the speakers.

"Hey, I got a love letter from someone today," I playfully said when he answered.

"You did? Who is he? I'll take him right here, right now," he said in his best, raging lunatic voice.

"Relax, I think he's harmless," I said, smiling.

"And who are you calling harmless, exactly?" he chimed back.

I laughed as I took a seat on a bench outside of my Banker's Hill apartment building.

"So, what are you doing tonight? Saturday night. Got any big plans?" he asked.

"Hmm, well I think we'll head out to the farm and go skinny dipping in the lake and hope Cranky Joe doesn't catch us," I said, smiling.

"What? Really?" he asked. A sense of surprise shot to his voice.

"No, I'm kidding. Where would I do that here? I wish though. Life was so much simpler back then," I confessed longingly.

"So, that's what you did for fun out in the sticks?" he chided.

"Doesn't it sound fun? Well, at least fun at seventeen, I guess?" I asked.

"The skinny dipping part doesn't sound half bad, but I'm not so sure I can say the same about the lake. Aren't there alligators in there?" he asked.

"What? Brady, it's Missouri, not Mississippi," I said, laughing.

"Crocodiles?" he asked, hesitantly.

"No," I said, still laughing.

"Oh, well," he said. "It's not all that bad, even if you can't go skinny dipping with the alligators or the crocks. You're on to bigger and better."

I paused for a moment without saying anything.

"Yeah, I guess you're right," I finally said softly, my smile fading slightly.

The weather was always beautiful. The palm trees were nice–don't get me wrong. And an ocean in your backyard–it doesn't really get any better than that. So, I'm not really sure why a lake in the middle of nowhere made me smile secretly to myself. Maybe it was the simplicity I missed–even if it came with an endearingly intrusive nature, like when you walk into the grocery store and the owner asks how your grandmother has been doing. It's funny, though. The ways of a small town seemed peculiar and almost foreign to me now, but nevertheless, there remained always a special place for their allure no matter how distant they became to me. This was the one thing that I wished Brady could understand or at least appreciate. Coming from Hamilton, a city in New York City's metropolitan area, Brady could relate very little to my youth. Though Hamilton was its own, little community, it surpassed New Milford's size over a hundred times. And Brady, to top it off, found no solace in small towns. Despite my subtle persuasions, he could see no benefits whatsoever of living in a place the size of "a pea," as he called it, secluded from major hospitals, booming businesses and towering high rises.

This bothered me on some level, even though I felt as if it shouldn't. After all, I too had escaped from my community's claustrophobic grip years ago, and I too couldn't imagine going back to live there permanently. But maybe I thought that somehow and somewhere along the line my small town had become a piece of me, and by Brady not appreciating it, it meant in some twisted way that he didn't appreciate me fully either. I knew that my meandering ponderings turned into misguided logic somewhere down the line, but nevertheless, try as I may, I couldn't shake the feeling of unintended rejection.

But even though Brady didn't comprehend me wholly, it was hardly enough to stunt how I felt about him, however. After all, I could never fully understand what it had been like to grow up in his life in New York either, and he had so many other ambitious qualities that more than made up for his inability to see the world retroactively through my sixteen-year-old eyes. In the end, he could have come from Mars and still have been Mr. Perfect. And anyway, I had always wanted more than a quiet existence in rural Missouri, and more importantly, in the end, I too had changed, and I knew that I couldn't expect someone to relate to a world that not even I wholly understood anymore.

"Bigger and better," I said again, expressionlessly into the phone, as my eyes caught the sails of a sailboat coming back into the harbor in the distance.

Fame

I had made it to Saturday morning, and my alarm had just reminded me of that fact. I quickly reached over and swatted at it. It continued to ring. I swatted at it again. Silence.

I rolled over, groaned, and in the meantime, somehow elbowed my roommate's cat in the head.

"Allie. I'm sorry, Kitty," I called after the frightened cat now scurrying out of the room.

Now, I was up, but I made no attempt to put the covers and pillows back together as I ventured out into the living room. April was still sleeping–or would be until the cat alerted her of my murder attempt.

I slid some open books over on the coffee table in search of the remote. I didn't find it there, so I turned to the couch and spotted a corner of it sticking out from underneath a throw blanket. I grabbed it and switched on the television, which was in the process of running a familiar commercial.

A big, sleepy yawn later, I made my way into the kitchen and reached into the cabinet for a small, white ceramic bowl.

"That's what I said," I mumbled, habitually reciting the catchy commercial jingle, while finding the box of frosted wheats in the pantry.

What do bunnies have to do with bread? I aimlessly wondered then as I poured the little white and tan bails into my ceramic bowl.

At the same time, I continued to passively listen to the television. *Good Morning Today* was just returning from the commercial break, and I quickly recognized the anchor's familiar voice.

"Mr. Shawn Neville, your lovely voice means Saturday morning. I love you," I said to no one listening then as I habitually grabbed the carton of milk from the refrigerator and poured it onto my cereal bails.

After I had filled the bowl halfway with milk, I stuffed the carton back into the refrigerator, scooped up the bowl and grabbed a spoon from a drawer.

Oh, music time. I hadn't missed it.

I made my way back into the living room and plopped down onto the soft couch, cereal bowl in one hand, spoon in the other.

My eyes, planted on the television's screen, followed the anchor's facial movements as I methodically crunched on the little, round bails, one by one.

"That's your news for this hour," I listened to Shawn Neville announce. "Now, we're going outside live to our concert series performance with anchor Heather Hughes."

I scooted closer to the edge of the couch and watched the camera's shot move from inside the studio to a stage just outside of it.

The live performances had long ago become my favorite part about morning news shows. I waited eagerly to see which band I would get to hear today. I think a part of me was still hoping to see that small band that Brady and I saw on what would become our first date those years ago. I really thought they would make it.

"So, Will, you were discovered in a small St. Louis pub. That doesn't happen everyday," my ears, without so much as a warning, heard the anchor remark.

Suddenly, I dropped the spoon into my cereal and let my bowl fall to my lap.

"What?" I heard myself ask out loud.

"No, I don't recon it does, but I'm happy and thankful to be here," the figure in dark jeans, a white shirt and a cowboy hat said from inside my screen.

I felt almost numb as I stared, mesmerized. I could see him standing there on the small stage and amongst a sea of people, holding his guitar across his body. I could see him, but the problem was that I was having a hard time believing it.

"Well, we've got a whole lot of people who are also thankful that you're here, and I'm sure they're ready for a song. So, why don't you take it away?" I listened to the anchor ask him.

"What?" I heard myself ask again. My words felt as if someone else were saying them. In fact, I felt as if someone else were me. I couldn't possibly be living this exact moment right now. I was beyond shocked, beyond confused. I was dreaming. I had to be dreaming. I must have gone to bed hungry, and now, I'm dreaming that I'm eating cereal, and Will is the weird thing in the dream that doesn't make sense. All dreams have that–the weird thing. Right?

For the next several minutes, I watched the handsome singer, captivated by his familiar, soothing voice as I listened to his lyrics flow from his lips to my ears. It was him. It was his voice. He was the singer on the stage. The singer was Will. I tried with everything I had to wrap my mind around the moment, the moment that was now transporting me back years to a summer night around a fire, a fall evening on his back porch–a hundred times in just as many places.

When the music stopped and the show went to a commercial break, I sat in the chair silently and as still as humanly possible for what felt like an eternity, allowing every piece–every image, every word–to sink deep into the depths of my self. And when I had convinced myself that what I had just seen was, in fact, real, I jumped up and darted into my room, coming out with my cell phone in hand.

My hands were shaking as I punched in Rachel's speed dial number.

I waited anxiously for her voice.

"Hey, what's up?" I heard her answer on the other end seconds later.

I didn't say anything. I had just noticed my words were gone.

"Hello? Julia?" I heard Rachel say.

"What, what is Will doing on my TV?" I somehow managed to get out, though I knew I sounded frazzled–like I had just woken up to a neon pink sky.

"Yeah, I've already seen it. I was going to call you, but I didn't want to wake you. I taped it. Didn't he look good?" she asked, obviously not at all as fazed as I was.

"Wait, Rach, back up. You knew about this?" I asked her, partially already accusing her of a lie by omission.

"Of course. Everybody did, including you. I told you about it last week," she said.

"Told me about what?" I demanded.

"That he was going to be on this morning," she said.

"That he was going to be on?" I questioned.

I grew completely silent for a second. It's confirmed. I'm dreaming. This can't possibly be real. What was she talking about?

"Rach, how did this all happen?" I asked.

"Well, his agent or recording company or something knew somebody who worked for the news station, and...," she started.

"No, I mean, how did this all happen?" I interrupted. "He's singing, and he has an agent–and he's singing. Will doesn't sing in front of people."

Rachel laughed.

"Well, he does now, honey," she said, with a smile in her voice. "Law school's really gotten to your head. I told you all of this."

"What? When?" I protested.

"I don't know–months ago, but nothing's really happened until recently," she said.

"What was I doing? Was I studying? Rach, I told you not to tell me things while I'm studying. Things like this happen, where I wake up to Will standing in my living room, and I have no idea how he got there. So, start over. How did all this happen?" I demanded again.

"Okay," she said patiently. "I'll start from the beginning. Will ran into an agent at The Home of Blues in St. Louis one night about six months ago. This guy recognized Will from the weekend before when he had filled in a gig for a friend at the same bar. The agent then eventually got Will and some other guys to record a demo. Then, a small label signed them a couple months later, and the rest is history, I guess."

"Wow," I said in a state of nothing but utter shock. "What changed his mind?"

"What?" Rachel asked.

I knew just enough of what was going on around me to tell that Rachel sounded distracted.

"He never wanted to sing like that. What changed his mind?" I asked her again.

"Oh, I'm not sure. Hey, Jules, I've got to call you back. Rover's getting into the cat food again."

"Yeah, okay. I'll talk to you later," I said, sounding defeated and the most puzzled you could possibly be–all at the same time.

I ended the call and let the phone drop to my lap as my attention rushed back to my television's screen and to the morning show returning from the commercial break. How had I not known? How could I have not known? My mind was in a frenzy of dizzying thoughts.

I watched intently as the camera panned back to the TV anchor, standing to the side of the outdoor stage. She was holding a microphone and gushing over the singer and his band, which was now softly playing in the background.

"If you know District 9's story, you know that they're a real fairy tale of some sorts," the anchor said enthusiastically.

District 9?

"Less than a year ago, they were randomly plucked from obscurity," the anchor continued. "Now, with the help of some great marketing and the release of their first album and one song in particular, they're here today. The next song they're going to sing for us is that song. Titled *Let Go*, the ballad rocketed to the top twenty and then topped the charts in a matter of a few, short weeks after the song hit national airwaves. And can you believe that most of the band members, including the lead singer, are firefighters? I guess you could say that they're all-American heroes," she said, as she turned away from the camera and back to the stage.

"Take it away. It's District 9," the suited woman then said to the gathered public as the assembled fans in the background cheered wildly.

After a short count, the band began playing. I watched fixedly, still frozen in my place. My heart had sped up by several more beats per minute by now. I listened to the words pour off of Will's lips as I watched his fingers strum the guitar's strings. From the looks of things this morning, it seemed as if he reveled in the spotlight. He looked happy up there. That was the only thing that seemed different about him—he looked happy to play in front of people. Everything else looked exactly the same. But I still was not completely convinced I wasn't dreaming either.

Will finished singing the last lyrics of the song, and the crowd erupted into applause and more cheers, which ultimately made me smile for the first time since I had noticed him on my television's set. The smile was completely involuntary. I had barely even noticed its presence.

He was handsome, standing on that small stage with his ivory, acoustic guitar swung across his muscular body. His eyes were a fierce shade of blue, and his hair was just long enough to show off his natural curls. And he was smiling. I had decided that he looked very much the part of a true rock star or should I say, country star.

Wow. Rachel's conversation had left me with so many unanswered questions. Like, when had he seriously contemplated becoming a professional musician? And, he was still a firefighter? As far as I knew, that's what he still had done, and the anchor had said it too. But how had he balanced it all? And how had he gone from playing melodies for me on his quiet back porch to playing songs for millions of screaming fans on my television screen? It was perplexing and amazing all at the same time, and I was mystified and so, so puzzled, to say the least.

"He did it," I whispered in amazement, still trying to convince myself that all of this was real. "He had done it," I said again, allowing it to sink in.

"But what was it that made you change your mind?" I whispered aloud to the handsome, blue-eyed signer inside my television's screen, as I leaned back and allowed the back of the chair to catch my fall.

Rachel's Novel

I was in the process of bringing up another load of dirty clothes to the laundry room when my phone, resting on the coffee table, burst into my favorite melody. As I walked toward the glass table, I shifted the plastic laundry basket onto my right hip and reached for the phone.

When I saw the familiar number, I flipped the cell open and continued again on my path to the small laundry room.

"Hey, Rach," I said into the phone.

"Hey, sorry I had to go so quickly. Rover gets sick if he eats the cat's food," she explained.

I snickered.

"It's fine," I said.

"So, you saw him? I can't believe you didn't know," she exclaimed.

"Yeah, me neither. But next time I don't respond to that big of news like you think I should, say it again," I said.

"I thought it was odd, but I know you've got your own stuff going on over there on the other side of the world. I just thought maybe you weren't interested in us cowpokes anymore," she said, with a smile in her voice.

"Rachel," I playfully scolded.

"I'm kidding. I'm kidding. Next time, I'll be more aware of your unawareness," she chided.

"Thanks," I said, laughing.

"He looked really good though, didn't he?" she asked.

"You're engaged, Rachel," I reminded her teasingly, countering her exaggerated enthusiasm.

"Girl, I know that, and happily engaged, but you're not," she jokingly jeered back.

"Rachel," I scolded, shaking my head, but continuing to smile.

"I know, I know. You're with Mr. Perfect. How is Mr. Med School, by the way? Isn't he coming to see you soon?" she asked–a hint of mischief mixed with excitement filled her voice.

"He's doing great," I said. "He's been pretty busy lately, but then again, so have I. And, yes, he's coming in fourteen days."

"I see you've got the countdown going already," Rachel said, pausing only to laugh. "Hey, I know you've got Mr. Perfect and that you two are going to get married and live in a big, beautiful mansion and have the whole, white picket fence and two-and-a-half-kids thing, which means you probably don't want to talk about Mr. Firefighter and Big-time Music Star, but…"

Rachel paused for dramatic effect before going on. "But," I said.

"But," she continued, "I would be doing a major injustice to you if I didn't at least tell you that I think he's still got a thing for you," she confessed, as if she had been holding the secret in a little box in her mind for ages, and now, she couldn't possibly bare to hold it in any longer.

"What?" I questioned puzzlingly. "Rachel, we've been through this a million times. That was high school. Everyone's moved on from it by now–except for you."

The whole soliloquy had elicited a grin from me because I half knew where it was all going. I, by now, had also gotten all of the clothes stuffed into the dryer from the previous washer load and had swung the lid closed. While using my shoulder to balance the phone against my ear, I turned the dryer dial to the *normal* setting with one hand before starting the machine with the other.

"No, no, I know, but I'm serious," she continued. "I talked to him at the reunion, which by the way, you are not weaseling out of in another five years. I am not going to another one of those without you. Janette Smith was unbearable. All she did was talk about her accountant boyfriend, who was just hired by the bank here in town and how he's so successful and blah de blah, and Will was sitting right there. I don't think she had any clue as to what he had done or what he was about to be. Hey, kind of like someone else I know."

"Funny, Rach," I interjected, as she continued.

"Anyway, I know that he's still the same old Will, but seriously, her and her big-time accountant boyfriend must live under a rock," she said. "In your defense, they should know. It's all over town. But anyway, I kept looking at

Will, waiting for him to say something, but he never did. He just sat back quietly and let her think that life hadn't changed for him since high school. It was actually pretty comical after awhile. But anyway, that being said, after Janette finally left, Will and I talked about his singing career and how he was doing and how his family was dealing with it and all, and then he asked where you were."

Rachel paused, and I waited for her to continue. When she didn't, I spoke up.

"So?" I asked wondering how that added up to Will still having a "thing" for me.

"Well, it wasn't the way he asked or even that he asked at all that was unusual. It was the way he reacted after I answered his question that struck me as odd," she continued.

"Okay," I said, now waiting to hear the "odd" part.

"He gave me that hollow-eyed stare he gives, and he just nodded his head," Rachel continued.

There was silence then, and I hesitated before speaking.

"Rachel," I stammered. "Honestly, you're going to have to come up with something better than that to make me a believer. He stared at you blankly and nodded his head? How does that tell you anything? Doesn't he do that all the time?"

"I'm being honest, Jules. He did the exact same thing when I asked him how he was holding up after you two broke up years ago, and I know he was a wreck then," she added.

"Rachel, it was his idea to break up," I reminded her.

My comment seemed to have hit a wall before it ever reached the other end of the phone. I waited for Rachel's response, but it never came, so I continued emptying my laundry basket of whites into the washing machine. Now, to both humor my friend and to satisfy my curiosity, I guess a little, I continued the conversation.

"Well, how did you answer him?" I asked, sounding only as if I were playing along and that was all.

"I told him that you were still in San Diego doing the whole law thing and that you would have loved to have been there–at the reunion, but that you had exams that day," she said.

"That's it? He knew half of that already. Anyway, I told you that I think he's dating someone, right?" I asked her.

She was quiet for a second.

"Remember?" I asked again. "I overheard his cousin say that he had found 'the one.'"

"That's right, I forgot about that. I haven't seen her. She wasn't there. He came alone. I'll keep my eyes peeled for you though," she happily offered.

"That's not necessary, Rach," I said, laughing.

"Okay, I'll keep my eyes peeled for myself then," she said, before pausing.

"Hey, Jon's calling. Let me take it and call you back," Rachel quickly rattled off.

"Okay, Miss Popular, I'll talk to you later," I said, still amused by the entire conversation I had just had with my friend.

I closed the phone and squeezed it back into my pants pocket.

Rachel's overly active imagination never ceased to amaze me, even after all of the years I had known her.

"Poor Jon," I said under my breath, smiling.

Jon was Rachel's fiancé. The two had just recently gotten engaged and had already set a wedding date for next spring. Rachel had met him in college. I had always thought that they complemented each other well. Jon was laid back, while Rachel was outgoing and always wanted to be in *the know*. He kept her grounded, while she kept him spirited. Spirit was probably the most endearing quality about my friend. Rachel's mind never stopped churning out new schemes and ideas that pertained to the love life of her friends. Her plots were all very playfully devious but always in good nature. I knew that she only wanted the best for those she rallied behind, and in the end, I was glad that Rachel was in my corner. Believing this, I knew that I couldn't be too hard on her when she brought up my former high school sweetheart. Rachel had always rooted for Team Julia and Will, and after we had broken up, she had taken it upon herself to follow the relationship to its absolute end, which Rachel didn't believe was reached until marriage, either to each other or to other people. Although I knew Rachel was pulling for the former as opposed to the latter, a part of me believed that she used my and Will's life as her real-life novel, only she had to discover the words on the page herself through crafty questions and careful observations. Nevertheless, I loved this part about Rachel. I only hoped she wouldn't be devastated when life ran its fateful, meandering course and I didn't end up with the man my friend had been rooting for all along.

Birthday Wishes

I couldn't see his face, but I knew him, and no doubt about it, loved him. He was fiery and familiar, strong and comfortable, and he held my hand with a firm gentleness, almost as if he promised in it that he'd love me honestly and never let me go. But who was he? I traced the contours in his abs and chest as we lay in the tall grass. Maybe it was the shadow the sun made as it bounced off of a nearby oak. Maybe he just didn't have a face at all. *Who are you?*

I continued to trace the paths etched out in his muscles as I lay my head onto his strong chest and listened to the soft echoes of his heart beating. His body was so familiar—not at all mysterious, though his identity still remained a mystery to me. *Who are you?* I persisted.

As I followed the rising and falling of his chest, I felt his other hand come to rest on top of mine. I felt safe, like I was home. I looked up then, and slowly, the shadow lifted from his face, and I smiled.

"Will," I whispered. "I knew it was you."

I drearily rolled over and reached for my cell phone blaring on my nightstand. It was eight in the morning.

"Speak of the devil," I mumbled, as I struggled to regain a worldly consciousness, at the same time, burying my head back into my pillow before answering.

"Hel-lo," I managed to get out. My voice was scratchy and deeper than usual.

"Good morning, and happy birthday!" I heard him shout on the other end of the phone, unfazed by my heavy-eyed greeting.

The call surprised me, though it wasn't completely out of the ordinary. We had always wished each other a happy birthday, and the tradition had continued even after we had parted ways romantically years ago.

"Thank you," I replied, pulling the phone slightly away from my ear and realizing that it was, in fact, my birthday. The thought made me smile. "And how have you been, rock star?" I playfully asked, now sitting up and starting to come to.

I had called him the day after I had seen him on TV for the first time. He had been somewhat short, but I had also expected that. Short conversations had been our forte for the past several years now.

"I've been doing great," he quickly rang back.

"Good," I softly replied.

"So, what are your plans today, birthday girl?" he asked cheerfully.

"Oh, nothing too much. Brady's flying in later, then dinner," I said, trying to downplay my excitement a little.

"The doctor?" he asked sarcastically.

"Yes, the doctor," I said, playing along.

"What about you?" I asked.

"What about me?" he shot back quickly.

"I heard that you met someone," I stated and asked at the same time. I sounded as thrilled and excited for him as humanly possible—under the circumstances and at eight in the morning, though I'm pretty sure it just came out sounding as forced as a *congratulations* to the winner after I had just been declared the loser.

"Where did you hear that from?" he rang back just as quickly. He sounded surprised by my statement.

"I overheard Kassi mimicking you at Mona's wedding," I explained nonchalantly.

Will remained silent. He seemed to have been formulating his next thought, but then I thought I heard him smile on the other end of the phone.

"Well, as a matter of fact, I have. I met her a little while ago," he replied confidently.

The words didn't come as a shock to me. After all, I had already known the answer. But I had to admit that hearing the words come from his mouth so easily surprised me at first—even cut a sliver into my heart a little. Nevertheless, I acted unfazed.

"She does realize that you're not just some big-time country star, right?" I playfully questioned him.

Will chuckled.

"Yeah, I'm pretty sure that deep down she just sees me as the small-town country bumpkin that I am," he confessed.

I laughed and shook my head. I neglected to press him for more details, though I desperately wanted to. I wanted to know where she was from, what she did, how he had met her, but in the end, I stifled my possibly never-ending barrage of questions. What stopped me from inquiring further was partially due to the fact that I was still half asleep and partially due to the overwhelming truth that, deep down, I didn't really want to talk about his budding love life on my birthday. After all, Brady would be arriving in several hours, and I had waited what seemed like an eternity to see him again.

"That's great, Will. I'm really happy for you," I half lied.

I tried to sound sincere. I think I might have just pulled it off.

He was quiet for a second.

"Thanks, Jules. It means a lot," he eventually said softly, before taking a deep breath in and then letting the air out slowly through his lips.

"Jules, I don't want you to take this the wrong way, and I'm just curious, but do you ever still think about us?" Will asked sheepishly, cautiously.

I hesitated.

"What do you mean?" I asked him, somewhat derailed by the drastic change in subject.

"I mean the little things we've shared, the times we've shared," he clarified.

I took a second.

"Sometimes," I quietly answered, remembering my dream.

Will paused, as if not expecting to hear that exact response. I panicked slightly. My bleeding heart had been exposed, and my head scrambled to pick up the pieces.

"I do think about how we were sometimes, and it makes me smile. We had some good times together, times that I'll probably never forget, but I also know now that things have changed–we have changed. We're not the same people we were in high school, and I've come to understand that, like I know you have too," I explained.

I stopped and waited for his response. Eventually, he spoke again.

"We did have some fun, didn't we?" Will asked and stated softly.

I could picture him gently smiling on the other end of the phone. I could almost see his lips widening across his strong, structured face, revealing his bright, white teeth and causing creases at the corners of his baby blue eyes in the words he spoke.

Then, he continued.

"You know, I was just thinking about it the other day, and I kept coming back to something. I know that people generally change the way they see the world as they grow, and I guess that changes some things, but I also kept coming back to the fact that I'm still the same person that I was when I was seventeen. I've just grown a little, seen a little bit more."

As Will finished his thoughts, I was again at a loss for words for a moment. Was he going somewhere with this? Then, just as quickly, my education in argumentation bolted wildly into the conversation like a wild mustang discovering freedom for the very first time.

"But isn't growing ultimately changing?" I asked. I wasn't even sure myself what I was talking about. It sounded kind of good, I rationalized.

Will paused. He didn't seem to agree exactly, but he refrained from voicing his opinion either way, opting to change the subject altogether once again instead.

"I was just curious as to how you felt about it, you being the philosophical expert out of the two of us," Will said jokingly.

Will's comment elicited a giggle from me, and then our conversation grew quiet again.

"Well, I hope you have a great birthday, Jules," Will said one last time, filling the silence.

"Thanks, and thanks for calling," I replied politely.

"Anytime, Jules," he softly said. "I'll talk to you soon."

"Bye, Will," I said.

I hung up the phone, paused and then pushed the thick comforter off my body and rolled out of bed.

"That was odd," I muttered.

I usually would have stopped to analyze the conversation, but this particular morning, a million errands scrolled through my mind. Brady would be here soon, and I still had to run to the grocery store, straighten up and take a shower. But for now, however, I settled on a quick jog around the neighborhood. I needed something that would wake me up quickly and get my blood flowing.

I threw on some running shorts, a tee shirt and tennis shoes and picked up my MP3 player off of the small, round table in the tiny hallway.

As I stepped out the door, I caught myself thinking that it was nice to hear from Will. I cherished the fact that we had continued to remain friends, even after the friendship had changed and shifted throughout the years. And I was happy for him, I admitted. I knew that deep, deep, deep down somewhere, I wanted only the best for him, which included him being just as happy with someone else as I was with Brady. Good for him, I tried to convince myself again. Good for him.

But that dream, on the other hand, I thought, remembering it again. I tried unsuccessfully to shake off its image—that feeling.

"You've got to stop haunting me like that, Will Stephens," I mumbled to myself, as I turned on the music player and started my jog down the concrete sidewalk of my neighborhood.

Fireflies

"**I** wish you didn't have to go," I said, as I took his bottle of water.

"I know," he softly said. "I'll miss you."

He faced me then and wrapped his arms around my frame.

"I'll miss you too," I said, following his lead and squeezing him tightly also. "Call me as soon as you land."

"Don't worry. I will, and I'll see you in a few weeks, right?" he asked. There was a hint of optimism in his voice as he pulled away from our embrace.

"Yeah, I can't wait already," I confessed, smiling.

"Okay, give me a kiss," he said. "This plane's going to take off with or without me."

"Would that be such a bad thing–without you, I mean?" I asked, smiling slightly still.

Brady smiled too.

I kissed Brady and then watched him throw his bag up onto the security belt. A part of me ached. I wanted to tell him not to leave me again. Maybe his flight would get cancelled. Maybe there would be a delay and he could stay for lunch or something–at the very least. Maybe there would be a surprise snow storm in the middle of September in Southern California. Or what about lightning or maybe the pilot overslept or they forgot to stock the cabin with peanuts–anything?

I let out a heavy sigh. I knew the odds were against me. If those things happened, they never happened when you wanted them to anyway. Plus, I knew he had to get back to school and his job. I had to get back to school too, but it didn't stop me from wishing I didn't and that there was still hope he would stay for just a little bit longer.

I continued to watch him as he slipped his shoes and his watch back on and then collected back his bag from the moving conveyor belt. He waved one last time, and I waved back before the escalator escorted him out of sight.

I continued to stare at the place on the moving stairs where he had disappeared into the vanishing corridor. Maybe he would reappear again. Maybe he would change his mind and stay for an extra day–maybe even forever.

Long seconds drew on, but Brady never reappeared. I sighed in defeat and then turned back toward the airport terminal's exit. This was going to be a long three weeks.

I reached home minutes later, and by then, I felt exhausted. Not only had Brady and I jam-packed a week's worth of activities into two days, a constant sense of missing him, even in the hours before he had left, had emotionally drained me.

"How was leaving your boy at the airport?" April shouted from upstairs when I walked into the apartment.

April had become a close companion while in law school. In fact, our friendship, in a way, made me feel like I had known her since childhood. Then again, law school had a way of doing that to people, I had figured out somewhere along the way. We shared a common suffering.

"It went okay, I guess. I miss him already, but he'll be back in three weeks or so," I replied, my voice fading as the sentence drew on. I was working hard to fight off the pain of missing him.

April's question satisfied, I sauntered into the kitchen, set my purse down onto a chair and dropped my keys onto the white countertop. Thoughts of my ever-present homework assignments loomed over my head as I gazed out onto the tiny piece of ocean that I could just barely see out of the window. It was the only piece we could afford. And I think it was by total accident that we could even see it at all. They had just torn down the high rise that would have obstructed our ocean view months before we moved in.

My thoughts slowly tapered away as my eyes caught a lighthouse coming to life in the far distance. Then, I spotted a tiny ship softly gliding on top of the ocean's gentle waves behind it. And before I knew it, my gaze had transformed into a stare, and my studious thoughts had completely faded to the back of my mind and were replaced with thoughts of Brady. I hoped that his flight would go well and that he would be able to take a nap on the plane before he would have to make the two-hour drive back to his apartment in Columbia. And I hoped that he had enjoyed his weekend with me, and I wondered if he missed me now as much as I missed him.

I noticed that, by now, the tiny ship had drifted behind a massive, asphalt-paved hill and out of sight, leaving only the modest lighthouse and the distant, soothing waves to my longing stare. I stood frozen in my place, entranced by the ocean's endless vastness. It was almost as if that miniscule piece of sea were calling out to me, at the same time that I was pleading with loneliness not to take me hostage. It was already too late though. The all-consuming creature had already stolen me away. I felt trapped, and I needed some air.

With that thought, I scurried into my room and grabbed a jacket.

"April, I'll be back," I quickly yelled upstairs.

And before April could question my mission, I was out the door and in my jeep.

After driving several miles down the 805, I pulled off the interstate and meandered down a winding, neighborhood street. Then, where civilization on my side of the border finally ceased, I brought the SUV to a halt at the dead end and paused for a moment to stare out over my steering wheel and into the horizon.

Chula Vista, California—the place where two worlds met. A sole land owner had owned the hundreds of acres of property along the California-Mexico border for most of his lifetime. Just recently, though, he had decided to sell the entire portion of it to a massive land development company. That company had since cleared all of the desert apricots and grasses and had left behind acres of barren, gently rolling hills of ginger-colored dirt, sparsely littered with parked land levelers and this road to nowhere. But just beyond the border, however, behind the obtrusive levy and massive fenced barrier, lay Tijuana. On that side of the world, houses, convenient stores, inns and abandoned buildings lay side-by-side–packed in tightly together.

"Hmm," I said reflectively, as I let out an audible sigh, marveling at the contrast.

Moments went by before I turned the volume dial on the radio up just a little more so that I could hear the music softly pouring through the speakers. And without missing a beat, I stepped out of my jeep and carefully crawled onto its hood. The evening air was just beginning to cool my surroundings. I could feel each chilling, gentle breeze as it passed over my body and tossed strands of my long hair across my face. When times got tough in law school or life, I always found myself here, at the end of this newly paved road, looking out over the vast emptiness of the rolling California hills and to the sea of Mexico. It wasn't much to look at during the daylight hours, but come night, the view completely transformed, taking on a magnificent and mysterious allure. It wasn't fireflies, but it was the closest thing I had now to the displays I remembered in my adolescence.

Off in the distance, a tiny herd of mountains to my left and the same piece of ocean that had called me there tonight to my right served as bookends that enclosed the scene in front of me. Evening shadows were just beginning to cast a blanket of darkness over the landscape as my eyes left the deserted California land. And then, something magical happened.

A sea of radiance sprang up. Millions of colorful lights jam-packed into one, tiny city just beginning to showcase Mexico's charm from where I lay boded farewell to the huge ball of red fire that had begun its descent into the ocean. New lights from homes, hotels, stores and bars were added every couple of seconds as the darkness grew around me. And tonight, my sky was Tijuana, and my stars, its lights.

I lay there silently, thinking about Brady, lakes, alligators and fireflies when one of Will's songs came gently pouring through my radio's speakers. A weighty smile found my lips then as I waited on the ebony sky to finally swallow me and then for the ever-appearing lights of Tijuana to rescue me from the darkness.

A Question

I pulled up to the first terminal in the airport and immediately spotted him. I gazed admirably at the tall, strawberry-blond figure. He looked so austere and handsome, even standing there with his little bags in hand. And as soon as I could, I brought the jeep to a stop alongside the curb and popped out.

"Hey, babe," Brady said, with a warm smile growing across his face.

"Hi, honey," I exclaimed. "How was your flight?"

He set his bags down and wrapped his arms around me.

Laura Miller

"It went okay. I can never get here fast enough though," he replied, his lips close to my ear, squeezing me tightly.

I too wrapped my arms around his muscular frame and squeezed him close. The embrace seemed strange and slightly forced, but it always had after we had gone weeks without seeing each other. It was hard to explain, but that first hug was like greeting someone you should know but secretly you don't know. It normally took a little while for us to warm up to each other again, but once we had, it was like we had never been apart.

Brady kissed me on my lips and then took a deep breath, as if taking in all of me in one inhale.

"Okay, let's get going," he said then, grabbing his carry-on and his small, rolling bag. "We've got reservations."

He threw his bags into the back of my jeep and then closed the hatch.

"Do you want me to drive?" Brady asked.

"Sure," I said, smiling. "Do you remember how to get there?"

"Oh course. How many times have we been there now?" he asked.

I smiled and then tossed Brady my keys and climbed quickly into the passenger's seat before the airport security guard could wave me down and tell me that I couldn't stop there. They were good at that.

It took roughly ten minutes to make it up the coast to La Jolla. Calvin's on the Cove was a quaint but elegant restaurant on the water in the small, coastal city just up Interstate 5. Brady and I had eaten there a few times before in Brady's several visits. The restaurant had

159

become, by far, our favorite dinner place—reserved for special occasions.

When we arrived in the center of La Jolla, Brady found a parking space on one of the town's narrow streets, not too far from Calvin's, and pulled in.

"I missed you, Julia," he said as he reached for my hand, pausing to look into my eyes, after putting the jeep into park.

"I missed you too," I said, smiling.

He kissed the top of my hand and then stepped out of the SUV. Meanwhile, I searched for my purse on the floorboard below my feet and noticed my cell phone had somehow fallen out and had landed on the opposite side of the floor. I grabbed my purse and then reached for the phone. Just as my hand felt its hard, boxy frame, I noticed the screen glow. I took a quick glance at the caller and felt my heart beat a little faster. It was Will. I hesitated for a second. I didn't know if it was out of habit or curiosity that I wanted to answer his call. Regardless, I wasn't going to answer it tonight, and I hastily pressed *Ignore* and stuffed the phone back into my purse just as Brady opened the passenger door.

"Thank ya, dear," I said, smiling and stepping onto the sidewalk—careful to disguise my knowledge of the call.

"Wait, Will, I want to leave my sunglasses in the car," I said as Brady attempted to close the door behind me.

Before I could even realize what I had said, he paused and caught my eyes.

"What did you say?" he asked. A puzzled look had lightninged across his face.

My thoughts stopped suddenly. Had I just said what I thought I had? It was an honest slip, and with it, my heart raced again.

"Will I need my sunglasses or should I leave them in the car?" I recited quickly, trying my best to recover.

"Oh," Brady said and then paused. "Probably not."

"Then, I'll leave them here," I said, throwing the glasses onto the seat and breathing a sigh of relief.

It wasn't the first time I had let it slip, and it also wasn't the first time I had successfully covered it up either. I despised, at times, that I was a living, breathing creature of habit and that my old habits died hard. I knew, however, that like most bad habits constantly corrected, this one too would eventually fade. I just wished that the whole process would speed up a little–at least for my relationship's sake.

I smiled at Brady and took his hand as we made our way to the restaurant, resting quietly on the water.

When we reached the front desk, the hostess seated us at a table next to the low railing on the ocean terrace. The sun was just beginning to set in the distance, and its warm colors had already started bleeding into the piece of the Pacific Ocean that Brady and I now viewed.

"This spot is perfect," I exclaimed. "I can see everything from here."

Brady only smiled.

When the waiter came over to the table to take our order, Brady recited from memory our favorite dishes.

"I'll have the steak, and my beautiful girlfriend will have the lemon tortellini," Brady rattled off to the waiter.

"You sure we just can't start with the chocolate cake?" I asked Brady teasingly, the corners of my mouth rising slightly.

Brady looked at me with a flushed expression. It made me stop short.

"Okay, I guess it can wait," I said, still smiling but now half questioning his severe reaction, while handing my menu to the waiter.

The man in black then disappeared to fill our request as Brady's face went back to a perfect, confident normal again.

"I love you," he said as if it were the first time he had ever said it to me.

My questioning look quickly dissolved into a warm smile.

"I love you too," I said.

Charm had always been his best quality, though I had to admit that it had matured over the years–or at least had come a long way since the sly trickery that had ultimately landed him our first date.

"I've never really liked the word *girlfriend*," Brady confessed then.

I looked at him puzzlingly.

"What's wrong with *girlfriend*?" I asked.

"I don't know," he said. "It's just a funny word."

I laughed softly.

"Okay," I surrendered.

"Can you believe that it's been four years?" he asked, changing the subject.

"Yeah, I'm so glad that law school is only three. I don't think I could have made it through another year," I said, looking slightly heavy-burdened.

Brady, seemingly puzzled, stared at me.

"No," he said, smirking. "I don't mean school. I mean us. We've been together for more than four years now–well, officially."

I cocked my head and stared into Brady's warm, brown eyes.

"Oh," I said, smiling again. "Wow, has it really been that long already?" I asked, now with a thought-provoking gaze. "It feels like just yesterday that you asked me to that concert. What was the name of that band again?"

"The All-American Saints," Brady replied, smiling.

"That's right," I said, nodding my head. "Gosh, it's crazy, but sometimes, it's all just a blur."

"It's called grad school, honey. It'll do that to you," Brady said, laughing.

"Yeah, I guess you're right," I said, starting to smile. "Well, here's to the beginning of the end," I said, raising my glass of wine.

"Of school, anyway," he snuck in.

"Of school," I confirmed, smiling.

Brady raised his glass also and brought it to mine.

The meal came soon after, and we sat under the few stars coming to life in the night's western sky, eating and catching up on the previous month of our lives. Then, after the meal, Brady subtly motioned for the waiter to come back over to our table.

"Can I interest you two in any dessert this lovely evening," the waiter sputtered off when he reached us.

I looked at Brady with big eyes and a wide smile.

"Yes, sir," Brady said in his suave, New York accent, while grinning back at me. His accent had yet to take on the Midwestern drawl, despite the fact that he had called Missouri his home for quite a few years now.

"I think we'll take the chocolate cake," he continued.

"You know me so well, honey," I said, smiling at Brady after the waiter had scurried away again.

"I should. I've known you for five years," Brady said, now with a big grin.

"That's right, and exactly why did it take you so long to finally ask me out?" I playfully questioned him.

"Well, frankly, you scared me," Brady said with the most serious look that he could conjure up.

"What?" I asked, slightly confused.

"You had those huge gloves and that big, puffy coat. You looked like the Abominable Snowwoman. Well, unless it was your perfect 80 degrees," Brady replied, starting to crack a smile.

"Okay, okay," I said, smirking and shaking my head. "And I see that you haven't lost that childlike charm either, have you?" I said, now laughing and setting my linen napkin onto the surface of the table.

Brady smiled, and then his smile slowly faded.

"But seriously, Julia, I don't know. I don't know why it took me so long," he said, looking me in the eyes.

The look in his eyes made me somehow uneasy—like he was about to tell me something severely serious.

"You were such a good friend and then before I knew it, you had become my best friend," I listened to him continue.

I smiled a soft but slightly uncomfortable smile.

"Your dessert," the waiter chimed in, setting a shiny, silver platter with a rounded covering on top of it in front of me.

I sat back in my chair, staring at the covered dish and wondering when, in my absence, had Calvin's upped the ante and changed its dessert presentation. My piece of cake normally came out on a white, ceramic plate decorated with chocolaty syrup swirls, and while the cake had easily appealed to the eyes in the past, tonight's staging effortlessly surpassed the normal delivery. Despite the change, however, I waited in anticipation for the waiter to raise his hand, which now held a knob on the top of the silver platter's covering, and to reveal to me my favorite chocolaty treat and, by far, my favorite part of dinner.

"Enjoy," the waiter said finally, removing the shiny, arched cover from the silver tray.

My face flushed white and then quickly turned back to a rosy rouge when I saw what had replaced my piece of cake on the serving dish. Then, a nervous shot of adrenalin sprinted rapidly throughout my body.

On the platter where my chocolate piece of cake had always sat in the past, was no chocolate cake at all. And in its place, sat a single, sable-colored, velvet box.

Managing to keep my wits about me on the outside, I uncontrollably panicked on the inside, and a feverish smile tumbled off my lips as I tried as best as I could to hide the uneasiness that I felt was seeping through my eyes and lips. It wasn't my birthday. It wasn't Christmas. It wasn't Valentine's Day. Was there another holiday that you might get little, velvet boxes?

Before I could grasp the full intensity of the moment, Brady was down on one knee beside me.

Then, I knew. This wasn't a holiday.

Clutching the black, velvet box, he gracefully removed the ring that was inside and gently took my left hand. The scene had, by now, attracted a large following, and before I knew it, I had been transported to a live, reality television show that every eye in the restaurant was thirsting to watch.

"Julia, you have been my rock, my joy, my safe place. I love you. Make me the happiest man in the world, and marry me," I heard Brady recite, with a soft smile on his face.

I stared at him with a blank expression and, again, flushed features. I was mad at myself that I had not even anticipated, much less contemplated that something like this could have happened tonight or even in the near future, for that matter. I had been agonizingly caught off-guard, and I knew that it was no one's fault but my own. Besides, he was right for asking me anyway. This was, after all, the next step in our relationship. I loved him. He loved me. He was brilliant and talented and charming. He was Mr. Perfect. Any girl would kill to have him. I really had nothing else to say but what I should say–what I must say. My mind raced as I spoke softly.

"I do," I stammered. "I will. I, I mean, yes," I sputtered, forcing a happy smile.

Brady smiled back and breathed a sigh of relief as he slipped the beautiful, one-karat diamond ring onto a finger that was attached to the hand in front of me. The crowd broke out into a burst of applause and cheers then, as Brady came off of one knee and kissed my lips as I sat in my chair, smiling, still trying to comprehend the previous few minutes of my life.

I wasn't sure what to do next. I looked at Brady and then at my left hand and at the new, sparkling adornment resting on my ring finger. My own hand looked foreign to me now. My old hand didn't have this shiny growth on it. My old hand didn't look as established or put together as this new hand. My old hand didn't belong to someone who belonged to anyone. I stumbled on the inside–like in a dream when you're uncontrollably falling but you never hit the ground. On the outside, however, I was a rock–a smiling rock–maintaining my shape even through the California earthquake.

Moments later, Brady asked for the check, paid the dinner tab and led me out of the restaurant to cheers and another round of applause by the reality TV audience. I felt like I was on some corny game show and a stage hand had just held up the *Applause* sign. I kept smiling nevertheless. In fact, somewhere between the restaurant's doors and my jeep, I had resolved to keep smiling–to soak it up and take it all in. It was the night of my engagement after all, and I had silently vowed to myself to make it a priority to be happy–at least appear peaceful– despite my hesitations. In the end, I knew that someday I would want to look back on it as an altogether joyful and happy experience–not a sad one. I would get used to the ring on my usually naked finger–that would be the easy part. And eventually I would get used to the idea of ever after as well. I just hadn't had enough time to think about it yet. There was, however, only one thing–one clear thought–that I just couldn't shake. For now–maybe because of my state of shock or delirium or denial or something–the only thing I really couldn't stop thinking about was that I never got my dessert. I never got my chocolate cake.

Wedding Plans

The day after the proposal, and after a good night's rest, I had already grown more comfortable with the idea of marrying Brady or marriage–period–I guess. I had accepted my initial nerves as a natural state of anxiety toward my next step in life. That's how Rachel had summed it up last night anyway. In fact, now that I had broken the news to my family and Rachel and April, I was surprisingly excited to be wearing Brady's big, beautiful ring, which he had picked out for me all by himself, on my once-naked finger.

Brady lost no time planning that next day either, I surmised, as I rounded the kitchen counter.

"Honey, how about April for the wedding?" he asked me, while he scrambled eggs in a bowl.

I stopped and looked up at him puzzlingly.

"April?" I questioned.

"Yeah, how about we have the wedding in April?" he repeated.

My eyes burned into my new fiancé–it would take me awhile to get used to the word fiancé, I noted–as I tried desperately to gauge his sincerity. Though he looked it, he couldn't possibly be serious.

"Brady, I can't plan a wedding in six months and in my last year of law school," I protested.

"I'll help you, of course," Brady replied, without the slightest loss of steam. "We'll do it together, and my parents can do most of the arranging."

"Your parents live in New York, Brady," I reminded him firmly.

"I know," he said patiently. "I thought we could have it at their country club there. It's a really nice place, and I'm sure they could get a really good deal on top of it."

I found myself growing more and more disheveled as our conversation continued. I had dreamed about my small, beautiful wedding overlooking the river in my little town since I was a little girl. It was going to be at the gazebo in the snow globe, but instead of grass or snow, it would be daisies that floated on the air. But now, I felt that Brady was single-handedly destroying that happy, childhood dream and stomping all over my pretty daisies.

"Brady, I don't want my wedding at your parents' country club," I softly protested. "Who said that we were going to get married there?"

Brady paused. I could tell he was a little caught off-guard by my reaction. I don't think he had considered that I would protest his well-thought-out plans.

He placed two pieces of bread onto the grill as he seemed to turn my words over in his head.

"Well, okay," he said finally. "We'll figure something out, honey. God willing, we'll be spending enough time in New York anyway," he said, now shaking something that looked like cinnamon onto the slices of bread.

I squinted my eyes in marvel and a growing irritation as my stare remained on Brady, who proceeded now to search for something inside of a drawer.

"What do you mean by that?" I asked, starting to feel myself grow impatient. As my impatience grew, so did the volume of my once soft, calm voice.

"Well, I just mean that if I get my top choice for residency, we'll be in New York for at least the next four years," he continued, not even looking up.

The marvel had by now left my face, but the irritation remained, and now it was fusing into anger and frustration.

"Brady, the farthest north this girl lives now is the southern United States, and I don't want to practice in New York anyway," I protested.

Brady paused from flipping the bread on the grill and looked up. His eyes looked hurt and shocked all at the same time and for the first time that morning. His reaction surprised me, yet so had his words.

We had always agreed on everything in the past, and I guess that he had somehow thought that this too would be an easy settlement.

His eyes eventually traveled to the floor, and after a long minute, they met mine again, and he began to speak.

"Honey, I love you, and I'm sorry," he confessed. "I should not have assumed that we wanted the exact same things for our wedding and even after. That would be boring after all, wouldn't it?"

Brady smiled at me, and despite the heavy weights that he had just unloaded onto me, a smile escaped from my lips as well–somehow.

"The truth is, those are small things compared to how much I love you and want to marry you. We'll figure all the small stuff out later," he continued.

Then he made his way over to me and wrapped his arms around my body.

I hesitated but then wrapped my arms around him as well, surrendering to his warm embrace.

The truth was, he was brilliant and just as determined as I was to follow a straight path to success. These were, after all, major reasons to why I loved him and why I had said *yes* in the end–that, and that he always found an elegant way out of every argument. In fact, that last trait just might be the quintessential key to my heart these days.

Even

"I'm so glad that you got a chance to get back here for a couple of days," Rachel gushed, throwing her purse down onto an empty chair in the tiny bar, with complete disregard as to where it landed.

"Yeah, me too. It's nice to be back," I said, as I pulled out a chair from the table and sat down.

Then, suddenly, from across the room came a familiar voice. It wasn't quite Southern. It was more like a country twang.

"Julia, are you lost, sweetheart?" the voice asked.

I looked up to see a tall, young, scruffy man approaching our table in the one-room bar.

"Ben," I exclaimed, smiling back at him and rising from my chair to meet his embrace.

"How have you been?" the burly character asked as he hugged me and then planted a wet kiss on my cheek.

"I've been well," I said, nodding my head as a happy smile sprang to my face. "How have you been? It's been, what, six years?"

"It's been awhile," he playfully said. "I didn't think you liked us anymore, Miss Lang."

I laughed softly.

"Now, why would you think that?" I asked.

"That's what Rachel told us," the burly figure said, elbowing Rachel's arm.

Rachel smiled and rolled her eyes at me.

"No dear, I told him that I didn't like him, not that you didn't," she explained.

"Oh, was that what it was?" the scruffy guy asked, chuckling. "Julia, take a seat. I got a quarter for your favorite song, and everything's on me tonight, ladies."

I laughed.

"I've forgotten how gentlemanly they make 'em in the Midwest," I said, eyeing Rachel.

"Jules, must I remind you that Ben, here, is the same Ben who once lined the girls' toilet seats with glue," Rachel interrupted. "It was even white, school glue. What was that supposed to do? Anyway, *gentlemanly* is not quite the word."

"That was you, wasn't it?" I asked, remembering and laughing as I playfully jabbed his arm.

The burly man ran off chuckling to the juke box while another lankier figure brought two drinks to our table and took a seat next to us.

"Now, Julia, does Will know you're in town?" he asked as if he didn't have time to mince words. Instead, he'd get straight to the point.

I looked at Rachel with a half-smirk.

"I don't know, Jeff," I said, shaking my head and shrugging my shoulders.

Rachel was shaking her head as well and half paying attention to the lanky figure as she thumbed through words on her phone's screen.

"No, I guess not," I replied, deciding to play along.

"Well, just to let ya know, when he's in town, he usually stops by here, and he's in town tonight," he said. "Do you want me to go dig out the disco ball in the basement and rig up the band's lights to make them swirl around and all that jazz?" He was making swirling movements with his hands as he spoke.

I laughed. Of course, that's what he was getting at.

"No, Jeff, we can probably skip all of that for now," I said, smiling.

"Jeff, don't you have a table to wait on or something?" Rachel interrupted, gesturing him away with the back of her hand.

"Speak of the devil," Jeff muttered softly then as his eyes darted toward the door.

Instantly, the rest of the eyes at the table turned toward the bar's screen door as well—just in time to catch it swing open and watch Will's six-foot-four, muscular frame walk inside.

I turned back around quickly and faced Rachel as Will made his way to the bar and Jeff left our table.

My body grew stiff and my heart raced as I massaged my diamond ring with my thumb under the table.

"Jules, are you okay?" Rachel asked from across the table. "You kind of have this deer-in-headlights look going on."

"What? No, I'm fine. Does he know?" I quickly whispered back to her, as I lifted my hand from underneath the table, exposing the shiny rock on my finger. My smile had completely faded.

Rachel glanced at Will, his back now turned toward us, and shook her head. "No," she whispered back to me. "I don't think so."

I took a deep breath and let out a nervous, heavy-hearted sigh.

"Jules," I suddenly heard Will's voice exclaim then.

I met Rachel's eyes, took another deep breath and then turned around in my chair to face him.

"What? When? How have ya been?" he asked, the words stumbling off his lips, as he made his way over to our table.

When he reached me, I pushed my chair out and stood up, meeting his embrace.

"I got in today. I'm only here for a couple of days," I rambled off, smiling and trying to hide the remnants of my miniature panic attack that took place just moments before.

He squeezed me tightly for several seconds.

"I see," he said, nodding his head and pulling away. "Hey, Rach. How are ya?" Will asked, as his eyes met Rachel's.

"Good, Will. Doing well. Jon says 'hi,' by the way," Rachel said, smiling.

"Okay, where's he tonight?" he asked.

"Hunting trip. Canada. Needless to say, I sat that one out," Rachel said, her eyebrows raised.

Just then, the juke box burst into my favorite 1960s song, and my face sprang to life.

I could tell that Will's eyes had caught my happy expression.

"You want to dance…for old time's sake?" he asked me then.

My eyes darted toward Rachel, who seemed to have read my mind.

"Ben, get your two, left feet over here and ask me to dance," Rachel shouted across the room.

Ben looked up from the juke box and smiled in Rachel's direction.

"You two, go ahead and catch up. I wish I could say I had steel-toed shoes on right now, but I'll survive, I guess," she said, eying up Ben at the juke box.

I laughed and looked back at Will.

"All right," I softly said, nodding my head.

Will put out his palm, face up, and I consciously gave him my right hand.

"I wasn't expecting to see you here tonight. I would have put on a clean shirt, and shaved and maybe worn some of that deodorant stuff," he said, grinning.

I smiled and looked down at the floor.

"You look great," I said, in a bashful way that even surprised myself.

"So do you, Jules," he countered, without missing a beat.

"Thanks," I said. This time, I managed to look into his bright blue eyes without wavering as I spoke.

"It's good to see you," I said, smiling warmly. "What have you been up to besides becoming famous these days?" I asked.

Will blushed as his gaze on me faltered slightly before returning.

"If I'm famous, it doesn't really feel any different," he muttered softly, honestly.

"That's probably because you were used to it already. You've been famous here since I've known you," I confessed.

Will laughed.

"Isn't everybody in a small town?" he asked.

My smile grew wider.

"I guess you're right," I conceded, as the conversation grew quiet.

"How's work?" I asked eventually, breaking the quiet lull.

"It's been good. You know I took off for awhile, but I worked the last couple of nights. It's good to be back. You know, not always traveling–though I'm not complaining."

"I know," I said, still smiling.

"So, you like it, though," I asked him.

"Like...?" he asked, as his word trailed off.

"The lights, the fans, the entertaining?" I asked cheerfully.

"Oh, that," he said. "I like playing my guitar, and I like that sometimes you can see that people really enjoy the words you're singin'–the same words that meant something to me when I wrote them. Now, the lights, on the other hand, I can do without them. They're bright and hot," he said, laughing.

I smiled a wide, happy smile.

"I told you so," I said, still grinning. "Well, minus the lights, I knew you'd like it."

"You were just itchin' to say that, weren't you?" he asked.

My smile grew wider.

"Maybe," I confessed.

"You never liked the firefighting idea, did you?" Will asked in a quiet voice with an endearing side-smile.

"What?" I asked, pausing from our dance to look into his face. "Why did you think that?"

"I didn't think. I knew, Jules," he whispered, still displaying his wry smile.

I hesitated for an instant.

"Will, you had to have picked the most dangerous career," I protested slightly, admitting defeat. "I wasn't exactly thrilled, but I was sincerely happy for you."

"I know. I know," he said, chuckling.

"Will, I would have done anything to make you happy…I still would," I said to him, smiling honestly.

We were dancing slower now. The song had changed sometime back. He gently held my right hand in his, and his other hand was on the small of my back.

"I mean, we were best friends, Will," I continued.

"Are best friends, Jules. We are best friends," he said in a quiet, confident voice.

I slowly nodded my head as our feet glided along the tiny dance floor.

"Are," I softly agreed, glancing back up at him with a smile.

He didn't say anything then, and neither did I. It felt good to be there, surrounded by old friends, talking to him. It was nice. It was comfortable, for now, anyway. The fact remained, however, that it was nice until they all found out how much I had changed since high school—until I got bored and needed the confines of sky scrapers and endless traffic. How my values had warped. I smiled as Will's voice caught my attention again.

"Jules, I've, uh, been doing some thinking, and I…," Will started to mumble as he reached for my other hand.

He stopped then, and I followed the path his eyes made to my left hand and then to my ring finger.

I swore my heart stopped for a second as the words fell from my mind and to the hard dance floor below.

"Jules, please tell me this is just a pretty ring," he pleaded.

My heart sank further–to the bottom most part of my soul, to the basement of the tiny bar–and nothing really seemed right to say, but I realized quickly that I had to say something, anything.

"It's not just a ring, Will," I softly muttered.

The words sounded still so foreign to me, almost as if I weren't saying them, but that someone in the far-off distance was saying them, instead, for me. The words sounded sad, yet confident.

Will continued to stare at my finger and the shiny, one-carrot diamond resting on it. His face turned a pale, flushed color, and for what seemed like a century, he said nothing. Then, he finally spoke.

"The doctor?" he softly asked, his eyes still cast on my ring.

My eyes slowly left my hand and followed a meandering path to his own weighty eyes.

"Yes," I mumbled. "The doctor."

"And I'm guessing this means you said *yes*?" he asked, softer still.

I nodded my head slowly. A half, awkward smile illuminated my face.

Silent seconds drew on.

"Well, I guess congrats are in order then," he said, sounding forced but positive.

"Thanks," I said, barely audibly, as I looked up at his hollowed face and then followed his gaze to the ring on my finger.

"Just tell me one thing, Jules," he said, returning his eyes to mine. He sounded serious.

"Okay," I said hesitantly, meeting his eyes again.

"Is he the one?" he asked.

I paused for a second again. It wasn't really a question I had been expecting. It was loaded, I knew, but I managed to stand strong behind my decision. I was wearing the ring after all. He must have already known my answer.

"He's good for me, Will," I finally said.

Silence crept into the conversation again as we continued to stand in the middle of the tiny bar, still hand in hand but not dancing; instead, just standing there.

"Well, that's what matters," he softly said.

The juke box page turned, and another song started playing then as I let out a thankful sigh. At the same time, Will found my gaze.

"It was really good to see you again," he said.

"It was nice to see you too," I said, wrapping my arms around his muscular frame. I didn't know exactly if the hug was force of habit or some kind of nervous impulse, but I embraced him tightly nevertheless, as he surrendered and wrapped his arms around me as well. I took a deep breath, breathing in his smell, free of cologne, a combination of sweat and laundry detergent. It was a familiar scent, one that instantly made me feel at peace again.

We held each other longer than usual. It was almost as if we both had an idea that our paths might never cross again. Then, he kissed me on the cheek and whispered into my ear.

"Take care, Jules," he said.

"You leaving?" I whispered.

"Yeah, I gotta work early tomorrow morning. The call of duty," he said, withdrawing from our embrace and tipping his baseball cap slightly in my direction. He flashed a side-smile and then turned to leave.

My eyes followed him to the door. I started after him, getting only a step in his direction, when I felt a hand on my shoulder.

"You tell him?" Rachel asked.

I turned back toward her and then nodded my head and tried to smile as best as I could.

"He'll be fine. He's a big boy, Jules," Rachel said, assuring me.

"I guess you're right," I softly said, turning my attention back to the closed screen door in the corner of the bar, as a set of headlights illuminated the dark world behind it.

Rachel gave me a hug.

"Don't look so sad. You're getting married to the perfect guy, honey," Rachel said.

"I know," I said.

"But no one has to know if you run after him," Rachel whispered.

"What?" I asked.

"Not a word," she said again as she motioned toward the screen door.

"Rachel, I'm not going to run after him," I said, shaking my head and now smiling again.

"You're going to tell me that you wouldn't take one more night with that sexy man?" she asked.

I stared at her in protest and with a questioning smile.

"No, Rach, I wouldn't," I said with conviction.

"But you've thought about it?" Rachel asked, with a half-smirk glued to her face.

I tilted my head and just barely cracked a grin.

"Rach, I think I love him too much," I softly said. "I just couldn't."

"Okay, well, can't say I didn't try," Rachel said, laughing. "Why don't you go give Mr. I Love Him Too Much a call?"

"What?" I asked her as she walked away.

"Give your fiancé a call," she said. "Say goodnight and then get back in here. I'll hold down the fort. And tell him I say 'hi.'"

"Rach, I didn't mean...," I started but noticed she could no longer hear me. "I didn't mean him," I whispered.

I stood there for a second, motionless, before I reached into my tight, blue jeans' pocket, pulled out my phone and slipped through the screen door. The slight chill in the air immediately made me shiver and forced my hand to my opposite arm as I found Brady's number and then hit *send*.

While I listened to the phone ring, I spotted several large rocks that were left sticking out of the loose-gravel parking lot, vulnerable to mischief, so I kicked each one of them with the toe of my shoe until I heard Brady's voice on the other end.

"Hey," he answered. His voice sounded raspy and tired.

"I'm sorry, honey. Did I wake you?" I asked.

"No, no, no. I'm awake. I was just resting my eyes," he exclaimed.

"Oh, okay," I said, laughing.

"Are you having fun?" he asked.

"Yeah..." My voice trailed off as I noticed a round object on the hood of Rachel's car.

"Babe," he said, noticing my short leave of absence.

"I'm here, I'm sorry. Yeah, I'm having fun. It's good to be back," I recovered, making my way to the car. "How was your day?"

I listened to him talk about his classes and something about his friend not showing up in time for something. I was too distracted by the object to give him my undivided attention.

"That sounds awful, honey. What happened to him?" I asked half-heartedly, still trying to remain, at the very least, a part of the conversation.

As I reached the car, I easily recognized that the round object was a volleyball. It looked old. Its seams were a deep brown, and it had taken on a yellowish tint. Carefully, I rolled it closer to me with one hand, while the other hand still held the phone to my ear. And within moments, I could faintly see that it had something written on it. I squinted and took a closer look, using the light from the phone to illuminate the ball's surface.

With my makeshift light source, I could just barely see that in a black, permanent marker was my name and my old volleyball number. My fingers retraced the faded letters and number as I remembered back to the day I had written them on the ball years ago. It was in high school. This was my ball. I had loved this ball. I had bought it with my summer babysitting money. But it had been years since I had last seen it.

I finished retracing the hand-written words, but as soon as I had, my eyes went to a set of unfamiliar letters below my original script. The new letters didn't look old and faded like the ones I had written those years ago now had. The new letters looked fresher and sharper—and they weren't in my handwriting.

I tilted the phone's screen a little closer to the ball, just far enough away from my ear that I could still hear

Brady's voice, continually fading into the background. My curiosity grew as my eyes feverishly darted to the new letters. I had just barely noticed that the ball had engulfed most of my attention when I felt a smile fighting its way to my face. The all-knowing grin had started in my stomach and had found its final resting place at the ends of my lips, and now, it made me beam with a silly, childlike joy as my eyes slowly followed over each word:

Now, we're even.

Goodbyes

"Jules, could you come here?" Brady called to me from inside his small, apartment kitchen.

His request made me stop short.

I had left San Diego eight hours earlier that day, and I was exhausted and in desperate need of a shower and some food, but nevertheless, I was excited to finally spend time with my fiancé again. It had been almost two months since our proposal and a month since we had last seen each other.

Brady lived in a small, older home in south Columbia with a friend he had met in medical school. The place was kept fairly well, and in the end, the fact that it was clean, for the most part, was really what mattered, I had concluded a long time ago. Because, truth be told, one could easily tell that two, college guys lived there. There were no pictures or photos on the walls. An oversized flag with the school's mascot plastered across its face hung above a worn-in, brown leather couch and was quite possibly the only effort at any kind of decorating. Well, that's if you didn't count the fake plant in the corner of the living room that I'm pretty sure also doubled as an end table. In fact, currently, the plant held a plastic cup from a familiar pizza joint in its fake potting soil and the remote in one of its branches. My face fell into a puzzled state as I stared bemused at the plant for a moment–until I heard Brady's voice again.

Slightly jolted, I set my carry-on bag down onto an aged, tan chair in Brady's living room and made my way to the kitchen where he stood.

"What did you call me?" I asked, as Brady came into view.

"Umm," he paused, seemingly to remember the last words that had just come out of his mouth. "Jules. Why?"

"Oh, it's nothing. I had just never heard you call me that before," I said, trying to sound unfazed by his reference.

Brady had always called me Julia. In fact, I hadn't been called anything different by a guy since Will. And for some reason, the name sounded odd and unsettling coming from Brady's lips. Of course, nothing had been exactly the same between us since the day after our engagement. Everything seemed a little more forced and a little less natural since then. We hadn't talked any more about when or where we were going to have the wedding, much less where we were going to live after we did get married. I suspected, however, that that was because Brady thought that in time I might change my mind. He had his heart set on New York, and I knew it. I could tell it by the way he had pushed his home state on me those weeks ago, and because of that, I hadn't brought up the topic either. Though, I knew the more and more I avoided it, the more and more other subjects became untouchable as well–like my plans after law school or even down to where we would spend the holidays. In fact, a part of me worried that maybe the two of us had become so wrapped up in our own, individual lives in the last few years that we hadn't paused to see if we could even coexist together in our futures. I mean, it wasn't that I feared that in the midst of all the hours apart and mounds of paperwork between us that we had lost each other, but instead, that we had never really found each other to begin with. Is that even possible for two people who had been together for years? Could I really not have taken the time to get to know him? Did he know me?

Despite the hope and excitement that I had initially put into my weekend with Brady, the next couple of days proved trying. My resolve started deteriorating early on. Each time Brady said something that hinted at our complicated future, my lighthearted walls crumbled a little bit more. Something that I couldn't explain began eating away at me so much so that I began to feel increasingly uneasy about my imminent life with Brady. It was almost as if he had transformed into a different person before my eyes in only two, short months, and more importantly, in the last couple of days. He was still compassionate and successful and handsome. I could still see those things. But something was different, and I had to figure out what it was.

What had changed? I wondered as I took a seat outside on Brady's back porch swing, while Brady took a shower upstairs. Had anything changed or was it all still the same and I was just now realizing the reality of the situation?

I stared at my cell phone in my hand for a long minute, then resolved to go in search of answers–answers from the one person I thought might have them.

"Hey," I said somberly when Rachel answered on the other end of the phone.

"Hey, what's going on? Aren't you in Missouri?" Rachel asked, excitedly.

"Yeah, I'm at Brady's," I answered, noticeably disheartened.

"What's wrong?" Rachel asked immediately.

Her voice sounded concerned.

I remained silent for an instant, gathering my words, until I could no longer hold it in.

"Rachel, why don't I have butterflies when I see him–and after almost a month?" I anxiously questioned my friend.

"What?" Rachel asked. I could tell she was a little taken aback by my seemingly out-of-place question–and rightfully so.

"I mean, I was excited to see him, but a different kind of excited. I was excited to get away from school for a couple of days and do something different, and I was excited because you should be excited to see your fiancé. And why does it sound so strange when he calls me Jules?" I rattled off unconsciously.

"Jules, he's Mr. Perfect, you know?" Rachel asked and stated.

"I know," I said. "Why am I such a mess? I have Mr. Perfect's huge ring on my finger, and for the first time in a long time, I'm miserable. I feel like I'm trapped in a life that's not my own, and I keep waiting for a breakthrough–for a change, but it hasn't come. Help me, Rachel. I need your words of wisdom. Just tell me I'm crazy. Tell me he's the love of my life, and we'll live happily ever after with our white, picket fence and two and a half kids."

Rachel laughed, but her laughter was short lived.

"Don't stress, Jules," she said in a more serious tone.

I could tell she was attempting to calm me down.

"Getting engaged can sometimes be a scary thing, especially if you're not completely prepared," Rachel went on. "Immediately, people start asking questions, like: 'How did he propose? When's the big day? Where are you going to live?' It can be pretty overwhelming, but at the end of the day, you've got to be able to know that he's the one. You've got to be able to know that you can be happy waking up every morning next this man. If he is the one, you should know or trust that you will know again once all of the dust has settled."

Rachel paused and took a deep breath and then slowly let it out.

"Jules," she continued. "Do you believe that deep down inside somewhere that Brady is the one? Yes, he is Mr. Perfect, but is he your Mr. Perfect?"

I was without words. I sat pondering my friend's questions for an anguishing, long, silent minute. I trusted Rachel, and I trusted that no matter how much Rachel felt one way about a particular subject or someone that she could always take herself out of the situation and become my objective voice of reason. Plus, I feared that I had already known the answer for which I was looking all along anyway, and when I finally spoke again, there were tears welling up in my eyes.

"I don't know," I softly said, "and that thought terrifies me."

The words frantically stumbled off my lips, as a warm saltiness streamed down my cheeks.

"He's amazing, and he's everything I ever wanted in a guy, and I don't know why I don't know, but I don't," I continued.

Rachel was quiet for an instant.

"Then, there's your answer, sweetheart," she softly said.

Moments after I ended my conversation with Rachel, Brady found me in my tears on the porch swing. He immediately took a seat next to me and put his arm around me.

"What's wrong, honey?" he softly asked. His voice trembled with concern.

I looked up at his face and saw the trepidation in his eyes. I hated what I had to do, and I hated myself for it, but I couldn't hold back my doubts any longer, and for better or worse, I knew I had to voice my thoughts. Maybe he could even change my mind, though somehow, I feared he couldn't.

"Brady, I'm nervous about getting married," I softly said, tears rolling down my cheeks and falling to my lap.

"It'll be okay, Julia. What are you nervous about?" Brady asked, squeezing me closer.

"I'm nervous that we want different things and that maybe we're not as similar as we thought we were," I confessed.

Brady took a second to let my words sink in. He had to have wondered what had triggered my tears and if there was still more I needed to say, I'm sure.

"Honey, sure, we may not always agree on everything, but that doesn't mean we can't make it work," he said, reassuring me.

"I know," I softly agreed. "But I know that living and practicing in New York closer to your parents means the world to you, and really, working in D.C. means the world to me right now. And I even think that we could somehow work around that, but I also feel that instead of growing closer these last couple years, we've only grown further apart."

Brady paused.

"Is it someone else?" he softly asked.

My face hastily turned up toward his.

"What?" I asked him, completely thrown off-guard. "No, of course not. Why would you ask that?"

He hesitated. He seemed to have been regrouping.

"Because I've never really felt like I've had all of you," he softly confessed.

My stare reached out to his sad eyes.

"Brady, I had no idea that you felt that way. Why didn't you ever say anything?" I asked.

"I don't know," he said. "I guess I just never wanted to hear the truth."

"Brady, there's no one else," I said. "That's not what this is about. This is about us—only us."

Brady sat on the swing, frozen in his place.

I let moments pass before I spoke again.

"Don't you think we've grown apart?" I gently asked him, eventually continuing the conversation.

I watched his eyes leave mine and settle on a spot in the far distance. I could tell he was thinking, and I grew more and more anxious as each moment of silence passed—until he finally spoke again.

"I love you, Julia," he said, avoiding my question.

My heart ached. He could have said anything else but that. And even with his tender words, I knew he saw what I saw. I knew that him not answering my question gave me my answer, and that answer crushed me more than I had anticipated. My salty tears uncontrollably rolled down my cheeks in tiny bucketfuls as I fought back the urge to take everything back.

"I'm so sorry, Brady. I know you see it too," I said as I slipped his ring off my finger and placed it in his hand, while I still had the courage to do it.

Brady tenderly protested for almost an hour thereafter. And in that hour, he was perfect, and gentlemanly and sweet, but his words seemed more like he was fighting not to fail, not to see me hurt, not to hurt himself, instead of for love. And by the end, even he could admit that there had been a change and was forced to surrender to our looming decline. And I knew that he knew deep down we both wanted different lives and that those lives, no matter how much forcing, could never coexist. More so, however, something that he saw in my eyes that last hour, those last days after the proposal and even, to some extent, every day before the engagement, made him believe that I needed something that he could never give me, he tried to explain. He said he had tried so hard to figure out what that something was all this time, but alas, was unsuccessful, he admitted. And like the true gentleman he was, he eventually told me that he understood, understood that I needed a different life than he could offer me, even though I could tell he felt as if he didn't fully understand why.

In the end, he had loved me with all that he had, believing that I hadn't ever given him all of myself. And maybe I hadn't or maybe that's all I had to give anymore. I wasn't sure. But I could tell that he realized that I had already made my decision, and regardless, to him, the outcome was the same–I didn't see him in my future, and he would never have my whole heart.

We sat on his porch swing with my packed bags in front of us in silence before leaving for the airport that day. And the tears were still streaming down my cheeks even two hours later as we pulled into a spot in the airport's parking lot and came to a halt. I met his eyes then. I could see in them that it pained him to see me so torn, and I just knew he wanted to make my world all better again, just like I wished I could his as well.

I tried to smile the best, sincere smile that I could muster up–one that said that we would both make it. I'm not really sure if I succeeded.

He softly smiled as well, but it was pained and not so assured. It pierced the outer wall of my already stabbed and beaten heart and forced my eyes to the floorboard. But in the next moment, I felt the top part of his hand under my chin gently lifting my face toward his.

"Whatever you're looking for, Julia, I hope you find it someday. You're much too beautiful for tears," he said, sincerely.

I could hear the sadness in his voice as I looked into his deep brown eyes. My heart continued to ache.

"I'm so sorry, Brady," I said, through my tears. "I'm so sorry."

A Date

"Life is funny," I said under my breath as I sat back in my office chair, wearing a somewhat heavy-hearted grin.

Graduation had come and gone and so had the bar exam. South Carolina wasn't exactly D.C. quite yet, but it was warm most of the year, and the beach was close and the water warm—a drastic difference from the icy cold waters of the Pacific. Most importantly, however, Charleston was home of the prestigious Summerton Law Group, a well-established firm that specialized in environmental law. As soon as I had passed the bar, I had put my first application into Summerton. I was beside myself the day the firm called me in for an interview. And then there was a second interview, and then a month later, I was on my way to the Palmetto State.

"What's funny?" I heard a voice come from out of nowhere, forcing my thoughts to a screeching halt.

I jumped slightly and sat straight up in my chair, just as a slender figure was planting his feet in the center of my office's doorway.

Anthony stood about six-foot-one, had olive skin, jet black hair and soft, brown eyes. He was model-like handsome, someone who naturally commanded attention whenever he walked into a room. I had worked intensively with him on a case for the last several months, and even so, his attractive self still made me nervous and slightly awkward in his presence at times. It's funny how many things I could actually drop, spill and ruin in one minute with him. That being said, I really got the impression that he had no idea just how attractive he was because he was also witty and smart and sweet. And he seemed to possess this certain silent courage in the face of adversity—this I had noticed early on in our working relationship, and I had admired him greatly for it. Best of all, Anthony hated politics, and while I loved learning about the law and how to apply it to my future cases and career and all of that, I could live without the politics. A lawyer who despised politics was hard to come by, and I had immediately seen Anthony as a pleasant breath of fresh air.

"Oh, nothing's funny,' I said, shaking my head and still smiling.

Anthony looked at me sideways. And I quickly connected the dots as I started to emerge from the place I like to call, My Own, Little World. Did I just tell Anthony Ravenel that I was laughing at something that wasn't funny? Yep, I'm crazy.

"I mean, I'm not laughing at anything. Well, I guess I am laughing–but at nothing in particular," I eventually spit out, trying my best to recover.

I noted that I should add *speak uncontrollably* to the list of things that I could do, without even trying, to embarrass myself around Anthony Ravenel.

I smiled at my own ineptness and trudged on.

"What are you still doing here?" I asked him.

"I just had a couple of things to finish up," he said. "I'm on my way out now. The real question is: What are you still doing here? The weekend started, oh, two hours ago," he said, glancing at his watch.

My smile grew for an instant and then faded.

"I know," I said, looking back down at my computer's screen. "I know, but I'm going to have to sit tonight out. I've got some catching up to do."

"Oh," he said, sounding defeated. "What about tomorrow night? You doing anything?"

"You're probably looking at it," I said, meeting his gaze again with a smile.

"Oh, come on, you'll need a break by tomorrow night," he assured me. "You and me. I'll take you to see some of the sights downtown–a tour of the city. It'll be fun."

I said nothing at first, as I took a deep breath. I looked at the figure in my doorway and then at my computer's screen. In the short months after my move to Charleston, I had thrown my focus into my work, and it wasn't hard to do so. I welcomed anything to keep my mind off of my recent past. Though I felt lately as if a weight had been lifted off my shoulders–like an impending fear of my future had strangely disappeared–it wasn't exactly as if it had been replaced by something much better. That was the catch. Had I made the right choice telling Brady I couldn't marry him? I felt as if I had done the right thing, but would I regret my decision later? I knew, in the end, only time would tell. For now, it was just one day at a time, picking up the pieces, moving forward.

A night out couldn't really hurt, I resolved, as I found a stray paper clip and proceeded to unwind it. In fact, it would probably do me some good to get out for a change–see the city for once. And I enjoyed Anthony's company. We were, after all, co-workers, good friends–nothing more, nothing less.

"Okay. Sure," I said, nodding. The corners of my lips rose slightly. "That sounds like a good idea."

"Good, I'll pick you up at seven then. Don't work too late," he playfully warned, as he tapped the inside of the door frame.

I smiled.

"I'll see you tomorrow," I said.

Evening Stroll

Anthony picked me up at seven sharp the next evening, and we made our way to Sophia's, a homey, little, Italian eatery, which sat in the heart of downtown Charleston, tucked away behind dozens of hanging emerald vines and stout, brick buildings that dated back to the 1700s.

Once we arrived, I followed the petite hostess as she skillfully weaved her way through a maze of outdoor tables, eventually selected one and placed onto its surface two menus.

I smiled, took a seat and waited for Anthony to sit down as the small girl vanished back into the maze again.

"How did you find this place? It's almost completely hidden," I asked Anthony as I opened the thick, hardcover menu.

"Oh, it's been here for years. Hang with me, and I'll let you in on all of Charleston's little secrets," he replied, with a soft, coy smile.

I smiled again also, trying desperately not to knock anything off of the table or trip someone or something–things I had, sadly, been known to do in his presence.

The dinner came, and we ate and talked about cases and our families and our college years, like we were old friends, remembering our glory days. And after dinner, we set out on a stroll on the narrow, limestone and shell sidewalks along the coble-stoned streets, past the shops and bars, taking in the sultry, evening air, along with the gentle, cooling breeze that rolled off the waves in the harbor.

I was doing a pretty good job of maneuvering my small heels over the broken places in the sidewalk. Charleston's sidewalks hadn't exactly faired the best on the ever-shifting surface of the sea-level city. Nevertheless, I was managing its tiny obstacles surprisingly well. Of course, that was until my eyes caught a man who looked like Brady seated at a table in a nearby restaurant. And in the two seconds that it took to realize that it wasn't him, one of my heels caught the edge of an aging piece of concrete. I stumbled but quickly caught myself. I don't even think Anthony noticed. My poise was still in tact–for now.

I returned my attention back to my uneven path, convinced now that every strawberry blonde served as a constant, but friendly reminder of what still seems to have been a misstep in this journey I so endearingly call *Life*.

I allowed a soft, inaudible sigh to escape my lips.

"Anthony, life eventually gets less complicated, right?" I playfully asked, smiling up at my friend.

Anthony stopped to look at my expression. I knew it had to appear, for the most part, happy, but still a little heavy-burdened.

He smiled.

"Yeah, I think it does, right before it gets interesting," he offered.

I paused for an instant and then laughed. I'd take interesting.

"Well, Miss Lang, where's our next stop?" he asked. "And we can ponder all of life's great mysteries."

I smiled at him and then lifted my eyes to the heavens as I contemplated our next adventure.

"How about…," I started.

I was beginning to feel an emotion that bordered carefree, and it was nice, for a change. In fact, for a minute there, Anthony had me forgetting completely about the complexities of life–forgetting about missteps and uneven sidewalks. But then, something changed again.

Before I could finish my sentence, my thoughts quickly hit a brick wall, as if the wall had just jetted up from the earth right in front of me.

"Will," I said so softly the word was barely audible.

I felt my breathing quicken, and for a moment, I said nothing. My words were too busy watching my past elbow its way to the forefront of my mind. But this time, it wasn't the so-recent past that haunted. It wasn't another strawberry blonde. No, this was a past of a more distant nature–and I neither expected it nor welcomed it;

though, I couldn't hate it either. It was just there, armored and now staring at me in the main corridor of my mind, and it was as if I were its prey, standing opposite of it— unprotected and vulnerable.

In an instant, my world had grown unmistakably silent, and the streets, the water, the skies had all turned painfully still as I dug my tiny heel into a small opening in the broken sidewalk. I had been taken prisoner, and now, the only thing that mattered in all the world was hearing the soft melody that poured from an unfamiliar, dark-colored sedan that rested nearly a block up from where Anthony and I stood.

"Julia, are you okay?" I could hear Anthony faintly ask in the background, battling against the melody's lyrics for my attention.

Though my body was numb, and my eyes were still locked onto the old sedan, I struggled desperately to form words—words, any words at all.

"Hmm?" I answered in a soft, unusually quiet voice, audibly distracted.

"Are you all right?" he asked again, cautiously.

I swallowed hard before I tried at speaking again.

"I'm sorry," I managed to say. "I just…that song."

Anthony hesitated.

"I hear the music. What about it?" he asked.

What about it? Only my world crashing in on me; my heart pounding holes into the walls of my chest; the sound my breaths made tunneling wildly through my lungs. I knew he hadn't heard any of those things, but it had felt as if he should have all the same.

"I know it," I replied, serene and slow. The melody still played in my ear like a time machine transporting me back years and onto a porch one particular, autumn night.

A part of me longed desperately to stay for awhile and find out what could have been had it really all been different; but alas, life was calling to me from the other side.

"Is this one your favorite" Life, also known as Anthony Ravenel, asked curiously.

"No," I softly lied. "It's not my favorite."

Anthony paused for a moment in what could have been reflection.

"Do you like the artist then?" he whispered back.

I unintentionally and tightly squeezed his hand. Yes, somewhere in there he had taken my hand. I'm not sure how. I'm not even sure when, and I'm definitely not sure why.

Anthony's question stung my heart, yet I continued to stare at the sedan, still straining to hear the melody over a set of horse hooves, people chatting off to the side and boat horns in the distance. I had heard the song before, or I had heard the first two stanzas before anyway. Regardless, I had heard it, and it had been my song–my song–and he had finished it. That's what had made all the difference. That's why I was standing breathless. That's why I was coming unraveled in the middle of a familiar, downtown sidewalk.

I labored to hear every last bit of the lyrics and the deep, seductive voice from my past, even as the traffic light flashed from red to green and my mobile juke box began pulling away.

Where was it going? I protested. *And why was it taking my song?*

My heart leapt toward the melody, now fading into the muffled sounds of its background. It took everything in me not to follow its lead. I watched the sedan longingly, my eyes chasing it deeper and deeper into the city. Then, just as quickly as it had come into my life and had stolen me away, it was gone and gone with it was my song, and all I could think about was how much I wanted it back.

Lyrics

I watched him walk away for a couple of seconds before I turned and slid my key into the lock.

I was smiling when I flung my purse onto the countertop. Anthony was the Southern-gentleman type, and I was sure that he had broken his fair share of hearts in his day. He was the kind of guy who made girls melt; the guy who had his date swooning over the sound of her first name with his last name by dessert. That was about the time that his big, puppy-dog, chocolate eyes were at their strongest and a thick, Southern accent was stumbling uncontrollably off his lips. I'm sure it was then that he usually had most girls won over. And despite my appreciation for his ability to capture a woman's heart, I wanted, in the end, no substantial part in it. Love was off limits until further notice, I had promised myself.

It had been almost a year since I had said my goodbyes to Brady, and although it surprised me at how quickly my heartache had faded, the night of our engagement still oddly lingered in my mind. What was love anyway, and what was its part in ever after? What kind of love does it have to be to make you want to say *yes* to happily ever after–to forever?

And sure, tonight sounded like a date. Anthony and I had, after all, spent the rest of the evening together on a wooden swing out on the pier, listening to the waves gently crash into the edges of the city and watching dozens of well-lit, tiny boats slowly pass under the Ravenel Bridge. But he had never tried to kiss me, and we had never talked about plans beyond the night. We just simply enjoyed each other's company, suspended over the water and beneath the stars still visible above the city's hundreds of tiny lamps. Though, he had held my hand that one time. I had almost forgotten about that.

I paused.

My smile quickly faded as the image of the dark-colored sedan from earlier that night flashed back into the forefront of my mind. And what had I really heard? It was Will's voice. It was a new song. But I had heard it before–a long time ago. But why again now? And what exactly had it said even?

I had often heard Will's songs in passing–in malls, local hang outs and, of course, on the radio. It had become almost second nature by now to hear his voice everywhere, so much so that it didn't faze me as much as it used to. But none of his songs I had heard in the last couple of years had been like the song I had heard tonight, however. This had been my song. Maybe that's why, this time, hearing it had made my heart skip a beat, my mind turn into mush and my hands feel like dead fish. Poor Anthony.

But the last time I had heard it, it had been without all of its lyrics, and it hadn't been on the radio or in a bar or blaring from someone's car stereo. Instead, it was that one chilly, September night years ago. I remembered it vividly. But maybe I hadn't heard it right tonight. It was late. There were people. There were other cars and carriages, boats and waves breaking against the city's walls. With all that commotion, I could have heard anything. I could have imagined anything. Right? I stared at a spot on the ivory wall in front of me for a solid minute, examining my thoughts as they danced circles in my head. And just when I thought that they were determined to make me dizzy, an idea took center stage.

Within an instant, all of my previous emotions–the racing heart, the quickened breaths–came rushing back and sent my body into a violent, physical motion in the direction of a small room, just down the hallway.

Against the inside wall of my den was a modest, wooden desk, shrouded with picture frames filled with images of my family and old friends. I quickly scurried to the shrine and fell into the black, leather office chair. At the same time, I swung open my laptop and frantically began typing the words *District 9* onto the small screen. After clicking *search*, a couple dozen websites appeared, and I clicked on the first official-looking site that I saw.

Anxiously scanning the songs by Will and his band, I found a sole love song, entitled *Butterfly*. With a hasty mouse click onto the song title, the same, memorable melody that I had heard years ago and also just hours before began seeping through my speakers and floating to my ears. Vocals followed, along with a sequence of carefully placed words, which tapered down my computer's small monitor. My eyes raced through the lyrics, even before my ears could hear the melody that went with them. The song's hauntings were unraveling what was left of my composure again. Its lyrics were a forgotten pleasure, and now that pleasure was stealing me away from my small, dark den and transporting me to a long-past, quiet, September night. My smile widened as my eyes continued to slowly scroll down the page– remembering a time, gone forever–as I read:

> *"It's a summer night*
> *And I can hear the crickets sing*
> *But otherwise, all the world's asleep*
> *While I can only lie awake and dream*
> *And every time I close my eyes*
> *A butterfly comes to me*
> *It has soft, green eyes*
> *A sweet soul*
> *Brave wings*
> *And each time, it hears me sing:*
>
> *Where have you been?*
> *I've missed you so*
> *Tell me of your travels*
> *Tell me you've seen the world*
> *Now, you've come back home*
> *Tell me you've carried me with you*
> *That you've held me close*
> *Tell me you've missed me*
> *Or that I'm not crazy for waiting 'cause*
> *Of all the butterflies that chose to stay,*
> *I'm in love with the one that got away*

Butterfly Weeds

Then in my dream it turns to me
And that butterfly smiles
And whispers in my ear:
Where have you been?
I've missed you so
My wings are tired
For I've carried you home
I've carried you through the mountains
I've carried you over the sea
Everywhere I went
I carried you with me

Then instead of spreading those brave wings
And flyin' far away again
That butterfly stays near instead
And whispers back to me:
Tell me again what you never said
And I sing again:
Where have you been?
I've missed you so
Tell me of your travels
Tell me you've seen the world
Now, you've come back home
Tell me you've carried me with you
That you've held me close
Tell me you've missed me
Or that I'm not crazy for waiting 'cause
Of all the butterflies that chose to stay,
I'm in love with the one that got away."

I was breathless.

The words on my screen had taken the air from my lungs. It was the rest of the song, and I couldn't stop staring at it. I mean, the pier was beautiful. The man was beautiful. The night was beautiful. Yet, somehow I had managed to find myself now in a corner of my dark den, curled up in my office chair, staring at lyrics on my laptop's tiny screen in a kind of sedative awe–my heart pounding, seemingly losing the battle, a loss for words– for the second time tonight. I could hardly believe what I was witnessing. I hadn't been mistaken. My ears hadn't lied. I resented the past for rearing its ugly head again, even as a warm smile jetted across my face. Will always had a way of throwing me off-guard at the oddest moments, but this was, by far, his fastest and most accurate curve ball. I wasn't expecting this one–not now, not tonight, not ever. In fact, I never expected to hear those words or his song ever again.

I commanded my hands to stop shaking, as my thoughts continued.

Even though the melody was mine, surely, the song was someone else's by now. He said he would finish it, but it had been years, many years, in fact, and surely he had forgotten his promise. Surely, I was overreacting. Though, I couldn't quite bring myself to stop. I wished I could just call him and ask him myself. But I knew that I couldn't. What would I say? How would I say it? What if it wasn't my song anymore, but instead, just some pretty lyrics?

Even that slight chance that the song reflected our time together still could mean only that our once-upon-a-time love story meant nothing more than a lucrative business move for the singer. I decided quickly that I wouldn't want to hear that truth. Plus, this was the last thing I needed right now. What I really needed was for him to stay in his world and for me to stay in mine. I've been down that road and so had he.

My eyes, which had fallen into an intense stare at the keyboard's letters, returned to the words still on the screen. And try as I might, I couldn't stop the cascading thoughts because despite what I tried to tell myself, I found it somewhat odd that a piece of me strangely wanted to believe that the melody and the lyrics were meant for me to hear. It would be sweet, anyway. But then again, it was dangerous, I knew. And if I've learned anything from my old flame's previous pitches, I've also learned that the past is a very determined ghost, haunting every chance it gets. Big events, small, mundane moments of the day, it doesn't matter. The past will find a way to squeeze into the present–if you let it.

I continued my awestruck stare into the screen, my breaths still short, as a phrase from my mother scrolled through my mind. She always used to say that the past is a relentless parasite in its quest, feeding off of the senses, looking for anything that will trigger a memory–forever there to complicate the present, forever there to remind us that it will always be a piece of us. I never had a clue as to what she meant, until now. Now, I understood fully, I feared, as I consciously commanded my heart to slow its pace. Any other time, I wouldn't have willingly entertained this so-called parasite. Most of the time, I wished it would just stay where it belonged–in the past. But this time, something was different. I was speechless, and I just couldn't bring myself to look away from its beautiful lyrics.

I listened to the song one last time before shutting down my laptop and folding the monitor over its keyboard.

Then, I reached for my phone in my pocket and scrolled through my contacts, settling on Will's name. I stared at the four-lettered word for a minute, before my fingers, absent the approval of my head, strayed to the phone's keyboard and formed a sentence:

I heard my song tonight.

My eyes traced over and over again each letter, each word of the sentence my fingers had just written. Then, I backspaced each letter until there were no words left in the message's screen and set the phone down.

And as if surrendering to the idea that I might never know for whom the sweet melody was actually intended, I stood up from my chair, switched off the den's lights and headed toward my bedroom. I had another date tonight, but this time, with my dreams, and I dared not keep them waiting on thoughts of my decided past and crazy what-ifs.

And, besides, in my dreams, it would be safe for the song to be mine.

Butterfly

I couldn't help but notice the minutes drag on. Seven couldn't come any sooner.

Resolving to bite the bullet and dive in–again–I began reading the paragraph at the top of my computer's screen for the third time that evening. But no sooner had I gotten through the first sentence, a familiar distraction came to my rescue.

My phone, jammed halfway under a stack of hand-written notes, suddenly burst to life. Without hesitation, I recovered the dancing device from under the stacks, glanced at its display window and brought the phone to my ear.

"Hey, Rach," I answered.

"Hey, Jules, what are you doing?" she asked, without missing a beat.

I paused to lean back in my chair and glance up at the clock on the wall.

"Uh, I'm finishing up some stuff at the office, and then I'm going home to get some sleep," I replied.

"Okay, well, book a ticket before you go to bed. Will is playing in New Milford next month, and you've got to come," Rachel said.

I could tell excitement was bursting from every part of her. I pictured fireworks coming out of her mouth and ears.

"Wait. What?" I asked, still trying to put the pieces together–after having been distracted by all of the fireworks.

Rachel refused to lose any steam by my question.

"Will is performing a benefit concert to help support flood victims. It's for a good cause, which I don't have to tell you about, and it would be so much fun if you could be there," she rambled off.

I was squinting my eyes as I turned my friend's request over in my head. I was well aware that the flooding had caused some major problems in my home state. As what happened about every ten years near the Missouri and Mississippi rivers, an unusually wet season had caused rain waters to exceed the rivers' banks and to flood nearby communities. And I knew firsthand what a levee break, four feet of water and six inches of silt could do to a home and a livelihood. I was seven when I watched my parents battle through it.

I picked up a pen and began aimlessly twirling it.

"A concert? Really?" I asked, somewhat surprised.

"Pretty good idea, huh?" Rachel asked.

I stopped twirling the pen.

"Yeah, pretty good idea," I said, nodding my head and smiling.

"Well…," Rachel went on, fishing for my answer.

"Well," I said, "that's really great he's doing that, and the concert does sound fun…"

"But…," she interrupted me.

"But," I continued, "it's just not the best time. I can send you a donation though, and you can make sure he gets it for me?"

I heard Rachel groan in protest on the other end of the phone.

"It wouldn't be the same, Jules. Plus, you haven't ever seen him play. He won't disappoint, I promise," she said, trying desperately to convince me.

"I'm sure he wouldn't," I said, laughing. "But I have so much to do here, and it's been so long anyway. I think it's just best if I just stay here."

"Julia," Rachel scolded.

Rachel very rarely called me by my birth name. She instead left the rare occasions for the times when she thought that I was acting exceptionally foolish. I had learned this a long time ago. And though I knew my friend's tactic well, I kept quiet as Rachel continued.

"Julia, you and I both know that if you really wanted to, you'd leave that stack of papers on your desk for a couple of days and fly your butt up here," she said.

I sighed.

"Rach, I just can't do it this time," I pleaded with her.

"Give me one good reason then," Rachel demanded.

I sighed again–this time, more audibly.

"I told you," I stammered patiently. "It's not the right time. I'm just too busy, and it's a long trip for just one day and one concert."

Rachel took a deep breath before continuing.

"What are you so afraid of, Jules?" she asked, sincerely. Patience had come back to her voice.

I paused for a second and allowed silent air waves to infiltrate the conversation. *What was I afraid of? What was I supposed to be afraid of?* I pondered Rachel's seemingly out-of-place cross-examination. Sure, the concert did sound fun. It would be nice to see my childhood friends again, and in the end, I knew that Rachel was ultimately right. I really could afford to leave the stack of papers for a couple of days and take the trip if I really wanted to, and the truth was that I really did want to. A piece of me ached to be there–to see him again, but I knew I shouldn't, and I wouldn't even allow myself to entertain the thought. Maybe I was a little afraid after all.

"I don't know," I said, after the brief break in the conversation. "It's just been a long time."

"What do you mean?" Rachel asked–remaining patient.

"I don't know. I tried so hard to forget, and then that song…," I said.

"Wait, forget what? And what song?" Rachel asked again, sounding puzzled.

"Just things I need to forget–that's all. And his last song. I heard it the other day," I confessed.

Rachel paused for a second.

"Oh yeah, that one," she said. She sounded as if she understood me completely now.

"Rach," I said and then stopped. I thought for a second as to how I should word my next question before I spoke again.

"Rach, I don't want this to sound conceited or anything. I'm just curious, but is the girl in the song…," I began.

"You?" Rachel finished my sentence.

"Yeah, I don't know," I stammered. "Some of it matches. I was just curious. I mean, I guess it's the whole butterfly thing. I think I'm just overreacting though."

"No, all of it matches," Rachel interjected. "But do I know for sure? No. I don't know. No one does. He hardly gets anything out about it in his interviews. It always looks and sounds like he wants to say something about it but nothing ever comes out. And you would think that someone here would know at least something. We're all curious–but honestly, Jules, no one knows. He keeps that part of his life pretty secret these days. I'm just waiting for him to show up wearing a wedding ring in an interview with Shawn Neville someday. That would be the first time that I would find out that he was even seeing anyone. And I would have said something about it earlier, but I didn't know if you had even heard it yet or if you even wanted to be bothered with it."

"Rach, really, when has that ever stopped you?" I asked, laughing.

Rachel laughed too.

"So, no one there even knows if he's dating anyone?" I asked, somewhat surprised.

"Nope, and I've asked," Rachel confessed.

"I'm sure you have," I said, smiling again. "That's really odd though–that no one knows."

"Yeah, I know it is, but what about the concert?" she asked, getting back to her mission. "I'll be there, and you don't even have to see him if you don't want to. Well, off the stage anyway," she reassured me.

I wanted to trust her, but something ultimately kept me from feeling completely convinced that I wouldn't be stepping outside of my comfort zone.

"Rachel, it's a long trip," I said in my last plea for her to surrender the battle.

"Okay, okay," Rachel said, backing off. "Just think about it. You wouldn't regret it."

I paused and smiled.

"Okay," I half-heartedly promised. "I'll think about it."

"All right, well, have a good night. Oh, and Julia…," she started.

"What?" I asked.

"Don't forget to wear something cute to bed…," she began.

"I know—because I could meet Prince Charming in my dreams or something like that," I finished.

"Yep, you said it. Okay, I'll talk to you later," she rambled off. And then, she was gone.

I smiled, knowing for certain that my friend had not changed a bit since high school, as I sat back in my chair and glared up at the spiteful clock on the wall again. Gone now was any desire to start the paragraph for the fourth time at the top of my computer's screen. By now, I knew my thoughts had scurried off to some place else, as a sigh fell through my lips and I wondered if I would ever really know the identity of the girl behind the song—or if it even truly mattered.

Seasoned Promise

The next couple of weeks flew by, and I hadn't so much as thought about the concert or the song or Will, for that matter. The case that had consumed my life since I had taken the job was edging to a close, and I reveled in the thought of never having to hear the words Snyder and erosive chemicals in the same sentence ever again as I sat on my screened-in porch sipping a sweet tea and listening to the couple of crickets in the tree outside of my apartment.

Though I tried not to think about it on my days off, my mind nevertheless would always slowly drift to thoughts about the case. Although the loose ends still needed tying up, for the most part, it had been a success.

The defendant, Snyder, had agreed to pay a small fortune in economic benefits to members of the fence-line communities affected by erosive chemical runoffs into a local marsh area. Justice had finally found its day, I thought, as I watched a pack of clouds move across the sky off in the distance.

I took another sip of tea and wondered if we would be so fortunate in our next case. But, of course, that was impossible to figure out now, and my mind reminded me of that by taking a violent u-turn in a whole, different direction.

What would it be like to see him again—to watch him on stage?

He had made it. The thought still sounded surreal and foreign in my head, but it didn't really surprise me. It had never really surprised me. I had always known that he had it in him, that one day, it would just take someone else finding it in him.

The sound of my phone ringing from inside my apartment halted my swirling thoughts. I set my glass of tea down onto the small, glass table beside me, crawled out of my comfortable lounge chair and scurried back inside and down the hallway, like a little lemming, following the sound of my ringer. By the time I had reached the other side of my bed, the ringing had stopped. Without hesitation, I picked up the phone. It was a text message from Rachel. My eyes followed over the letters as I read:

Still thinking? It'll be fun!

I smiled and held the phone in my hand as I slipped away into another thoughtful trance. Rachel couldn't let it go, wouldn't let it go, I knew. It was a valiant effort, but a valiant effort in vain all the same. The case was too close to being finished. Sure, I didn't have to be present to tie up the loose ends. Most of my work was done through emails and faxes anyway now. However, I felt better being able to run to the office if I really needed to, and besides, it would be good for me to get a head start on research for my next case. Flying home for one day to see a concert one night just didn't sound that practical right now.

I set the phone back down onto the bedside table and picked up a pair of pumps that I had carelessly strewn onto the floor the day before. I usually functioned best in a livable chaos; though, I often wondered how I found everything I needed when I needed it.

With the shiny, black heels in one hand, I looked up for the miniature string of tiny, round beads that dangled from a light fixture in my walk-in closet. When I spotted it, I gently pulled the cord, forcing the light to illuminate the small room.

On the floor, under a bar full of black, gray, navy and tan pant and skirt suits, I found a new home for the shiny, black shoes. Pleased with my efforts at attempting to restore a normal sense of order back into my little apartment, I reached for the string of metal beads again. I paused, however, when my eyes caught a shoe box with a tiny word etched across the side of its pink lid. In permanent, black marker, I read: *Pieces.*

Before I could stop myself, my hands left the metal strand and made a beeline for the small box, located slightly above my head. My fingers slowly pushed over the letters on the lid, and then without another thought, my hands carefully slid the shoe box out from underneath the stack of other boxes and blankets that lined the shelf.

I towed the pink box to my bed and fell onto the fluffy comforter, at the same time, positioning the container squarely on my lap. Slowly opening the lid, my thoughts raced back to college and then to high school and to the treasured few memories that sat tucked away in the little box.

Inside, I found my old, high school diploma, a *friends forever* necklace that Rachel had given me our freshmen year and a messy pile of letters, aged ticket stubs and old, fading photos. I took a second to take in the memories sitting at the top of the small pile. A stub for a film that debuted more than a decade ago rested proudly in clear view on top of a Valentine's Day card with two dancing hearts on its cover. The card shifted my eyes toward the sloppy stack of stationery.

"My last pieces of you," I whispered under my breath, as I smiled and let out a deep, heartfelt sigh.

I vaguely recognized each card as my fingers slowly flipped through the pile. Each one had a little, heartfelt note scribbled inside, below the printed message, and all of them were signed: *Love always and forever, Will.* I smiled as I read an inscription:

I'll always be your Spider-Man, my Mary Jane.

Another read:

At times, the road will be hard, the days will be long, and the journey you've traveled won't feel like a song. But know that I'll always love you, and with love, all is certain.

My smile widened.

"We really were head over heels–and so, so young," I heard myself say out loud.

Then, my smile faded, and my heart paused when I came across one, specific piece of memory I had all but forgotten about. I stared into the tiny, pink shoe box for almost a minute before I picked up the small, four-by-six-inch photo. The color in the picture had, by now, faded to dull greens and blues, and time had frayed the photo's edges, but it didn't matter. The memory was still visible.

The picture had been taken the day that I had left for college. Will was standing next to me with his arm around my waist, and in my hands were his orange flowers–his butterfly weeds. I knew the flowers had ultimately found their final resting place in a cardboard box, most likely covered with dust, along with the rest of my treasured memories stored in the back of a closet in New Milford.

As I stared at every detail in the photo, I remembered back to the day that Will had given me the timeless flowers. I remembered that I had promised him that I would never forget him. A smile widened across my face again when I realized that, just my luck, I had held up my part of the bargain–despite my efforts not to. I had not forgotten him, though he had also made that part nearly impossible. These days, he graced my television screen, my car radio and even the conversations that came out of my all-endearing, yet meddling best friend. Nevertheless, I had kept my promise. I had kept all of my promises I had made to him thus far–except for one, I suddenly remembered.

My heart raced as the memory of the first night I had heard the melody of his now-famous love song came flooding back to me. That fall night, on his back porch, his hand on mine, I had made a promise.

I sat as still as humanly possible then, staring into my bedroom's beige walls and then back at the faded photo, still resting in my hand. My revelation motivated me and frightened me all at the same time. I continued to sit frozen and silent, until I finally came to one, solid, whole thought.

I had to keep my promise.

It wasn't like me to go bad on my word–not to him– not to anyone.

"I'll buy the ticket. I'll go, and then I'll come back home," I confirmed aloud, as if someone else were in the room to hear me.

At the same time, I tried my best to convince myself that the trip would be uneventful–simply a quest to fulfill a vow made years ago.

It could be that simple–but it could also be severely complicated also, I knew. Sure, I could show up and leave without so much as any controversy, but what I could take home with me in my little carry-on could be lasting. If I did end up seeing him, how would he react? Would he be happy to see me? Would it be awkward? Would he bring up my broken engagement? Did he even know? I couldn't help but question if I was intentionally walking into the lion's den–a lemming in a lion's den. The thought made me cringe.

And though I didn't know why, the thought of hearing Will's song again without the option to turn the station made me strangely nervous. I just wanted to be rid of my past. I moved across the country to start anew, not to rehash what-could-have-beens. I had no time to get wrapped up in my past again, and frankly, no real desire. I had treasured our time together, and it would be nice to know that he had treasured it as well, but it had ended a long time ago and that was that.

I carefully returned the photo to the top of the stack of treasured memories, now with permanent residences in the pink shoe box, and then closed the lid and slid the box back into its place on the closet shelf. I then shuffled back to the screened-in porch, took a seat in my cushioned lounge chair and grabbed my laptop.

Within only a couple of minutes, I had booked a round-trip ticket to St. Louis. I let out a deep sigh of relief mixed with anxiousness and then sat back into my chair.

I was his friend too, in some way, shape or form. And I had just as much duty as any one of his other friends to be there and to support him in his success. Right? And plus, I guessed, whether I liked it or not, a promise was a promise.

The Song

As I edged closer to my hometown, I could feel my heart beating faster and faster as my nerves ran wild and loose throughout my body, kind of like children who had just discovered they had a snow day. And my mind was the mother, with no control of the weather, much less the children.

It's a concert, for God's sake. Get yourself together, I recited in my head over and over again, just as one of Will's songs came pouring through my rental car's speakers.

I flipped the station. Now, even my own radio taunted me. Wasn't it enough that I was on my way–that eight hours ago I had left civilization for corn fields and cattle? Was it too much to ask not to be haunted by my past now on my last stretch of normalcy?

I switched my driving hand again and sat deeper into the driver's seat. The late afternoon had by now given way to evening, and the sun had begun its descent into the horizon. It was my final leg of the trip, my last bit of highway, and sooner than I had wished, I would be there and in his presence for the first time in years. The thought kind of terrified me. And a big part of me wondered what I had gotten myself into, while the other part wondered what he was doing now. Was he nervous or was he sitting back and laughing with friends, soaking it all up? Would he suspect that I would be coming tonight? Would he notice me there? Would it even matter? I hadn't really thought of that. Would it hurt me more if my coming didn't matter at all? Had he even remembered my promise? With my mind suddenly sent spinning into overdrive, I forced myself to refocus on my mission.

It didn't matter. He wouldn't know that I had been there anyway, if I could help it. I hadn't told anyone, not even my best friend, about my last-minute, nine-hundred-mile journey. Rachel will kill me, I know, but Will would surely have found out if I had let even her in on my little secret. Nothing stays a secret in a small town; I knew that much. I only wanted to fulfill my vow and then be back on my way to civilization, back to Charleston, back to my own life.

A little before eight, I arrived at a grassy field and slowly pulled onto a dirt path. The ground was uneven and made the rental tilt and shift as it maneuvered over the rough patches. I'm pretty sure off-roading wasn't in the rental agreement. We'll just keep this part a secret, I thought to myself, as I tapped the gas.

Very soon, I came to a tiny stand that temporarily housed a middle-aged man whom I didn't recognize. He was taking donations, so I handed him a bill and then continued on my way.

After rolling over a couple more uneven spots in the ground's surface and thinking that I might very well have to return the rental in not just one, but several different pieces, I finally pulled into the grass and put the car into park. A row of cars had already formed a long, meandering line across the front of the field, and another several rows were beyond that row. From the cars, it looked like a lot of people for a concert in New Milford.

I threw my keys into my purse and stepped out onto the soft soil. The ground was an unused pasture that belonged to an old farmer who lived a mile up the highway. Though, it didn't look much like a pasture now. Rows and rows of plastic, white chairs lined and spread out from a tiny, makeshift stage. I squinted my eyes. From what I could see through the fading daylight, it looked like the stage was the bed of a tractor trailer. And probably for good reason—it most likely was. I pictured Will insisting on using the tractor trailer instead of his usual stage with which he often traveled. It was less "fuss," I could hear him saying even now. Either way, I guessed, it did fit in nicely with the acres of fields and the usual dusting of trees that surrounded it.

I took a deep breath before taking another step. I could see that no one was on stage, but I could already hear the buzz of the crowd, the soft roar of a couple thousand people talking and laughing and carrying on. Where did all of these people come from?

Strands of faces, young and old, wrapped around the base of the small stage and stretched back more than a hundred meters. Most of their backs were toward me, and most eyes seemed to be toward the stage, and by the look of things, no one seemed to notice me at all. The thought made me smile sheepishly on the inside, but it didn't stop my heart from starting its now, all-too-familiar pounding pattern in my chest.

I slowly made my way through the grassy parking lot and to a temporary shack that sat directly behind the crowd. The tiny stand had caught my attention, and it would serve to distract me for the time being anyway.

Hanging tee shirts lined the tiny walls and a miniature cash register rested near the front of the small, six-by-five-foot box.

"Hey, miss, do you want to buy a tee shirt? All proceeds go to help support Missouri flood victims," a freckled-face boy, who looked as if he was still in junior high, called out to me as I neared him.

I smiled at the boy as I walked toward the hut.

"How much?" I asked.

"Ten dollars," the freckled-face boy replied.

I rifled through my purse, pulled out my wallet and then a twenty-dollar bill and handed it to the cheery boy.

"You can keep the change," I said, smiling.

"Thanks," the boy replied, handing me a white tee shirt with the words *Support Flood Relief* in red letters across its front. I looked at the top and then squeezed it on over the shirt I was already wearing. At least, I'd blend in.

With no visible distractions remaining, I set out again toward the throng in the middle of the pasture. Each step toward the crowd made my breathing quicken. And by the time I had reached the last row of white, plastic chairs, I noticed that my palms had grown clammy as well. I rubbed them against the hips of my jeans and stealthily slid into an aisle a couple of rows up.

As quickly as I could and trying desperately not to bring any attention to myself, I claimed a seat as if just finding one made me safe from my own uneasiness. The plastic chair a couple of seats down the row was my temporary hiding place. Once hidden, I took a quick scan of the people around me. To my surprise, no one looked even the slightest bit familiar. I was in New Milford, right?

I situated my purse onto an open, plastic chair next to me and slid my arms into my leather jacket. The air was cooling now, though it was still fairly warm for October. I then pulled my long hair out from underneath the jacket and glanced forward toward the stage, peering in between the shifting heads and swaying bodies. I could just barely see the group of people who lined the front of the platform but not enough to make anyone out. I rose up on tiptoes, still trying to catch a glimpse of Rachel's head in the crowd.

Then, without warning, the soft background music stopped and the few lights that had subtly lit the makeshift stage grew dimmer and dimmer, until what was on the stage was no longer visible. And within seconds, several dozen beaming, bright ivory and blue lights that hung over the stage on little, metal structures illuminated four figures in the darkness–a young, tattooed drummer, a clean-cut pianist, a burly base guitarist and a tall, boyishly handsome guy donning a cowboy hat and an acoustic six-string across his chest.

I hardly recognized the man holding the six-string. The lights, the crowd, the band–seeing him now made it all strangely real. And for the first time, he wasn't the boy

I had remembered him to be anymore. He wasn't the boy who climbed old windmills for fun or even the boy I had watched grow smaller and smaller in my rearview mirror the day I had left for college. He wasn't a boy anymore.

My heart fluttered as the figure holding the guitar sauntered up to the microphone stand in the center of the stage. He looked very similar to how I had remembered seeing him years ago on *Good Morning Today*, but somehow seeing him up on stage, live, and within a football-field length of me, made everything different–made me oddly breathless. He looked really good. He had on dark denim jeans and a white tee shirt that looked exactly like the one I had just bought from the freckled-face boy in the hut.

"How are ya doin', New Milford?" Will shouted from the stage.

A wide smile lit up his face as he spoke to the crowd. I could tell that he was happy to be where he was. Even from a distance, I remembered that smile–it was as if everything in the world were right.

The crowd cheered and screamed. Then, Will and his band started right in on their first song, and then their second, until they were cruising right along, hitting each song like they had done it a million times before. Every once in a while, though, Will would take a break, mostly to remind everyone why they were there, and then, another song would follow.

When I closed my eyes, I could almost picture myself on Will's back porch at the end of a warm, July day, listening to his voice, believing that there was nothing in the world more soothing. In fact, his voice was just as beautiful to me now as it had been all those years ago. Although, something did seem a little different tonight with the way he sang. Tonight, he commanded so much attention. So many people seemed to love him and his band and its music. And I knew that most people still looked at Will like they always had. He was the same old Will to them–the same Will who still played pick-up basketball games in the high school's gymnasium, fished on the weekends and put fires out during the week. I knew this much, mostly from Rachel, of course. However, to the few who didn't know him that well–and I would suspect that was a lot of the people now standing around me–he was every bit as famous as the last celebrity. I could see in the faces nearest to me, at least, that that was exactly how they saw him. Those next to me donned tee shirts proudly displaying Will's profile, and they gushed enthusiastically over his every word. And tonight, I had to admit, there was a tiny part of me that kind of felt like them. After all, he really was a celebrity in his own right, and he very much looked the part tonight. And I was proud of him and happy that he had gotten the chance to follow his apparent dreams thus far. Most of all, however, I was happy that the world had gotten a chance to hear him sing.

After the band wrapped up its last song, the crowd broke out into a loud round of applause. Will and his band members took a bow and walked off the left side of the stage, disappearing behind a long, black curtain. The multitude grew ever noisier, yet stood still then, waiting anxiously for the band's encore. And not to disappoint, moments later, Will reemerged again from the left side of the stage. This time, however, he wasn't holding his six-string, and not all of his band members followed him. Only the pianist trailed him, finally taking a seat on the bench behind the piano in the back corner of the stage. Will, on the other hand, walked to the front of the platform with only a microphone in hand and a spotlight guiding his path. He stopped at a stool centered on the stage and took a seat, anchoring one leg on the ground, the other on one of the stool's rungs.

It only took a matter of seconds before the massive crowd's buzz faded and then went silent. And then, he had everyone's attention.

"I've saved this one for last," Will finally spoke in a soft, deep voice. "I wrote it years ago, but this is going to be the first time anyone's ever heard it."

His words came out raspy and almost shy.

Then, he paused and removed his cowboy hat, while a melody from the piano began to play softly in the background.

It was his last song of the night, and his first words came spoken—not sung.

"I couldn't stop at one. This one's for you too, Julia," he said.

I stifled a gasp by covering my mouth with the inside of my hand. I swore my heart stopped for an instant—or at least, it came the closest it had ever come to completely stopping.

What had he said? My mind raced, and I panicked.

I could hear every breath I took, as if I were in some sort of strange space vacuum on some strange planet in another world. In reality, I had heard what he had said, but what was really real anymore? I couldn't tell. The line was constantly blurring these days.

I couldn't think of anything else but his last words. Nothing else mattered and nothing else came to mind.

I listened to the girls in the crowd scream and then grow quiet again before Will bowed his head in the center of the stage and a beaming ray of light left him and spotlighted the piano player, who continued his soothing solo.

A tear slipped past my eyelid and slid down my polished cheek, at the same time, my legs grew strangely weak. I was melting–uncontrollably malfunctioning. I wanted to sit down, but I couldn't take my eyes off of the singer, so I simply remained motionless–frozen where I stood–a tall weed in the all-too-crowded field. My stare never left him as my eyes strained to see his figure in the dark now. I could just barely see that his gaze now focused on a spot in the far distance. And as the piano solo drew to a close, the ivory light returned to Will, and Will began a soft melody:

"The sun's a settin' on Cedar Lake
While that autumn fog settles in
The fish aren't bitin'
Crickets sing
Just me and an old friend
Remembering the good ol' days
When we were just kids
Startin' trouble, chasin' old flames
The what-ifs, the what-might-have-beens
Until slowly the conversation dies
And I know that he knows
Cause the next thing he says
Is, buddy, don't tell me lies,
How does the story really go?

Does she ever cross your mind?
Does she ever steal your nights?
Is she still a part of you?
Do you ever wish she were still by your side?
And what would you do?
If she walked up here tomorrow
And told you that she loved you?

Butterfly Weeds

Would you drop it all and run to her?
Would you tell her you love her too?
Or would you simply send her home?
And tell her you've moved on?
Tell me, buddy, what would you do?

Then I looked at him with two sad eyes
And I said,
More than every once in a while,
More than most dreams,
More than just my heart,
More than anything,
More than you know,
And more than I can say,
I've loved her more
Every passing day

And every time I close my eyes,
She's here with me
Her soft, green eyes,
Her hand in mine
It's her I see
And I tell him,
I wish your dreams kept you close
Or that one led you back to me
And that I'd trade it all
For the day he didn't have to ask me,
Tell me, buddy, what would you do?

Now, I'm tellin' you,
Julia, My Butterfly,
More than every once in a while,
More than most dreams,
More than just my heart,

More than anything,
More than you know,
And more than I can say,
I've loved you more
Every passing day
Julia, I've loved you more
Every passing day."

I let a breath of unsteady air pass cautiously through my lips as the ballad ended, the piano ceased its playing and the stage lights dimmed. I felt as if I had held the air prisoner in my chest for the duration of the song. I could hear the crowd erupt as Will exited the stage for the last time that night. I watched his figure walk slowly, head down to the edge of the dark curtains and eventually disappear. And though I heard the crowd's cheers, they weren't loud enough to block out the racing thoughts in my head or the thudding of my pounding heart in my chest.

What had I just heard? What had just happened? And what had he meant? He said my name, right? It was my name. It wasn't anyone else's? I was Julia, right?

Not even able to form anything resembling a whole, logical thought, I unlocked my eyes from my deep stare into the stage that, by now, held no one. My heart was in pieces, and tears had welled up in my eyes, forcing a gradual mist to escape down my flushed cheeks. I hadn't taken my eyes off of the singer the entire night. I was so entranced by his voice and the sweet words he had sung. And I knew it sounded crazy, but I felt almost as if it had just been only the two of us standing in the field together all alone, alone and together like so many times years before. But this time, I was speechless and uncontrollably breathless. I tried desperately to regain my thoughts first and then my composure. How had a simple song unraveled me so much?

It was that one, five-letter word that had made me lose myself. My own name had caused me to shatter into a million, tiny pieces, and now, I lay broken amongst the grass and dirt in a Missouri field. I hadn't suspected this turn of events in the least bit as I had made my way back to my hometown earlier in the evening.

I slowly lowered myself back into the chair behind me. I would have involuntarily fallen into the seat within moments anyway if I hadn't forced myself to its plastic surface.

It was my name. He had said my name. I wasn't crazy. I couldn't be dreaming. I could physically feel the wet tears that I was now frantically wiping off my face with the back of my hand. The buzz of the crowd was so clear and so audible. I could even smell the grass and soil beneath my feet that now mixed with an assortment of colognes and perfumes. I wasn't dreaming, which also meant that I couldn't wake up.

The thought made me feel somewhat claustrophobic. Now, I wished more than anything that I were next to Rachel, though I'd take anyone familiar now. I just needed, at the very least, some validation, but I knew I wasn't getting any of that anytime soon. I didn't know anyone around me, and more importantly, no one knew me.

With that realization, my thoughts immediately turned toward my escape. I needed only to get to my car across the grassy parking lot before anyone could see my disheveled state, before the crowd around me started leaving, pouring past me.

Searching for my leather handbag still on the chair next to me, I noticed a woman who was probably in her forties looking dead at me and whispering to someone who could have been the woman's husband. My glance quickly left the stranger then and refocused straight ahead. Great. I had been spotted. The soggy girl in the back, crying her eyes out, had officially been detected.

Just get to the car.

I put my head down and dashed toward the sedan parked in the temporary parking lot at the edge of the field. I was making some headway, but I couldn't help but catch the whispers as I fled past the lingering few who had filed in after the concert had started.

"Is that her?" I heard at different times as I fled, still feverishly trying to wipe the tears from my cheeks with the back of my hand. I was too well aware of my physical and emotional state not to think that they weren't talking about me.

But maybe they would just think I was allergic to corn or dirt or grass–or love songs with my name in them, written by old flames.

It took me less than a minute to reach my rented car. Once there, I jumped into the driver's seat and forced the key into the ignition. A quick turn purred the engine to a start. My hands were shaking as I slid the gear shaft into reverse and then drive.

A slight sense of relief came over me as I made my escape from the dirt path and back onto the highway.

Safe.

I let out a sigh.

Though my getaway lent only but a little solace, it was enough to get my hands to stop shaking. I drove deliberately; though, the faster I drove, the more my heart pounded in my chest. And my thoughts continued to turn awful-looking cartwheels in my head. It was like someone had just put a four-year-old up in my mind and told her to play the outfield.

"What just happened?" I spoke out loud, uncontrollably babbling. "Is he serious? Why would he do this? What does it mean? He couldn't have waited this long, but had he? Why wouldn't he have told me sooner? What was it exactly that he had told me anyway? Did he even know I was there? I was engaged, Will. I was engaged a year ago. You knew that. I could be married now."

I spoke as if someone were in the passenger's seat next to me. I spoke as if he were in the passenger's seat next to me, though my words fell to the hard, unforgiving floorboard instead.

"I am being ridiculous, and I am definitely not crying," I tried to convince myself. "These are silly tears, and they mean nothing. They mean nothing," I pleaded as the salty wetness poured down my face.

I slowed as I turned onto a gravel road. My heart literally ached, though I still wondered why. It didn't seem possible that he could still shake me like this. Thoughts cascaded through my mind one after the other. At the same time, an old habit guided me down the winding, gravel road and to a familiar, almost-forgotten place.

Confessions

I brought the rented sedan to rest at the graveled area where tonight a handful of fireflies had already begun their dance around the open, grass fields. A black lull had just engulfed the countryside no more than an hour ago, leaving a silent blanket of darkness behind. Tree frogs echoed crickets in the nearby brush, and I could hear the creek behind me gently pouring over a bed of limestone as I turned the key and silenced the engine.

It would otherwise be a completely tranquil experience, but tonight, the peacefulness of my surroundings did little to calm the battle that was already in progress in my mind.

I gripped the steering wheel with both hands and then let out a deep sigh. I caught myself questioning how I had even gotten there. I tried to recall the path—the turns, the winding roads—that had led me to the spot to convince myself I hadn't just teleported there. I couldn't conjure up any images, so I quickly gave up. Pure instinct or habit had led me to where I was.

"What just happened?" I whispered one more time—to no one.

I took another deep breath and then slowly and uneasily let it fall through my lips. Then, I lifted the door handle and slid out of the car. After pausing a second to take in the vast sky above me and the thousands of tiny stars now exponentially springing to life, I smiled slightly for the first time in what seemed like an eternity.

"God, I missed you guys," I said to the heavens as if the stars could hear my confession. To me, they offered the peace I needed—for the meantime.

Slowly, I rested my hands on the top of the sedan's hood, pushing gently, testing its stability. My jeep had always held me, and so had Will's SUV. The sedan shouldn't be any different, I rationalized or at least, I hoped, as I climbed carefully onto the hood and made myself comfortable. It had, after all, survived the grass parking lot.

The air was still slightly warm but now carried with it a northwest chill in its breeze. What looked like millions of proud, tiny stars now littered the sky, and tonight, the half-moon shone as bright as it could without its other half; though, it still left the world below somewhat sheltered by a quiet, deep shadow.

I hopelessly tried to make out the facial features of the man in the moon, as the image of the night of my first kiss bounced to the forefront of my memory and froze there. This was all I needed right now–the thought of my first kiss with the boy who had just transformed into a man before my eyes and had just dropped a confession heavier than the world's weight onto my heart just moments ago. That was just what I needed.

The lingering memory made me smile for a moment nonetheless. The thought was poison, though. It only led to a flood of similar memories–starry nights like this one, talking about nothing really at all, holding hands, no worries, no cares.

"Life was so simple then," I whispered through a smile.

Lost in the distracting hauntings of my past, I suddenly spotted two headlights off in the far distance. They startled me slightly.

"That's strange," I softly whispered.

In all the times I had ever been there, I had never once seen another car traveling down the same, secluded path. I squinted to try and make out the image behind the lights as they crept closer and closer toward me. I could tell they were slowing.

It wasn't until the mysterious vehicle followed a bend in the road that I could clearly make out its make and model. And what I saw left me breathless–again. It was an old, small SUV–his old SUV. But how had he found me? And had he even meant to find me?

I lifted my back up from the windshield and sat up as the vehicle came to rest next to my rented car. I quickly wiped the remainder of the drying tears from under my eyes and brushed my cheeks with the back of my hand.

My heart pounded again–the feeling was becoming familiar–and I felt now as if it could leap out of my chest at any second.

He stepped out of the SUV, and I could see the outline of his figure. He was wearing the same blue jeans but a different tee shirt from when I had seen him on the stage no more than an hour ago. This shirt was navy, and something I couldn't make out in the shadows was printed in bold letters across his chest. And now, instead of a cowboy hat, he wore a baseball cap. And he was holding something, but I couldn't quite tell what it was either.

"Hi, Jules," Will said, as a genuine smile tenderly lit up his face.

I paused for a moment and quietly cleared my throat. It should be awkward, but somehow it seemed somewhat natural–him being there.

"Hi," I spoke softly, but cheerfully, trying to appear completely unnerved, feeling like my efforts just might be miraculously working.

Will smiled wider and continued to walk closer to me.

"Mind if I take a seat?" he asked when he reached the sedan.

"Not at all; it's a rental," I said, jokingly. Those acting classes I never took were paying off.

Will carefully climbed on top of the car's hood and leaned his back against the windshield next to me, leaving a good foot between us.

"Did you know I was here?" I asked him as he made himself comfortable. I hoped that it was just dark enough that he couldn't see my soppy eyes.

Will hesitated for a second, and then with a big grin on his face, he settled his eyes on mine.

"Of course. Where else would you be?" he asked.

I paused.

"But how…I never…," I started. My eyes were narrow, and I looked puzzled, I knew.

"Oh, you want to know how I knew you came at all?" he jumped in.

"That would be a start," I said, nodding, the corners of my mouth rising.

"You promised," he said.

I froze for an instant.

"You remembered that?" I asked, somewhat surprised.

"Of course, and from the looks of it, you did too," he said, leaning over and gently elbowing my arm.

"A promise is a promise," I softly said, secretly recalling my reasoning for being there. "But seriously, how could you have known?"

Will smiled. He had a mischievous look on his face.

"Did you see the camera guy scanning the crowd?" he asked. He held a half-grin on his lips.

"Umm…yeah, I guess I noticed him," I said.

"Before the show, I gave him a photo and asked him to look for you," he said.

"You didn't?" I demanded.

"I did. And turns out, he's got a good eye," he said.

I let my head fall softly back onto the windshield again as I laughed—a sincere and almost comfortable laugh, miraculously allowing some of my nerves to fly away.

"You never cease to amaze me, Will Stephens," I confessed.

The conversation stopped then, and a wall of silence filled its place as we both stared into the heavens. A million questions ran through my mind, but I didn't know which one was more important—besides, the silence was comfortable and almost freeing. Eventually, though, Will broke the quiet.

"Did you hear the last song?" he asked. His voice was soft and deep.

"I did," I said, in almost a whisper.

"I finished writing it about a year ago. I meant every word of it," he confessed.

His words hit my ears and sunk deep down into my chest and then out to my limbs, reaching every part of my body that didn't even feel like my own anymore. I felt like I was completely outside of my situation and only just looking on.

And as I waited for his news to settle, I tried desperately to process it piece by piece. At that point, I had been pretty sure that he hadn't been referring to anyone else named *Julia*. But hearing it confirmed, I strangely felt a fresh wave of nervous joy and curiosity overtake me, which left me only with more questions–questions that I knew would have to wait for now, at least.

"It's a beautiful song, Will," I said, slowly nodding my head. My response was safe, I knew.

Will nodded his head but remained silent.

"And how does 'the one' feel about this song?" I asked him pointedly, slowly beginning my quest for answers.

Will softly chuckled.

"I don't know, Jules, how do you feel?" he asked.

Startled by his reply, my breaths stopped for an instant. My investigation had backfired. What was he talking about? I turned my head toward the rugged boy from my youth who was now the handsome man beside me. I could see his piercing blue eyes and a subtle, five-o-clock shadow on his chin and cheeks as a single ray of moonlight danced on his face. His stare remained straight ahead as his sea-blue eyes pierced a spot in the distant sky. Yet, a smile lingered on his lips, and I suddenly felt as if we were sitting around a fire, and I was noticing his blue eyes for the very first time.

I let out a slow, uneasy breath before I looked forward again, locking my own stare on the moon. There was no man in the moon tonight. No, it was definitely just Will and I–just the two of us, looking our past square in the face.

My eyes pierced the night as Will's voice solicited my attention again.

"You're the one, Jules, and I should have told you when you asked those years ago, but I knew it wasn't the right time. I knew that you weren't ready yet," he confessed then.

"Ready?" I mumbled. My word was almost inaudible. I was noticeably shaken as my stare fell from the sky and to his structured face.

Will paused and took a deep breath, though his eyes never left the heavens. He seemed to have heard my mumble.

"Jules, you've always been the only one for me. I let life get in the way of us only to realize that I didn't really have life without you in it. I didn't take the record deal in search of some kind of fame or elusive fortune or anything like that. I didn't take it for me, Jules. It's been great. You were right; it's all been great. But you know that I would have been just as happy to spend the rest of my days playing my guitar for my number-one fan," he said.

Will stopped and smiled as he turned his head and caught my frozen stare, which hadn't left him.

Had he answered my question? What had I even asked? His words were the sound of heaven hitting earth, if it were a perfect world and if we hadn't just lived the last ten years apart.

"But when I realized that I might not even get that dream—my dream of playing for you for the rest of my life—I remembered a promise you had made to me," he continued.

My heart leapt, though I still didn't quite know how to react. Had he really done all of this for me? Was that even possible? His confession made me either want to pull him close to me and be held in his arms even for just one last time or want to push him away and hate him for the rest of my days for keeping his secret all of these years.

"Why did you wait so long to tell me this?" I asked, puzzled and grateful and flattered and angry with him all at the same time. The words just seemed to fall out of my mouth. "I almost got married. You know that." A sternness lingered in my voice.

Will turned on his side and rested his head on his hand.

"Yeah, I know," he said. "That hurt a little." He now wore a half-grin. "You know, Jules, after I had cooled off from the night I saw you wearing that ring, I had booked a ticket to San Diego to see you—to talk to you, to plead with you to give me another chance."

"A ticket?" I whispered, puzzled.

His eyes caught mine again before he spoke.

"I did, but then I ran into Rachel the next day, and she told me that you had broken it off. Jules, I wish I could say that I knew all along that you wouldn't go through with it, but I didn't know for sure. I just prayed like hell you wouldn't."

A smile cracked my stoic exterior.

"Thanks, Will. I'm glad I had your best wishes," I said, scolding him, half-playfully, half-seriously.

"I'm so sorry, Jules. I hadn't really realized how fast everything had gone until it was too late. I was so busy trying to find a way to get you back that I kind of got lost along the way. And in the end, I decided not to go to San Diego. I thought it might be too much–you dealing with everything and me. I decided to give you some time. I know that whole situation couldn't have been that much fun," he added.

"It wasn't, but I've moved past it," I reassured him. My tone was even and to the point.

Will paused for a moment, and silence filled the air again. Then, he spoke.

"In the end, Jules, I knew you had wings–wings like no one I have ever met. You had your dreams, and they were bigger than this town, and they were bigger than me. I knew that, and I knew you. I would have loved to follow you and to be with you when you graduated college or got into law school or passed the bar. You passed, right?" he playfully asked.

I turned my face toward his and gently smiled.

"I know," he said, smiling back at me. "See, I would have loved to be there with you living your dreams. It kills me that I wasn't. But I knew that I would have only slowed you down because my place was here. This was my calling," he said, lightly tugging on the bottom of his shirt below the small letters that I could now see that read: *St. Louis Fire Department*.

Will paused and looked down at my hand for the first time that night. He seemed to have noticed through the glimpses of light as the clouds rolled over the moon that my left hand now bore no ring, and he smiled slightly. I aimed to stifle his smile. There were still unanswered questions.

"It hurt, Will. You gave up on us. You stopped trying, and at the very end, when it mattered the most, you never even fought for us–or at least, I never had known that you had even tried," I said firmly, without wavering.

I surprised myself at how quickly my voice enveloped with passion–at how quickly I had jumped back through the years. It had been so long ago. How could this all still matter to me?

"I was foolish, Jules," he said. "I shouldn't have let you walk out of my life. I should have protested. I should have fought for you, but I was young, and I thought you would change your mind in a short while and come back to me. And more than that, I was selfish. I wanted all of you, and I wanted you to want me too. And, believe me, I wanted to tell you. God knows I wanted to tell you so many times, but you see, I had to wait. I loved you too much to lose you twice."

My heart broke at his words, and tears welled up in my eyes again as I fought to keep them locked within my eyelids. Some piece of me was rebelling against my body, even as I silently begged it not to.

"Will, I loved you," I softly said.

There was no turning back then, I knew. The conversation I had both longed for and dreaded for most of my adult life had begun. Closure had begun.

"But you made me a different person, Will," I softly confessed. "I was fighting for survival in the last days we were together."

I paused to look at Will's face. His baby blue eyes looked as if his heart were breaking.

"You made me never want to hurt like that again," I continued, almost as if it had been a long-awaited confession.

"I'm so sorry, Jules," Will said, his eyes pleading with me. "But you've got to know that the longer I waited for you, the more my heart broke. My ship sank, Jules, and my plan failed, and before I knew it, I was lost without you back then. Even though I could no longer wrap you in my arms or kiss your pretty forehead, I still saw you."

He paused for a moment before continuing.

"You haunted my nights and then even my days. I lived for sleep at times when you would come to me, and it would be just like you had never left. Dreams would always end with you, and then mornings would steal you away with a cruelty that haunted my days. The start of each new day pained me as I opened my eyes only to face my merciless reality. No matter how hard I tried to push you to the back of my mind, you always found a way back to the forefront," he said.

He hesitated and then looked down, locking his stare on his black, leather boots.

I kept my gaze on his face. I could see an indescribable pain that I had never seen on him before radiating from his eyes and lips. I knew he was sincere. I wanted to pull him close–even if it was out of habit–but I commanded my hands to stay on the sedan instead.

He continued.

"I eventually learned to live as normally as possible again," he went on. "I learned to get out of bed and put on a smile every day, though even in my laughter, my heart ached. I learned to hide my hurt when someone asked about you or mentioned your name, which they often did and still do. I slowly learned to live a quiet existence without you by my side, carrying the heavy burden that was my secret."

Will paused, and then he returned his eyes to mine.

"Then one day, I received an answer to my prayers, and it came in the form of a business card. It sounds crazy, I know, but it was almost as if fate had conspired for us, Jules. It took me a little while to realize it, but once I had, I was on a mission. Jules, I took the offer for you. All of this–the performing, the tours, the songs–is for you. I did it all to bring you back to me."

"What?" I softly questioned.

If that were even possible, I wondered how he had collaborated all of it in his favor. Here I was, and here he was right next to me. It had been years, and he was now telling me that all it had taken to get us back in the same time zone, in the same place, was a business card, a prayer and what had to have been a whole lot of faith.

I still hated him for letting me go and for not telling me anytime in the last decade that he was still in love with me. But could there have been some truth to his words? Does timing really play into this at all? Had I never had gone to law school or worked at the firm if I hadn't at least got the chance to spread my wings–outside of New Milford? And had he not tried to tell me several times, even through Rachel at times, that he still had feelings for me? I was starting to believe that I wasn't completely innocent either. And the truth was, after I had left my hometown in search of new adventures those years ago, I had never really looked back. And he eventually became a beautiful piece of my past, like the rest of it, to which I could not return. I had shut him out–not completely–but just enough to make it count, and I had forgotten what it felt like to be his. But it had been so long, and so much had changed. I had changed.

My silent thoughts again failed to reach his ears, as he continued his soliloquy. He was telling a story, and it seemed to be one of his favorites.

"I had just finished my first album, and I knew that it would only be a matter of time before you'd come back. After all, you promised," he said.

A confident smile danced to life on his face as he gazed into my eyes again.

"Jules, I've already waited too long to tell you this," he continued.

He reached behind him and held out an object, which slowly became visible in the moonlight, between the two of us. I involuntarily panicked for a moment. The weight of his confession was hitting me.

"Julia, when I said that I would love you until the last petal falls, I meant it," he said, serenely and self-assured. "You're the answer to my every prayer."

A little more of my heart melted then, and as I looked at the tiny, little flowers nestled in his rough hand, my heart also ached. I recognized the small, hand-written note attached to the flower's stem by a fine, white ribbon. It had been the same butterfly weed that he had given to me almost a decade earlier. Its color had faded to a pale peach color now, and it didn't look as new and as vibrant as it once had, but nevertheless, it still had all of its silk petals.

"Where did you find this?" I asked, taking the stem into my hands. A certain surprise filled my voice.

"Under that raggedy, old teddy bear of yours and some track medals," he said, smiling. "I had some help."

I smiled too. Then, I remembered. It all came flooding back to me as if it had been a repressed memory nearly forgotten. I remembered how heartbroken and how loved I had felt when his same, sad eyes first handed me the flower those many years ago. My own eyes had welled up with tears then as they threatened to do now. My heart throbbed as I recalled driving my jeep farther and farther away from my high school sweetheart that day. For some reason, me driving away had always been the last memory I had associated with our storied love, and it had always left me feeling bitter sweet.

I stared into the flower's silk petals as my heart beat wildly and my mind raced with thoughts—thoughts from when I was sixteen to the present. Within a night, my whole world had unfolded, revealing to me the innermost pieces of my heart. The memory of how I had felt to be loved by him had finally squeezed out of its box that had been stored in the furthest part of my mind. And it sounded crazy, even to me, but I wanted to tell him immediately how much I had loved him and that I would always love him in some way. Maybe it was because I thought it would bring some kind of closure or maybe it was only to make his sad eyes happy again. I wasn't quite sure. I loved him for the memories he had given me and for showing me that true and honest love was possible. He had been mine once for awhile, and he had been my best friend. I knew that I would always save a piece of my heart for him, and I wanted desperately to let him know that, but I knew that telling him wasn't practical, and it wouldn't be that easy. In the end, I realized the moment had long passed. Now, too much time had gone by, too much life had been lived and too much change had changed us. We weren't kids anymore. Now was the time to be realistic—to realize moving on was just a necessary part of life.

My silence seemed to have discouraged Will's already bleeding heart. It looked as if pain like needles stung the inside of his chest as he tried desperately not to fall to pieces from both, what seemed like, fearing and preparing for the worst.

"Will," I said, still trying to gather my thoughts and my words so that they would match when they fell off my lips. I stared straight ahead so as not to be distracted by his handsome features and his own seductive lips.

"I'm not the same person I was when we were in high school. You don't even really know me anymore," I softly said.

Will seemed taken aback for a moment.

"Well, Jules, if you haven't noticed, I'm not exactly the same person that I was ten years ago either," he said with a half-smile. "I'm here fighting for you, aren't I?"

A coy smile slipped across my face.

"I'm just trying to tell you that you might not be saying all of these things if you really knew me now," I said.

"Hmm," Will said, nodding his head.

"Then, just who is the new Miss Julia Lang?" he asked, sincerely, yet also with a hint of playfulness in his voice.

"Well, okay," I said, pausing, then taking a deep breath before exhaling. I wasn't quite sure how to answer him. I wasn't expecting him to call me out on my statement. I started in hesitantly.

"Well, I'm a vegetarian and a staunch independent," I said and then stopped to gauge his expression.

It hadn't changed. He was still wearing that goofy grin of his, as if everything in the world were right all of a sudden. So, I continued.

"I make a living arguing, and I don't believe that there is a perfect someone for anyone," I finished.

Will sat back against the windshield again, and then his eyes left me and began a tranquil stare off into the distance.

I too returned my gaze to the night sky.

When he finally spoke again, I could see out of the corner of my eye that he was nodding his head.

"A vegetarian. Really?" he remarked.

He sounded surprised.

"That is a big change all right–but I'm afraid that you're going to have to do better than that if you want to scare me off, Miss Lang," he said.

My eyes returned to him. I should have known it wouldn't be that easy.

"Jules, as long as you haven't taken to eating people– and I'm pretty sure that's against the vegetarian bylaws–I could care less if you order the garden salad instead of the prime rib."

Then, he paused.

"Vegetarians don't eat people, right?" he asked me, chuckling.

I looked into his big, blue eyes and smiled.

"See, my dear, you've still got most of your morals, at least," Will said, smirking at me.

I laughed.

"But, seriously, Jules, it really is simple," he said. "See, I'm in love with the person you can never outrun. I'm in love with you, Julia."

I took a deep breath in and then slowly let it out. I didn't know if it were his words or the way he so seductively said them that left my lips speechless and my mind a cluttered mess.

You're a lawyer for God's sake, Julia. Pull yourself together.

I took a few moments, let his words settle in, and then I ineptly scrambled in search of my own words.

"Will," I finally said. I spoke softly, my eyes locked on the butterfly weed pressed in between my fingers. I took another deep breath and slowly let the air escape from my lungs and then through my dry lips. I could feel every painful heartbeat in my chest as I formulated what I knew I had to say.

"I just think," I started and then stopped.

"I think that it has been a long time," I continued. "We're two, different people now, despite what you might think. We're not two sixteen-year-olds. You have your life here, and I have mine in Charleston," I said, gaining steam. "You fight fires and have an amazing, singing career. And I have a great job doing something I love also, and then there's D.C. and work there someday possibly. You see, no matter how you look at it, our lives just don't match up anymore."

I paused before continuing. The words had come out as if I had recited them over and over in my head at least a hundred times before, and in that instant, I almost wondered if I had, in fact, subconsciously recited them. Then, I looked into Will's eyes, which were now cast down on a spot near the edge of the car's hood.

"I just don't think it would ever work, Will," I pleaded with him. "We're living our realities now."

Hearing my own words echo back stabbed my heart; but nevertheless, I found a blind courage to continue.

"But I promise you that you'll be with me in my dreams. When I lay my head down on my pillow each night, when time is all my own to escape the world and dream, I'll meet you there. We'll both be sixteen, and we'll be happy, and we'll do all the things we used to do. What we had belongs in dreams and meeting there each night seems to work well anyway," I said with a soft smile. "But as for us in this lifetime, we've just changed too much, become two, different people and followed two, different paths. It's life, Will, not a fairy tale."

I finished, and the two of us sat in silence for what felt like an eternity. Then, he finally spoke.

"Why did you come back, Jules?" he soberly asked.

"I made a promise," I softly said.

"But why now?" he asked.

"It's a good cause, Will," I stammered.

It was a lie—for the most part. It was a good cause, but I also knew that it wasn't the cause or the promise that had brought me back.

Will didn't reply. He just sat there, seemingly defeated. Then, he turned and faced me and took my hand in his and kissed my slightly tanned skin.

"Julia, you have been my world since I first laid eyes on you, and you may not realize it, but I have taken you with me every day in the last decade. Please know that there is not one moment that I stopped loving you. You are the reason for my smiles and my songs. You are my hope and my inspiration. My heart has only beaten for you. I do admit that I had my doubts, none of which involved my love for you. I did worry that you had forgotten me and that you had forgotten what we had, but just being here with you now, it's proof. It proves to me that you haven't. I see no change in your eyes, and it's the most comforting feeling I've ever known. Jules, please know that I will love you unceasingly for many lifetimes to come."

He took a deep breath and then slowly let it out before he continued.

"Jules, but no matter what big dreams you're living or what lucky guy you end up marrying…," he said, as his words trailed off.

I heard him clear his throat, as silence filled the thick air around us.

"Please know that I love you. Even if I have to do it in secret–or in dreams–I'll love you forever," he finished.

Then, he set my hand gently back down onto my bended knee and methodically slid down the hood of my rented sedan.

When his feet met the ground below, he turned back toward my motionless figure.

"I guess I'll be seeing you in my dreams," he said, with a saddened smile, while touching his finger to the bill of his baseball cap.

Then, he started to turn but hesitated.

"And, Jules," he began and then stopped.

My eyes met his.

"I believe that there is a perfect someone for everyone, and I know that you still believe that too. There is a perfect someone, even if the road to that someone isn't all that perfect," he added.

His deep blue eyes pierced mine as he spoke. And though I could barely see his eyes through the shadow of his cap, I did see the hand that inconspicuously brushed his cheek. He had tears escaping from his eyes. I had never seen him cry.

Then, he slowly turned and made his way back to his SUV, pausing before lifting the door handle but never looking back. Instead, he opened the door and slowly slid into the driver's seat.

Though I remained steadfast in my convictions, my eyes had joined my heart and now rebelled against me as well, slowly and involuntarily releasing salty tears onto my already red cheeks again. Watching him walk away, I yearned to pull him back and to bring his muscular body close to mine. And for an instant, I sat up from the windshield and almost followed after him, but I miraculously resisted the urge, allowing my head to guide my actions.

Then, I watched him stare for a minute into his steering wheel, start the ignition and eventually and slowly pull away. I could just barely see through my misty eyes his tires kicking up gravel and dust in the glow from his taillights as his SUV faded further and further into obscurity. And then, he was gone.

Collisions

I sat frozen on the hood of my rented sedan. I couldn't help but feel as if a piece of my heart had jumped out of my chest and had followed Will as he drove farther and farther away from me just moments ago. I still held his pale peach flowers locked within my fingertips, and now, I tried desperately to hold back the constant flow of tears that threatened to flood my eyelids. The moment felt as if I had just let the tiny, happy, boxed-up memory of my high school sweetheart walk out of my life with him tonight. And in reality, it had. Could it have been that that memory had given me the security–albeit a false sense, but security all the same–that I needed to believe that everything in every part of my life would always be okay? As long as I had the memory of us at seventeen, a piece of me always felt like I still had him as well, I think. But now that I was almost certain that in the future I could, try as I might, only be able to conjure up the lasting image of his SUV fading into the distance, I felt helpless. Now, only a hollow shell remained where our last, miniature piece of love had been stored. With him, my jovial memory of the slice of life that we had shared together had disappeared from my life completely, and it was more than I could bear. Hurt and an inexplicable heartache overwhelmed me, but I had done the right thing. We had parted ways for a reason, and in time, my heart would heal again.

I wiped my rebellious tears away as I sat staring up into the black sky, spattered with dashes of light, most of which were now obscured by the mist in my eyes. The lights had attracted my already divided attention, and though they appeared somewhat blurry to me now, a few stars quickly became my main focal point. I watched, entranced, as the few soon became dozens, and then the dozens, hundreds, and then they all worked together to bring character to the dark and empty background that was tonight's sky. It was beautiful–just as I had left it years ago. I inhaled deeply again through my nose and smelled the familiar mixture of tall grasses and aged maple. I knew the smell well. It had always been the aroma that I had associated with the country, untouched by smog or pollution, just a mixture of trees and wildlife.

My fingers then carefully caressed the flower's petals in front of me, while my eyes glanced over the note that dangled from its stem. I read again the hand-written inscription: *I'll love you until the last petal falls, Jules.*

"Hmm," I said, letting out a deep, thoughtful sigh.

All life had shown me when it had come to love was that it was far from a fairy tale. It was what it was—a lot of planning and strategy and compatibility. Not much risk was involved after the age of eighteen. After that, time never really stopped, and a day planner became your best friend.

It almost seemed as if that hope for perfect love I had always heard about in fairy tales and movies while growing up had turned out to be more like a perfect phantom instead. You see it in everything you watch or read, but you can never find it yourself—not in real life anyway, I knew. True, I had been in love at least a couple of times, but in perfect love, only but once. It seemed perfect anyway—carefree, hopeful, risky—but at the same time, it can't be perfect unless it lasts forever. This, I also knew.

I remembered perfect love, albeit its memory had grown faint throughout the years. Perfect love was that kind of love that made no sense but made everything else make sense somehow. It was raw and unscripted, turbulent and slightly unpredictable. I remembered how it had made me feel. I remembered the butterflies, the comfort, the warmth; but most of all, I remembered that at the same time that I had had perfect love, I had also had a belief in happily ever after. And maybe it was because I had no reason to believe otherwise at the time. Probably.

I locked my eyes again on the starlit sky above me. They remained there, until my cell phone broke my attention. I quickly reached for it in my pocket and glanced at its screen. In the display window, in bold, capitalized letters read: *ANTHONY*. I thought about answering it, then silenced it instead and slid it back into my pocket.

"Time to get back to life," I said aloud.

I took a deep breath and sighed again. Then, I looked down at the small, gold watch on my hand and took note of the time. My flight was at six the next morning. My parents would kill me if they found out that I was in town and didn't stop by, but now, it was late and time to go. I'd have to take that chance. I made a mental note to plan a trip back home to see them soon and looked one last time into the vastness of the open sky. You didn't get this view everyday or just anywhere. Then, I slid off the sedan's hood and made my way back into the car. I had roughly two hours to sort out my thoughts before I reached St. Louis. It was going to be a long two hours.

If I could have closed my eyes driving back through town and past the field where the concert had been just hours before, I would have. The best I could do now, however, was keep my eyes planted only on the yellow and white stripes directly in front of me. And that's just what I did.

It was a half an hour before I allowed my eyes to venture away from my direct path for a split second. I reached for the dial on the radio and turned up the volume so that it was audible again. I needed a break from my thoughts.

"This is 98.7 Wolf Country and this is Jason David sitting here with local heartthrob Will Stephens," I heard the voice say before it continued. "Will, tell us what it felt like to sing for the first time in front of your hometown."

"You're kidding me," I exclaimed, as the words from my stereo flooded my ears. Though, I knew I shouldn't be the slightest bit surprised anymore about what flowed from my radio.

I reached for the tuner to change the station to something that triggered my emotions just a little less but then paused. I was curious. It couldn't possibly hurt anymore. I had just heard the most gut-wrenching confession I will probably ever hear. What did I have to lose now?

"Well, it was a pleasure," I heard Will say through my speakers. "I had my mom and dad and my grandma in the first row, and I looked down one time, and even through the lights, I could see my grandma bustin' some moves."

"So, that was Grandma down there. I thought that was your sister," the radio announcer said, through laughter.

I could hear Will chuckling in the background as well.

"No, seriously, it was great, a real treat for me to be here and to play for all the people who have supported me to this point," Will went on.

I listened as the announcer spoke again.

"Now, let us not forget what this whole concert is about. It's about raising some support for those victims of the recent floods, right? Tell us a little about that," he said.

"Yeah, Jason, this whole night was for those who have been affected by the flooding," Will said. "My heart goes out to all those who have lost homes or livelihoods, and I'm just asking everyone, even after tonight, to continue to give to local efforts to support victims and to remember to keep them in their prayers."

"Well, thanks so much, Will, for coming out and speaking with us tonight," the announcer went on. "It's definitely a great cause to support. I just have one more question. You didn't think you'd get out of this interview without me asking it, did you?"

Will softly chuckled.

"No, I suppose not. Fire away," Will said.

"Well," said the radio personality, "Will, we've never heard that last song, and it was pretty obvious to me that it was about a special girl in your life. Care to tell us about that?"

The airwaves grew quiet for a moment. I clenched the steering wheel with one hand and reached for the volume with the other and slowly turned it up.

"Well, it was for a special girl. She was my high school sweetheart," Will said.

"Was she here tonight?" I heard the announcer ask.

"Uh, yes, she was," Will said.

"Well, where is she now?" the DJ asked.

There was silence again.

"Well, I recon she's on her way back to South Carolina," Will replied.

His voice had grown somber.

"South Carolina, huh? So, does this mean you're still on the market, for all those ladies listening tonight?" the announcer asked.

Now, both hands were clenching my steering wheel.

"Not that I think there would be any of those ladies here," Will said, chuckling again. "See, they all knew me in junior high."

The DJ joined in Will's laughter.

"But no, sir, to answer your question. I'm taken, and I have been since I was sixteen," Will confessed.

"All right, well, if she's listening now, is there something you'd like to say to her?" the DJ asked.

The airways went silent. My fingers reached for the volume button and increased it yet again.

Still nothing.

Then, eventually, his voice came pouring through the speakers.

"I just want her to know that she's still the same beautiful, after all these years, and that I'm here–always," Will said.

My heart ached, and I again felt the enormous urge to cry. I should never say never. It only gets me into trouble. Of course I could hurt more. What was I thinking? I slowed and carefully pulled off the highway and onto the gravel shoulder. Both hands on the wheel, my eyes began to well up with tears. I didn't want to leave, yet I had no reason to stay. I had no reason to stay, yet somehow, for the first time, I wanted to have a reason to stay. I had done it hundreds of times before, yet tonight, I just couldn't do it. I couldn't bring myself to step on the gas pedal, to keep on going. And for the first time, it seemed natural, yet completely crazy to just stop.

And suddenly, and without warning, a new confidence sprinted wildly through my body, and for the first time in years, my thoughts were completely contrary to what made sense. They were risky and uncalculated, clumsy and childlike, but they were all focused on one, definite truth. And in an instant, not only all the world, but my world was right again. Well, almost.

I made a u-turn back onto the empty, two-lane highway, forcing myself back down the path I had just come. I was surely crazy, but what about this night wasn't?

Home

Before I knew it, I was pulling back into the grass parking lot, the rental swaying back and forth, threatening to split into two again.

Still with both hands on the steering wheel, I stared at the dimly lit scene in front of me. There were hundreds of white, plastic chairs still set up in neatly made rows. A flatbed truck now sat next to one row of chairs on the far right, but I could see no one in sight.

I put the car into park, then slowly got out and gently closed the door behind me. I sighed and released a sad exhale from my lips, even though, for a moment, I felt almost relieved to find no one.

Within seconds, however, my heart ached again, reminding me of my quest. He could be anywhere by now. I took another deep breath and then cautiously made my way to the last row of chairs and took a seat. I was nervous. My hands were shaking, yet I found it strange that at the same time, I never felt surer of myself.

I looked around. The scene in front of me looked different now than it had just hours before. In fact, the field had almost returned to its natural state. I mean, it was still littered with chairs and a stage and a few people who I could now see behind the stage–none of whom were Will–bustling around, unplugging cords and loading instruments and lights. But now, tree frogs had replaced the hum of a crowd of people; a sole white light had taken over for the blues and greens; and the smell of weeds had replaced the odor of bottled perfumes.

Seconds drew on in near silence as I methodically observed the men and women dance around in the distance. It was as if I weren't there at all. I was an invisible fly on their wall. The feeling was comfortable–almost euphoric. I reveled in it until a familiar sound penetrated the air.

"Julia," a voice called out from behind me.

I turned in my chair and then quickly stood up when I saw him.

"Did you forget something?" he asked, sincerely.

I didn't immediately say anything. I couldn't say anything. For a moment, I had no words.

"Yes," I finally managed to mumble.

I watched his muscular chest rise and fall, feeling his blue eyes pierce my inner being as I rallied up my courage.

"I forgot how much I love you," I sheepishly said, with a messy, post-tears smile.

He looked shocked and almost as if he were going to say something. Though, he remained speechless, motionless.

"Could you use a hand?" I asked, as I grasped tightly the back of a plastic chair, so he wouldn't see my hands shaking, praying he'd say something.

Will continued to show off a weighty expression as he stood there, staring at me staring at him.

"You're beautiful," he finally said, his face melting into a happy grin.

I breathed a blissful sigh of relief. And though I disagreed with his statement, I didn't protest. I stood before him with hair tossed around moist eyes, make-up in shambles, in my tee shirt and dark blue jeans, not even having the slightest idea of what to do next.

"You're even more beautiful than in dreams, though I'm still prayin' like crazy this isn't one," he said, in a low, soft voice, as he took a couple steps in my direction.

Then, as if the world had been set on some kind of slow motion option, I watched him bend down and lower one knee to the ground. As he did this, he pulled a small box from his pants pocket and lifted its lid toward me. Inside was a diamond ring.

"Julia Austin Lang," he began, "I love you more than anything in this world, and I could never imagine spending a second more of my life without you, and I've more than learned life's lesson. I'm not gonna let you get away again.

Jules, will you marry me—some day very soon?"

My left hand had found my face and was now pressed against my lips as he finished.

And speechless and breathless, I managed to nod.

Will smiled, gently took my hand from my lips and slipped the ring onto my finger. Then, he stood and scooped me up into his arms.

"Thanks for coming back to me, Jules," I heard him whisper into my ear.

The tears welled up in my eyes once more as I surrendered to his embrace, but this time, they were tears of relief, of having finally won the battle for my heart. And this time, I let them fall.

I was home. I was safe. I was happy. I was sixteen.

"I told you I'd come back," I whispered as I too wrapped my arms around him and rested my head against his strong chest, breathing in the scent of comfort. "I'm sorry I took so long."

Those words–the words that had held me captive for so long now instantly freed me, and I felt as if my whole life had changed in that instant. I smiled and closed my eyes, inhaling a deep breath of my new-found freedom. It smelled like a mixture of his cologne, sweat and aftershave, and it was, to me, just short of heavenly.

And as he held me, I realized that there had never been another for me. I had always been his, and he had always been mine, and in that moment, my heartbeat slowed, and my hands stopped shaking, and I melted into his strong arms, like I had never said goodbye. I had found him again, and with him, my world had become completely unwound. It was messy and impulsive, naïve and irrational, and somehow, right again.

Epilogue

I pause from my thoughts for a moment as I let my pen lie idly over the words on the page and look up to the painter's colors in the big sea above me. A tear trickles down my aging skin, getting caught in a silver strand of my hair. All around me, the world appears utterly peaceful–almost painfully–because I know that it will not last forever. It never does.

Tall grasses mixed with dandelions and butterfly weeds give way slightly to the soothing breeze, and the hum of a perfect silence rings gently in my ears like waves breaking in a far-off ocean. Perhaps, they are the waves that I viewed outside of April's and my little apartment in Banker's Hill or the Southern ones from

Charleston that often brought me comfort in my former life.

I watch the colors above me fade into deep blues and dark grays as night touches first the picket fence and then the base of the earth in the distance.

The smell of lilac brushes over my cheek bones as I close my eyes and take a deep breath, filling my tired lungs with as much of the freshest of air I can possibly fit into them at one time. Where there are grandmothers, there are lilac bushes, I think to myself and smile knowingly. I hold the breath hostage for a moment and then slowly let it escape through my lips, allowing my chest to fall gradually, leisurely.

Then, slowly letting my eyelids fall over my eyes, feeling every gentle gust, I relax in the quiet, the calm, consciously feeling my chest rise and fall.

Eventually, I command my fingers back to life again and close my pen into my old, tattered diary. Then, I take out the few photos I keep safely tucked within the journal's pages, and my tired eyes follow aged fingers as they trace the images of my love and I side by side. We are in our high school caps and gowns. He's standing beside me, playfully gnawing on my kelly green and white tassel above my head.

Our faces are vibrant and so full of life. We were so young then.

I finish tracing the images in the photo and then slide it behind another photo. Then, for a second time, I find my fingers methodically following the outlines of the snapshot. This time, I'm in a white gown and looking into his eyes. I'm smiling as if nothing in the world could ever make me sad. We look so happy and still so young. And now, even though I can still feel every wild emotion of the young girl in the photo, I resemble her no longer.

God, I feel like it was yesterday that I was standing there so excited for my new life. It goes so fast.

I take a shallow breath and let it out slowly as I look deeper into the photo, recapturing every slightest detail, reliving every simple moment. Then, I slip the photos back inside the journal's pages and softly sit the notebook onto my lap and continue my stare off into the distance at the lavender and crimson sunset fading into a tree-lined horizon. The sun would soon disappear. My arthritic hands ached from the writing, but I had said everything that I had wanted to say today, and I was happy that my ailing hands had allowed me to do at least that. It had been awhile since I had gotten the chance to write in the journal. It had become a habit of mine, in these last years, of taking the final moments of daylight to reflect on my days here on earth.

My lungs let out a sigh of contentment as I observe the scarlet sun sinking lower and lower into the tops of the farthest, emerald, leaf-filled trees. I watch the butterfly weeds dance in the breeze alongside the lake in the distance as the sky fades into a darker shade of blue. Above me, the dusk-to-dawn light flickers off and then on again. After several tries, the light finally remains lit and illuminates the place where I sit. Now, it is getting late. The thought has crossed my mind several times already that I had better be heading back inside before it gets too dark to see the path back to the house. The thought of leaving this scene saddens me a little, but I know that my already weary eyes will thank me later for the little light still left to get me home.

I take one last look at the colors in the sky fading into deeper shades before I start my journey. Then, I prop my left hand onto the arm of the chair in preparation of lifting my body from the chair's surface.

These days even the smallest of tasks become valiant efforts. As I brace myself on the chair's arm, I use my other hand to pick up the tattered journal that rests in my lap and to move it toward the tiny table next to me. But when I bring the journal closer to the table top, its corner knocks the edge, sending it, the photos and the pen tumbling to the grassy ground below.

Frustrated by my clumsiness, I sigh and then slowly bend over in my chair and stretch my fingers toward the fallen photos. I pause, however, when I see a tri-folded piece of nicely pressed stationery next to the fallen journal, resting on the ends of the short spikes of grass. My eyes immediately leave the photos as my fragile fingers go instead toward the folded note. I hadn't remembered putting anything loose into the journal, except for the photos and the pen. Although, the piece of paper could be anything. My memory doesn't exactly serve me well these days.

Curious about the mysterious note, I gently gather up the pages and sit back into my chair again. I then carefully unfold the sheets of stationery with both hands and then slide my glasses back to the edge of my nose. The hand-written words on the page become clearer as my eyes sluggishly adjust to the dimmer lighting, and though I have never seen the letter before, I immediately recognize the hand writing. The realization makes me gasp, and as I bring my fingers to my lips, I can feel my creased hands grow clammy, shaky. It had been a month since the love of my life passed away, and instantly, my eyes anxiously, yet meticulously, follow over the words on the page:

My Sweet Jules,

Don't be frightened by this letter. I had some time, and I wanted to

273

make sure you remembered some things—all of which I have told you before, but none of which I could tell you now without the help of this letter today.

First of all, though I am not able to sit with you tonight and watch the violets and pinks fade into the tree-covered horizon or the butterfly weeds dance their dance along the lakeside, please know that I am still with you and that my love will never leave you. Though I am not there beside you, continue to live your life like you always have—full of emotion and passion and drive. If you get lonely, think about when we were sixteen, when life was all our own, and we made the most of it. Remember our first kiss on that gravel road outside of town. Remember the first time that I told you that I loved you. You looked so beautiful that night with the fireworks reflecting off of your big, green eyes.

Jules, best of all, remember when you came back to me. You were my butterfly, Jules. You told me later that you were terrified and trembling as you stood in that field after the concert, but that's not how I saw you. You looked beautiful and so sure of yourself in your blue jeans and tee shirt and blond curls. Though your eyes were damp, radiance beamed off of you like nothing I had ever seen. You were so brave, and I was so happy in that moment. You had come back to me, Jules, and I knew it. I never stopped thanking God for that day, and for you. I had missed you in those years that we were apart like I miss you now.

But, Jules, life only got better from there. From here on out, if you ever feel alone, think of our wedding day amongst the trees trying to hold onto their luscious, emerald leaves but losing the fight to tangerines and saffrons. I can still see you gathering the layers of your white silk into one hand and readjusting the bouquet of crimson daisies and tangerine butterfly weeds—exactly what you wanted—in the other. I was the happiest man alive watching you glide down that pearl-colored aisle runner leading to the gazebo along the riverfront. Jules, you were beautiful that day, and you only got more gorgeous to me as the years went on. And remember when you handed me that tiny note scribbled on that piece of ivory napkin. Do you remember what it said, Jules? I remember it like it was yesterday: "Since my wish has come true, I guess I can tell you now. It was for you—for always. Love, Jules."

And it had been years, but I knew exactly what you had meant. I knew that you were talking about your wish that night under the stars—the same night that inspired my love songs to you.

Then, my sweet Jules, remember the years that we spent making up for lost time. Those were good years, Jules. We raised three, very wonderful, successful children, who all take after you. They have your same passion for life, and they're so headstrong. You were and are a wonderful mother to them. They'll do what's right, Jules. Don't spend your days worrying about them. They'll be fine, sweetheart.

Lastly, but by no means least, Julia Austin Stephens, my life began and ended with you. You were my world since I first laid eyes on you, and you may not realize it, but I carried you with me every day since that moment, and yes, my sweet Jules, I carry you with me even now. I never stopped loving you since the day that I met you, and though I can no longer hold your soft hand by your side, I love you no less than the day that I met you. You were the reason for my happy smiles and my heartfelt songs. You made me the man that I was proud to be, Jules. You were my hope and my inspiration and my every answer to prayer.

Now, you and I both know that I'll wait a lifetime for you— remember, Butterfly Weeds never give up—so take your time down there. And tonight, as you watch that big, orange sun disappear into the earth and your world gradually grow dark, I'll help God turn on the stars, and I'll wait for my dawn—when you return to me, Julia Stephens.

I love you, My Butterfly. You'll always be my endless song.

Love always and forever,
Your one and only Butterfly Weed, Will

P.S. Make a wish for me.

Tears well up in my eyes, as I lose myself in his soulful words from another world.

"My last piece of you," I whisper as I gently kiss the letter, then bring it to my chest and press it against my racing heart.

After a moment, I let my hand slowly fall to my lap as I tightly close my tired eyes and take a frail, labored breath, feeling my lungs gradually fill with air. Then, slowly again, I exhale, and feel the sensation of every quickened heartbeat in my chest.

"I carried you with me as well," I whisper, as the tears trickle down my wrinkled cheeks. "Thank you for giving me wings, Will Stephens, and thank you for guiding me home."

I pause, as my heartbeat slows to a normal pace again. I allow myself to relax, though my tears continue to squeeze past my closed, weary eyelids.

"I miss you," I say quietly into the breeze.

I sit motionless in my chair for a while then, letting the gentle, warm, evening gusts glide softly across my aging face. I replay Will's timeless love song again in my head, and eventually, all of my quietly held heartache melts away.

When I open my eyes again, I notice that the sun has finally escaped back into the earth and that the world has grown vastly quiet except for the few tree frogs and crickets beginning their night songs in the oaks surrounding me. The brightest stars have now also popped out of the darkness, while the moon has taken its place in the eastern sky.

I gaze at the heavens in awe of its vastness, and I wonder then if Will is somewhere up there too looking down on me watching him tonight. I wonder if he's smiling that goofy grin of his.

A few moments go by, and I notice that the blanket of blackness above me had in the meantime sprung thousands of tiny lights, and I catch a glimpse just in time to see a burning star streak across the night sky. Almost by instinct, I close my eyes, then lower my head and silently recite a wish. When I finish, I open my eyes and cautiously turn my face toward the world above me. And with my creased hands, I press the love letter up against my beating heart one more time and recount his fateful words: *"More than every once in a while. More than most dreams. More than just my heart. More than anything."*

As I say them, I lean back in my chair and once again close my weary eyes, and in my mind, I am sixteen, and he is just a small-town boy, hoping this small-town girl says *yes.* And in that moment, there are no hurts, no what-ifs, no regrets. Life is just beginning as a soft, peaceful lull covers the world, butterfly weeds sway their dance in the distance and a soft gust wiggles free a page from my journal and sends my last words tossing around in the wind:

Life didn't go how I had planned, but I couldn't have planned a better life. Somewhere in between the beginning and eternity, I fought the war that we all must fight—the journey that in taking, forces us to come face to face with our own realities. My reality was that I was, is and will always be madly and hopelessly in love with you. You are my love of loves, my dream of dreams, my hope of hopes, and I would take the journey all over again because it led me to you, because it's our story—the story of us.

As for the war, I surrendered.

The End

ACKNOWLEDGMENTS

Thank you to God, first and foremost, for giving me the chance to write for you.

And to my husband, who, if it weren't for him, this book might still be just pages of black ink tucked away somewhere, long forgotten. I will be forever grateful for your constant support. I love you and am blessed to have you every day in my life.

To my mother, father, sisters and family who were brave enough and patient enough to read the rough draft of my first novel in its entirety and who were kind in their criticisms and ever enthusiastic about my dreams of a stable career in writing.

To those mentors in my life who were passionate in their profession and who taught me that the perfect word is powerful.

And finally, to all those loyal friends along life's journey who have served as my inspiration and who were never anything but encouraging–even as we fought alongside each other each day to discover our dreams.

To each one of you, Thank you.

OTHER BOOKS BY LAURA MILLER

My Butterfly
For All You Have Left
By Way of Accident

★★★★★

"THIS IS PURE ROMANCE AT ITS BEST."

~Romantic Reading Escapes on *My Butterfly*

"Just amazing, angsty, gut-wrenching."

~Gutter Girls Book Reviews on *My Butterfly*

"This is certainly one of my favorite love stories ever."
~A Novel Review Blog on *For All You Have Left*

"It takes you back to the innocence and joy of falling in love."
~She Reads New Adult on *For All You Have Left*

"A classic, All-American, enchanting love story."
~Southern Belle Book Blog on *By Way of Accident*

A LOOK AT MY BUTTERFLY!

William Stephens has a story to tell as well. Find out what he was doing while Julia was away and discover the untold events that Julia left out.

Please turn this page for a preview of

My Butterfly

Breakfast

I opened my eyes to white ceiling tiles and what sounded like a loose wheel on some type of cart or something rambling past the room. I closed my eyes again and tried to recall how I had gotten there. There was a call, a fire and then...there was Julia. My eyes shot open. She was still asleep on my chest, and my arm was still around her. I tried to rest my hand on her arm, but I couldn't feel my hand. It must have fallen asleep. My eyes darted back to her face as I watched her nuzzle her head deeper into my chest. I froze then and became conscious of my every movement out of fear that the slightest flinch would wake her. I couldn't help but want to watch her sleep. She looked so peaceful. She always looked peaceful when she slept, and while I wasn't quite convinced that this would be the last time I would ever get this moment—to watch her dream—I had learned something yesterday—that no moment is guaranteed.

I caught her head move again, and then I noticed her eyes flutter open. I quickly forced my eyelids over my eyes again and pretended to be asleep.

She was still for a few more seconds, but then she quickly sat up. I peeked out of one eye and saw her reaching for something on the floor. It looked as if it might be her shoes maybe. *Where was she going?*

"Good morning, sunshine," I said, pretending to wake up.

I stretched my good arm toward the ceiling and started to sit up but then fell back with a groan.

"God, what happened to me?" I asked, faintly smiling.

Her face angled back toward mine.

"You'd think I had fallen through a burning building or something," I continued.

She laughed once.

"Careful there, Spider-Man. You're probably going to be a little sore," she said, as she sent a smile my way and then went back to putting on her shoes.

"Where are you going?" I asked.

"I am going to get us some breakfast," she said, in a way that made it sound as if it were an announcement.

She paused for a moment, glanced back at me again and then softy smiled. It didn't seem like a happy smile.

"And then, I've got to get home," she said.

My heart sank, but I forced a smile anyway.

"This hospital bed not homey enough for you?" I asked.

Her lips started to edge up her face just a little more, as she sarcastically batted her eyelashes at me.

"You have bed head," she said then, snickering.

I playfully narrowed my eyes but then smiled as I noticed the long second that her gaze lingered in mine.

"There's a doughnut shop across the street," she said, eventually dropping her eyes from mine and then grabbing her purse from a table at the foot of the bed.

I watched her make her way to the door, but before she disappeared behind the curtain, she stopped and turned toward me.

"Chocolate Long Johns with sprinkles?" she asked.

I flashed her a wide smile, which I guessed was all the confirmation she needed because she turned then and escaped past the tall curtain and out of the room.

I waited for almost a minute, staring at the door, just in case she had forgotten something and popped back in. Then, my eyes darted toward the television at the front of the room. I had to strain my neck a little in order to see my reflection in its black screen and even then, I was still just a shadowy outline. But it would have to do. I quickly ran my fingers through my hair, then suddenly, I felt a muscle in my back pull tight, and it made me flinch. I groaned and then returned to the same position on the bed in which I had been for the last twelve hours or so and raked over my hair one, last time.

After I had done the best I could with my bed head or whatever she liked to call it when my hair spiked up every which way, I spotted a glass of water on the table next to my bed. I picked it up, took a big swig and swished it around my mouth. Then, I looked around the room for anything that resembled toothpaste or a toothbrush. Nothing. My eyes eventually landed on a small bouquet of flowers on the little table. I guessed they were mine. *Could I eat a flower? Would that even help?* Thankfully, I spotted a bag of mint chocolate candies next to the vase and scooped it up. I popped a couple of the chocolates into my mouth and chewed them. Then, I took another big swig of water and set the glass back down.

The room was quiet and still without Jules in it. My eyes began a slow scan of the space around me. There was a window to my right, and there was a little sliver of light pouring through it. But the only view out of it and to the world was the empty side of a red, brick building. Besides that, there was a chair near the window, a small table at the foot of the bed, the television and then a trash can near the big curtain to my left, but that was it.

I let out a breath of air, as my eyes lowered to my hands again. And just then, I got an idea. I quickly rolled the candy wrappers into tiny balls. Then, I sent them, one at a time, flying toward the trash can across the room. But I missed both times, and both times, the foiled paper rolled to a final resting place on the tiles near the basket. I sighed and then looked around the room for something else to do to kill the time until Julia returned. Besides the few standard things, the tiny place was empty and mostly dark, and the air smelled kind of stale. I was happy that I hadn't had to spend the night alone in it.

My mind got stuck on that thought, as I replayed in my head waking up next to Jules. I wasn't sure how many more buildings I could fall through and still be all right, but if that were all it took to get Julia Lang next to me again, I also wasn't sure I'd think twice about doing something stupid the next time.

I heard the loose wheel on that cart again outside the room. It sounded as if it slowed when it reached my door and then continued on. When I couldn't hear the sound of the wheel any longer, my gaze fell to the white sheets that were turned every which way at my feet. Then suddenly, a shiny object near the middle of the bed caught my eye. It was the guardian angel. I cautiously reached for it, being conscious of my sore back. Then, when I was close enough to touch it, I clasped my fingers around it and brought it close to my heart. And after several seconds, I rested my head back against my pillow and stared up at the white tiles, until eventually, my eyelids fell over my eyes.

"Two chocolate Long Johns with sprinkles and some milk."

Startled, I forced my eyes open. Then, I watched Jules make her way over to my bedside and set a paper bag and a small container of milk into my lap.

I smiled.

"Thanks, dear," I said, grabbing at the top of the bag.

I stole a quick glance at her. She was staring at me sideways, just as I had suspected she would be. I watched her eyes do that playful, sarcastic thing, which drove me wild, and I held out for what I knew was coming next. Wait for it. Wait for it. There it was—a smile.

"I mean Jules," I said, finally.

I went back to rummaging through the doughnuts in the bag as she took a seat on the bed next to my midsection and faced me.

"So, how long do you have to be here anyway?" she asked.

"Uh, I think they'll let me go today," I said, starting to grin. "I'm pretty sure they were just waiting to make sure nothing else was wrong with me."

She slowly nodded her head.

"Good," she said, through a soft smile.

An Excerpt from MY BUTTERFLY

I watched her then, as she lowered her eyes and reached her hand into her purse. Her hair was pulled together, and it sat in a pile near the top of her head. It looked kind of messy, but it had always been my favorite look on her.

She eventually found what she had been looking for in her purse, I guessed, because she pulled out a short stick and smeared its contents onto her lips.

"Jules," I finally said, setting the bag of doughnuts and the milk onto the bed beside me.

She lowered the chap stick from her lips and met my gaze.

"Thank you," I said.

I rested my hand on hers. Her eyes darted toward my hand, but she didn't move.

"I lied last night," I said.

I watched her head tilt a little to the side, as if she might be interested in what I had to say.

"I didn't just put you as my emergency contact out of habit," I went on. "I did it because…"

"Where is that lucky bastard?" I suddenly heard a familiar voice come from behind the curtain. "Better be decent. I brought your girl."

My eyes rushed toward the door, and within seconds, the curtain flew open, revealing a tall, lanky guy and a petite brunette. Almost at the same time, I felt Julia's hand quickly escape from underneath mine, and before I knew it, she was standing at the bedside, fidgeting with the hair on top of her head.

"Oh, hey, Julia," Jeff said, stopping short and staring at her with big eyes.

Julia looked up for an instant and bashfully smiled at him.

"I didn't know you had company," Jeff said, meeting my stare.

I didn't say anything. I just stared back at him with a defeated expression. And after a moment, he swallowed hard and carried on.

"Well, you dead yet, buddy?" he asked.

I found Julia again. Her eyes were searching the floor at her feet, but she eventually caught my stare and sent me an awkward smile. My eyes traveled back to the curtain then, but Jeff had already made his way over to a monitor near my head and was now poking at buttons. And Jessica was standing at the foot of the bed, looking shy, with flowers clutched within her small fingers.

"No, Jeff, not dead yet," I mumbled.

"I heard what happened," Jessica said. "Are you okay?"

Her voice was timid but sweet. And suddenly, it felt like New Year's Eve those years ago all over again—with Julia and Jessica in the same room. Only this time, I hadn't been holding the brunette's hand when Julia had entered the doorway. This time, it had been Julia's hand and Jessica had appeared, but somehow, it didn't seem to make a difference—not to Julia anyway.

"Yeah," I said, looking up at Jessica. "It's just a broken wrist. I'll be fine."

My eyes left Jessica when I noticed Julia in the corner of the room, rifling through her purse again. I watched her pull out a set of keys and then turn back toward the three of us—me; Jeff, playing with some cords at my head; and Jessica, now sitting in the spot on the bed next to me where Julia had been just moments ago.

"I should be going," Julia said.

Jeff stopped playing with the cords and looked up.

"What? No. Stay," he said, stuffing a Long John into his mouth. "We were just about to see if Will needs all of these cords to live."

Julia's eyes fell onto mine, and she sweetly smiled. Then, she looked back up at Jeff.

"I really need to get going," she said, starting toward the curtain.

"Jules," I called out after her.

She stopped and turned.

"You don't have to go," I said.

A half-smile slowly found its way to her face.

"I do," she said, nodding her head. "Take care, Will."

Then, she turned again, disappeared behind the curtain and was gone.

Photo by Marc Mayes

LAURA MILLER is the national bestselling author of the novels, *Butterfly Weeds*, *My Butterfly* and *For All You Have Left*. She grew up in eastern Missouri, graduated from the University of Missouri-Columbia and worked as a newspaper government reporter prior to writing fiction. Laura currently lives in the Midwest with her husband. Visit her and learn more about her books at LauraMillerBooks.com.

Made in the USA
Lexington, KY
05 April 2017